HEARTS IN WINTER

CARRIE ELKS

❧   I   ❧

*H*er ex-husband leaned close, making her heart leap in her chest. "Can I talk with you later?" he asked her. "In private?"

Alarm bells clattered in her ears. "I don't think I'll have the time today. I'm the maid of honor. I have a lot to do."

His gaze flickered to hers. "It's important."

She frowned. "It can't be that important. I haven't seen you for years."

Dylan exhaled heavily, his beautiful lips parting. "It's really important, Evie. We have a problem we need to sort out."

Evie. Only Dylan had ever called her that. She felt her cheeks flush.

"What kind of problem?"

He leaned closer, his breath tickling her ear. His voice was low and smooth, and made her shiver. But not as much as his words did. Because they were the last thing she expected to hear as his sweet voice caressed her skin.

"A really big problem. We're still married."

. . .

The bride looked beautiful, the groom devastatingly handsome, and the Inn was perfectly decorated for a winter wedding. Everley looked around the grand ballroom, a smile pulling at her lips.

The whole day had been perfect, and her cousin Holly deserved that. She and her groom were the golden couple of Winterville, after having fallen in love last year as they battled over the town's future, before they settled down to build it together.

In the corner some of the older townsfolk were clustered together. Everley couldn't help but grin at their outfits. Some of their tuxedos had to date back to the nineteen sixties, and only came out for weddings every few years.

Her sister, Alaska, slid a full glass of champagne in front of her. She was wearing the same dress that Everley was. Red velvet, with white roses woven into their hair. The theme continued on the tables, with centerpieces of red rose petals floating in vases, the glass lit by flickering candles that surrounded them. The hall itself was tastefully decked with red and green wreaths that their cousin, North, had created at his Christmas tree farm. Even though it was only November, it made Everley feel festive just looking at them.

"Okay," Alaska said, leaning across the table so that Everley could hear her above the band. "Spill. What's Dylan doing here and what did he say to you in line?"

Everley took a large mouthful of champagne. The bubbles went up her nose and made her choke. She doubled over as she sprayed the expensive wine over the tablecloth, much to her sister's amusement.

"Was it *that* bad?" Alaska asked.

Against her will, Everley looked across the room to where she knew her ex-husband was sitting. He was wearing a dark blue suit that matched his coloring perfectly. His hair was pushed back from his face, and the flickering candlelight was warming his skin. His long, muscled legs were stretched out as he sat at a table.

And he was looking right at her, a smirk pulling at his lips.

Dammit, he'd seen her choke. That was so typical. It was the first time she'd seen her ex-husband in eight years and she'd already looked like an idiot in front of him.

Except he's not your ex-husband.

She blinked at that thought. Then took another mouthful of champagne, praying to god that this one went down the right hole.

"You okay?" Alaska asked, her eyes wide at Everley's reaction.

"I'm fine," Everley said, putting her glass down. "And I'm also still married."

Alaska blinked, her mouth dropping open as she stared at Everley. "What?" she managed, before shaking her head, apparently muted by Everley's revelation.

"That's why Dylan's here. Apparently, we're still married. He whispered it in my ear after the wedding. He wants to talk to me about it." And she really didn't want to talk to him. She hadn't prepared herself for it. And Dylan Shaw was the kind of man you needed to prepare yourself for.

Once upon a time, the man had been the love of her life. He'd stopped her in her tracks when she was eighteen years old. He'd been a medical student then. Older than her, more experienced, and stupidly attractive. With one look, he'd swept her off her feet.

"Still married? Wow." Alaska took a big gulp of champagne, swallowing it quickly. "Are you absolutely sure?"

"Dylan was." Everley sighed. "Apparently the paperwork never went through."

"So what are you going to do?" Alaska asked her.

"Get another divorce I guess." Everley sighed. The last divorce had been hard enough. She'd cried for weeks.

Months, even. But she'd been younger then, and so in love, despite their separation. It was fine, she was older and wiser now. Now it was just a piece of paper they needed to get taken care of. The emotions were behind her. "I assume that's why he wants to talk."

Alaska glanced over her shoulder to where Dylan was sitting. "Damn, he looks better than ever," she said, a sigh in her voice. "What is it with guys and suits?"

Everley wrinkled her nose. She knew exactly how Alaska felt. "It's primordial biology. If a guy wears a suit our lizard brain thinks he's rich and successful and it makes us want to have babies with him." Everley shook her head. She really didn't want to think about making babies when her ex-husband was in the room.

It was too weird.

"Well you and Dylan sure would have made pretty babies." Alaska pulled her lip between her teeth. "I'm sorry, that was a stupid thing to say."

Everley laughed. "It's a stupid situation." It really was. Never in her wildest dreams did she imagine she'd see Dylan here today, let alone discover they were still technically husband and wife. She had so many questions, but she wasn't sure she wanted to know the answers.

"Can you do me a favor?" she asked her sister. "Can we keep this between us for now? I don't want the town gossiping about this. Or for it to ruin Holly and Josh's day."

"You're not going to tell Holly?" Alaska asked, her brows lifting. "But you tell each other everything."

"She's flying to Hawaii in the morning. I don't want her worrying about me on her honeymoon. And hopefully by the time she's back it'll all be taken care of." And Everley would be a single woman again.

Then Dylan could fly back to where he came from and

she wouldn't have to be aware of him staring at her every few minutes.

The band stopped playing for a moment, as the MC stepped up to the microphone.

"Ladies and gentlemen, please welcome the bride and groom for their first dance."

Josh held his hand out to the bride, his eyes full of love as she placed her palm into his. Everley felt her chest contract as Josh gently pulled Holly into his arms, brushing a lock of stray hair behind her ear.

The band started to play. She recognized the song. It was a cover of one of Gray Hartson's, their favorite singer. "The River" had been his first hit, about losing your first love and finding it again, and it felt completely appropriate for Josh and Holly who'd found each other again after years apart.

Remember when we were kids? And everything we did? The days we spent at school right by the river.
The day that love died. And everybody cried. We held each other tight by the river.
The day I walked along the river was the day we said goodbye.
The day we walked along the river was the day I made you cry.
Now I sit here all alone and all I think about is then.
Why can't we walk along the river again?

Without thinking, she glanced over at Dylan. A little jolt of electricity rushed through her as she realized he was looking straight at her. The MC spoke into the microphone again, inviting the parents and bridal party to join them. She danced with North for a few minutes, then with Gabe, while Alaska and North danced. When the song was over, more couples joined the floor, and Gabe glanced over her shoulder at the bar. She smiled because she knew he was dying to get back there and stop dancing. It had never been his favorite pastime.

"You can go," she told him. "You've done your duty."

"You sure?"

She nodded. "Positive."

Gabe led her to the edge of the dance floor and she watched his back as he approached the bar. Then, as though drawn by a magnet, her gaze slid to where Dylan was sitting, the clash of their eyes making her chest feel tight. Without breaking her gaze, he stood and walked toward where she was standing at the edge of the floor, exuding the kind of masculine confidence it was impossible to learn.

When he reached her, she had to lift her head to look at him. At six foot two, he'd always towered over her, even in heels.

His face was serious as he held out his hand and asked, "Will you dance with me now?"

Dylan's head was pounding to the beat of the music. His body was still on Central African time, where it was the middle of the night. It had taken him fourteen hours in the air, plus connections, for him to get back to his small home town in the Allegheny Mountains, and he was beyond exhausted.

It felt strange to be back here. Not just because he was used to the intense heat of Africa instead of the achingly cold breezes that always seemed to dance around Winterville at this time of year. But because *she* was in his arms. His ex-wife. Or his wife, if you wanted to be pedantic about it.

And she molded against him perfectly, the way she always did.

It had been eight years since he'd touched her. Back then

they'd been kids, playing at being adults. He'd thought he had everything it took to make her happy, to protect her.

And he'd been so damn wrong it was laughable.

The song came to an end, and the band segued into a Christmas song that made him smile. He looked down at Everley, and she smiled back. He exhaled, feeling lighter. She didn't look mad at him, though he felt mad at himself.

"Christmas in November?" he asked her, wanting to hear her voice again.

"That's what we do." She shrugged. "You must have seen the town sign when you arrived. It hasn't changed since you lived here."

Welcome to Winterville. Where Every Day Is Christmas

"Dad tells me you've taken over at the theater," he said, his conversation light as he moved her around the dance floor. Her body was lithe and warm, her hand curled around his. He kept his other low on her back so that he didn't touch the enticing skin that was exposed by her strapless dress.

"That's right. We're rehearsing for our first production right now."

"A Christmas show?"

She smiled. "Yeah. The Revue. We open in December. We've modernized it a bit since you last saw it."

"How are rehearsals going?" He knew enough about the theater industry to keep a conversation going. He'd been by her side as she attended drama school, and at the front of the auditorium for her first show. And right now he wanted her relaxed. He knew he'd sprung their lack of divorce onto her in the most shocking of ways. And he also knew he should have kept his mouth shut until a more appropriate time. But too late now.

"It's going pretty well. We only started a couple of weeks ago. We premier on December first, so there's still lots to do before then."

"I'm impressed. You always said you wanted your own theater." He could feel the heat of her skin through the fabric of her dress. "I'm proud of you."

She tipped her head to the side, exposing her elegant neck. "Thank you." A smile played at her lips. "How's your work going?"

"Good." Since his medical school days, he'd specialized in treating HIV and AIDS patients. His fellowship had involved spending time in both the Atlanta hospital he worked at, and volunteering in Sub Saharan Africa. And for the past few years he'd spent his time almost permanently there, working to treat the local community, and train local medics so that they would be able to take over the project. "That's one of the reasons I'm here. We're trying to secure funding for a medical center and I have to meet with some donors."

"One of the reasons?" Her golden hair caught in the light from the chandeliers, and he wanted to touch it.

"I was owed some time off. About eight weeks, actually. I wanted to spend it with my dad, we never see enough of each other. Plus there's the little problem of our divorce to sort out."

Everley winced at the words.

"What's wrong?" he asked her, his eyes catching hers.

"It's just weird hearing you say it."

"You don't want to talk about getting divorced?" That was why he was here, after all.

"I'm not sure it's good luck to talk about divorce at a wedding. Is it even okay to say the word here?" She grimaced. "I don't want to give Holly and Josh any bad voodoo."

He bit down a smile. "You think if we say it three times Beetlejuice will come running through the Inn and demand Holly and Josh separate?"

Everley started laughing. "Anything's possible." Her face was soft and smooth, her lips full as she bit down her amusement. "But maybe we could talk about this another day. Are you free tomorrow?"

He nodded. "Yeah. Come over to my dad's place. That's where I'm staying."

"Does nine work?"

"Nine is fine."

She looked away from his gaze, nodding gently. "Okay then." She was biting her bottom lip and damn if that didn't make him remember how sweet she used to taste. How she'd fall apart in his arms.

He forced that memory from his brain, trying to think of something to say. Anything to stop him from thinking about kissing her.

"So how have you been?" As soon as the words escaped he realized how stupid they were.

"In the past eight years?" She was almost laughing again.

He smiled. "Yeah."

"I've been good. How about you?"

"Good, too." Well this was going well. "Dad tells me you guys own Winterville now."

"Kind of. We don't own it. A trust does. We're directors of the trust, but really the whole town is part of it. It's been a wonderful thing, Grandma would have approved."

"I was sorry to hear about your grandma," he said softly. Candy Winter had founded this town, and she'd been close to all of her grandchildren, but especially Everley. He knew it had to be hard on her to lose the parent figure her grandmother had been.

She looked up at him again, her eyes glassy. "Thank you."

He wanted to tell her he was sorry he hadn't been there for her, but that was inappropriate. They were nothing to each other anymore.

You're husband and wife.

What a mess. The sooner they sorted this whole thing,

the better. Because he didn't need this messing with his head. He'd long since reconciled himself to the mistakes he'd made. Starting with getting married at the age of twenty-four.

The music came to an end, and Everley relaxed in his arms, as though relieved she wouldn't have to touch him anymore.

"Thank you for the dance." She stepped back, pulling her hand from his. "I'll see you in the morning."

He nodded. "At nine."

She spun on her heel and walked across the dance floor, her hips swinging in a way that made his body tense.

It was only muscle memory, that was all. And a severe lack of any action for months. As soon as they finalized their divorce and he went back to Africa, he'd forget all about her.

As far as he was concerned, that couldn't happen fast enough.

$$\maltese \quad 2 \quad \maltese$$

"That was a great wedding, right?" Everley's middle cousin Gabe had insisted on walking her home from the Winterville Inn, even though it was less than ten minutes to get to her cottage in the center of town.

"It was." She smiled, remembering how Josh had carried Holly out of the Inn and down to the limo he'd ordered to take them away to a mystery hotel before they caught their honeymoon flight the next morning. He'd been adamant that they wouldn't stay in the Inn for their first married night, and Everley couldn't blame him. Half the town would probably be pressing their ears to the door to confirm the marriage had been consummated.

"It was good to see Dylan, too," Gabe said.

Dylan and her boy cousins had been close growing up, even though he was a few years older than Gabe. It didn't matter when you were a kid in a small town like Winterville – you hung around with anybody who wasn't an adult.

After their dance, she hadn't spoken with Dylan again, though she'd been all too painfully aware that he was in the room. Every now and then she'd look over and their eyes would catch and she'd quickly turn them away again.

Gabe glanced at her from the corner of his eye. He was a little unsteady on his feet. Not that it mattered, because she was too, and somehow their lurches seemed to cancel each other out.

"Yeah, it was great to see him," Everley said.

Gabe lifted a brow. "Was that sarcasm?"

She sighed, reaching down to pull off the stupidly high heels she was wearing. They were hurting her feet way too much. Sure, it was November and freezing as heck, but she could cope with that. And she'd rather not have blistered up feet next week when they were rehearsing at the Jingle Bell Theater.

"It wasn't sarcasm," she said, hooping the straps of her shoes around her fingers. She'd lost about four inches, and now her head only came to the top of Gabe's shoulders. "It was... I don't know." She scrunched her nose. "Despair?"

"Despair?" Gabe was trying not to laugh. "That's pretty dramatic. I thought you were over him."

"So did I. And then I found out that officially I'm not."

Gabe blinked. "I have no idea what you're talking about. Did you drink some of Charlie Shaw's moonshine?"

Everley pulled her lip between her teeth. "If I tell you something, do you promise not to tell anybody else? Especially not North." Her eldest cousin – Gabe's big brother – was notorious for his overprotectiveness. And she couldn't deal with that right now.

"Sure." Gabe shrugged. "I'm leaving soon anyway. And after the amount of alcohol I've drunk, I'll be lucky to remember anything in the morning."

"Dylan and I are still married."

Gabe stopped suddenly, his eyes wide as he turned around

to look at her. "What?" He shook his head. "How can that be? You got divorced years ago."

"That's what we both thought. But apparently not. I don't have all the details but I don't think he'd lie about this." Gabe looked as upset about it as she was.

"Wow. That's crazy." He tipped his head to the side, considering her words. They'd almost made it to the town square. Even in the dark you could see that the center of it was under construction. In a few days the annual Christmas tree would be up, along with the huge decorations they'd bought for this year. "Hey, does that mean you've been cheating on him?"

"What?" Her mouth dropped open.

"The guys you've dated since. Technically, you've been cheating." Gabe started to laugh, and she hit him on the arm.

"That's a horrible thing to say." But technically, he was right. Her stomach did a little flip flop. "It's not really cheating, is it?" she asked him, suddenly worried.

"Nah. I was kidding, I promise. But don't tell Alex the fireman that you were already married. That guy was already cuckoo about you."

Ugh, the less said about him the better. Just one of her many mistakes in life. "You're right though. It doesn't matter whether I knew it or not, I was actually breaking my vows."

"Nah, you did nothing wrong." Gabe put his arm around her shoulders, pulling her tight against his coat. They'd started walking again, mostly because her feet couldn't bear to be against the cold concrete for too long. "And if it makes you feel any better, Dylan's broken your vows, too. I can guarantee he hasn't been a monk all these years."

"Ugh." She screwed her nose up. She really didn't want to think about that. It made her stomach feel weird.

"So what are you going to do about it?" Gabe asked her, as they turned the corner into her street. It was picture postcard perfect, lined with pretty cottages that all have porches at the front. In summer, their yards were filled with bright flowers. She'd bought this place years ago, though at the time it was her hideaway for when she was living in New York. But now she was here permanently, and she loved it.

"I'm going to see him tomorrow to discuss it," she said as they climbed up the steps to her front door. She turned to look at Gabe. His face was illuminated by her porch light. Damn, he was disgustingly good looking, just like his brothers. And he knew it.

So did half the women in Winterville and the surrounding towns. The less she thought about that, the better.

Gabe patted her shoulder. "It'll be okay. You two will sort it out. Then you can have sex again without worrying about being an adulterer."

"Gabe!"

He laughed at her expression. "Sorry, Ev. You chose the wrong cousin to confide in. I'm never good at giving out advice. Or relationships."

"Join the club." She slid the key into the door. "You coming in for a drink? I could put some coffee on."

"Hell no. I'm not having coffee after midnight with a married woman. What would the town have to say about that?"

3

Dylan was drinking coffee in the small kitchen of the home he'd grown up in. His dad walked in, wearing overalls, with *Cold Start Garage, Winterville* embroidered across the chest pocket. "I'm off to work. You got everything you need here?"

"I'm good. I have coffee." Dylan lifted his half-full mug. He was still a little hung over from last night's wedding. On top of that, he hadn't slept too well. He'd been thinking about Everley's reaction to his revelation. And the fact that she'd be coming over this morning to discuss it.

He wanted to make this as easy as possible on her. God knew, he'd hurt her enough eight years ago. If he could have sorted out their divorce without involving her he probably would have. But his lawyer had already told him it wasn't possible.

"You want one?" Dylan asked, standing to grab another mug from the cupboard.

"Nah, I'll get one from Dolores on the way to work." Dolores ran the Cold Fingers Café at the center of town. She and his dad had always been a little sweet on each other.

His dad pulled something out of a drawer. A pack of cigarettes.

"Are you smoking again?" Dylan swallowed a sigh as his dad stuffed the pack into his pocket.

"Sometimes." His dad looked shifty, like a kid being caught with his hand in the cookie jar.

Dylan put his mug on the table. "You know that's the worst thing you can do, right? For your heart, your lungs, your mouth..."

"I don't have any other vices."

Dylan sighed. "Dad, you make moonshine. You eat way too much processed food. You have all the damn vices it's possible to have."

"Okay then, I don't have company. Is that better? I get lonely, and the cigarettes make me feel... less alone."

Dylan winced. *Touché.* "I'm sorry. I should be around more." He came to see his dad when he could, but between his work in Africa, and his affiliation to a hospital in Atlanta, it was never as often as he would like. Once or twice a year at most. He'd choose those times carefully, too, making sure that Everley wasn't in town, being sure not to bump into her family or friends. It was like walking a tightrope, but it was for the best.

Until now, at least.

"You don't need to be sorry, son. I'm damn proud of what you do. Your job is important, you save lives every day. I'm a grown man, I don't need my son to keep me company."

"You should date."

His dad shook his head. "No."

"Mom left a long time ago." About seventeen years, to be precise.

"I know that." His dad shifted his feet. "I'm not waiting for her to come back."

"You should go on a dating app or something." Dylan

shrugged. "What about Dolores? You two have always been close."

"Dolores is a friend. You don't mess with friends." His dad's voice was resolute. "Now I need to go to work."

"Try to smoke a bit less at least. Okay?"

"I'm not addicted." His dad sighed, pulling the pack out of his pocket and shoving it back into the kitchen drawer. "Happy?" he asked Dylan.

"Kind of."

He shook his head and grabbed the door. "Damn kids thinking they know everything."

"Have a good day."

His dad let out a gruff snort and walked out of the door, leaving Dylan to his coffee. Tonight he'd check if the pack was still in the drawer.

He was almost certain it wouldn't be.

The cold November air wrapped around Everley as she left her cottage and headed into the town square. A team of men from North's Christmas tree farm were working away in there, making the ground ready for the giant fir tree that was on its side on the bed of a huge logging truck. They'd already decorated the rest of the square. Garlands were festooned between candy cane lampposts, and although it was almost eight weeks until Christmas Day, she couldn't help but smile.

The decorations were Holly's doing. She'd updated them all, keeping to their Grandma's aim of making Winterville a place where it was Christmas every day.

The Cold Fingers Café was already open. Usually Everley would stop in on her way to the theater and grab an Americano to go, needing the caffeine injection to face rehearsals. But if she bought herself a coffee, she'd have to buy one for

Dylan, too. And she had no idea if he still liked Americanos as much as she did.

The thought made her feel wistful. There was a time when she knew everything about Dylan Shaw. His hopes, his dreams. The little cluster of freckles on his hip. The dips and rises of his body.

How to make his breath catch in his throat, in that sexy, guttural way.

It felt strange thinking about that now. Of course their split had been painful. And yes, she'd been hurt, and she'd wallowed for a while. But she'd also thrown herself into her career, into friendships, and little by little she'd pushed the memory of him away.

And now he was back and she couldn't ignore him or their past. It was like reopening an old wound and discovering it hadn't healed as well as you'd thought. Sure, the skin had repaired and there was a pretty little scar, but underneath...

It needed some work.

She passed The Cold Start Garage. Usually she'd pop in to say hi to Charlie, but today she was on a mission. Instead she walked on, turning the corner onto the Shaw's block, the small white house appearing in the distance.

Dylan answered as soon as she rapped her knuckles on the door, as though he'd been waiting for her to arrive. His hair was wet, brushed back from his face to reveal a line of paler skin where the sun hadn't tanned him. He was wearing a soft, grey sweater and jeans. He stepped aside for her to pass, and she could smell the lime and cedar tones of his cologne.

"Have you had breakfast?" he asked, as she followed him down the cramped hallway.

"I'm not hungry. But I'd kill for a coffee."

"You still like it black?" He lifted the carafe, pouring out a generous mugful.

"Yeah, I do." She smiled. "Just like my soul."

He laughed and inclined his head to the living room. "Take a seat, I'll bring the drinks through."

She sat on Charlie's old, threadbare sofa, the familiarity of the room overwhelming her. She could be nineteen years old again, tangled with Dylan as they made out like crazy while he was home during a break from med school.

"There you go."

Dylan placed the coffee cup in her hands, his fingertips brushing hers.

"Thank you." She took a sip. It was hot and strong.

"How did you find out we aren't divorced?" she asked, as Dylan sat on the chair opposite, his long, denim clad legs stretching out. He was scrutinizing her over the rim of his coffee cup.

"I was rewriting my will. My lawyer did some digging and discovered the papers had never been filed."

"Are you certain?"

"Yep." He smiled wryly. "We're definitely still married."

"So what do we do?"

"We get divorced again." He shrugged. "Or for the first time, technically."

"Is it that simple?"

Dylan nodded. "According to my lawyer, because you've been a resident in West Virginia for more than a year, we can file here. And we've been living apart for eight years, so we can have a no-fault divorce."

"So we don't have to find a reason?" She sighed with relief.

"Nope." He tipped his head to the side. "Did you think we would?"

"I was worried." She shifted again, pulling her lip between her teeth, remembering Gabe's teasing. "I haven't been faithful to you. Even though we were married, I mean."

Dylan didn't move an inch. He stared at her, his lips slightly parted, taking in her words. "Of course you haven't.

We haven't been together for eight years. I assumed you haven't sworn off all men for good." There was a tic in his jaw. "Neither of us knew we were still married." He looked her straight in the eye. "This is my fault, I should have checked and I didn't. I'm getting it rectified now."

It was typical of him to take control. Once upon a time it might have rankled her, but she had a show to put on and didn't have time to do all the work. This time she'd let him do what he needed to.

"How long will the divorce take?" she asked him.

"I want to get it handled before I leave. My lawyer's writing up the papers and will bring the draft over in a few days for me to approve. After that, he'll send through the official documents. Do you want to check the drafts?"

"Will there be any surprises in there?" Everley asked him.

"No. Not unless you want any of my assets. I assume you don't."

She shook her head. "No, I don't. I assume you won't want any of mine?"

His eyes flickered down her body, then he quickly pulled his gaze back up. "You have assets?"

"I have savings. And I own an interest in the town, plus part of the theater."

"Okay. Well no, I don't want any of them. Though it'll be easier if you list them and send them to my lawyer. Just so he has all the details to file before the court."

"Should I get my own lawyer?"

A smile tugged at his lips. "If you want to. Or we can both use Jeff. I'm not trying to pull the wool over your eyes, Evie. I just want to get this thing over with. The same way you probably do."

He called her Evie. And it made her feel like she was eighteen years old again.

"Okay. I'll probably get somebody to look over the final papers once you have them. Just to make sure."

"Fine by me."

She emptied her coffee cup and put it on the coffee table. It was worn and covered with water rings, but she still used a coaster. "I should go. I have to be at the theater. We have rehearsals."

"Are you performing in the show?" He sounded genuinely interested.

"I'm the director. But yes, I'm performing as well."

His brows lifted, as though he was impressed. "I'd like to come watch."

"Give my name at the box office and they'll comp you some tickets," she said softly.

"I can pay."

A smile flitted over her lips. "I know you can. But since you're my husband, you should get some perks."

He chuckled. "It's weird, right? All these years we thought it was done with, yet here we are, still married."

"And they said we wouldn't last." She raised a brow.

He laughed again. "We proved them wrong, hey?"

"So very much. We should invite them all to our anniversary party. What is it, our ninth this year?"

"It feels like a lot less," he joined in, amused. "The time's flown."

"It really has."

There was a bang from the kitchen. Dylan blinked and turned his head. "It took him less time than I thought," he muttered, the smile melting from his lips.

"Who? What?" Everley blinked.

"Dad left his cigarettes behind this morning. Said he didn't need them. I guess he changed his mind."

"Charlie are you smoking again?" Everley yelled. A red

faced Charlie peeked through the kitchen opening, a smile pulling at his lips when he saw Everley there.

"I'm not addicted. Just a social thing."

Everley lifted a brow. "Those things are gonna kill you."

"Tell me something I don't know." He looked over at his son, then back at Everley, his expression softening. "It's nice to see you here, sweetheart."

"Dylan and I are talking about our divorce."

Dylan's eyes widened, and she realized he hadn't told his dad about their situation.

Charlie's face turned a darker shade. "You're what?"

"Um, we found out we're still technically married," she stuttered, widening her eyes at Dylan in apology. "Just a little paperwork issue. It should be solved very soon."

"Paperwork?" Charlie's voice was thin. He swallowed hard. "I don't know anything about that."

"I didn't say you did." Everley's eyes met Dylan's. She could see in the depths of them that he was thinking the same thing.

Charlie was looking way too shifty.

"Do you know something about this?" Dylan asked Charlie, his voice low.

"Why would I know anything about it?" Charlie stepped back, not meeting their gazes. "It has nothing to do with me."

Dylan stood, his height towering over his dad. "What happened back then?" he asked, his jaw ticking. "You were the one who was supposed to send the papers off. I was traveling to Atlanta, and Everley was heading to New York. You told us you'd take care of it."

"I just..." Charlie shook his head. "I thought you should give it more time. That's all."

Everley put her hand over her mouth to hide her gasp. "Oh my God, Charlie. What did you do?"

The older man glanced at her, his face red. "I kind of

forgot to send the papers off. And I might have told your lawyer at the time that you'd changed your mind."

Everley wanted to feel angry, but Charlie's face was way too funny. She had to bite down a smile because this was so damn stupid. This was so typical Charlie.

"You two were perfect for each other," he grumbled. "Everybody could see it. I thought you just needed time to work things out."

"So you knew we were married all these years and you never told us? Everley's been worried sick that she's been unfaithful to me."

Well, she wouldn't say worried sick. Just slightly perturbed. But whatever.

"You don't have to worry about that, sweetheart." Charlie gave her a weak smile. "He drove you to it."

Now she was laughing. Dear Lord, could this get any worse?

Dylan wasn't though. "Do you realize how crazy this is?" he asked his dad. "What if I'd asked another woman to marry me? I could have been a bigamist. Or Everley could."

"No you couldn't." Charlie shook his head resolutely.

"Yes we could!"

"Nope." Charlie folded his arms across his chest. "Neither one of you would marry somebody else. Because whether you know it or not, you're soul mates. That's why you're both in your thirties and still single. It's not my fault you're too dumb to see it."

Dylan looked appalled. His expression made her want to laugh all over again. His eyes fell on Everley's and she felt her chest jolt.

Damn, he had such expressive eyes. Hazel with green flecks. Her favorite.

"You're an old romantic, Charlie," she said, shaking her head.

"He's definitely something," Dylan muttered.

"I think I'll go and have a smoke," Charlie said, holding up his cigarette pack like a shield. "Leave you two to sort things out."

"The divorce. We're sorting the divorce out." Dylan narrowed his eyes.

"Mmmhmm."

"And I won't be asking you to take the papers to the lawyer this time," Dylan added.

"Okay." Charlie shrugged. "On your own head be it." He turned on his heels and walked toward the back door. "I'll be back around six, if you want to share a pizza for dinner."

The door slammed behind him. Everley bit down her lip, but it was no good, because another wave of laughter over took her. Her chest shook, her eyes watered, and the hand she put over her mouth did nothing to stop the giggles from escaping.

"You think this is funny?" Dylan was leaning against the sofa, a frown pulling at his lips.

"I'm sorry." She wiped her eyes. "It's just so stupid. I can't believe he did that."

"I can't either." Dylan's teeth were gritting together. "I'll be talking to him about it later."

She breathed in, trying to get control of her amusement. "Don't be hard on him. He's a sweet man."

"He's a fool. What did he think he was doing? As though you and I ever had a chance." Dylan shook his head. "We were doomed from the start."

She stood, ignoring the stab of pain in her chest from his words. "I should go. I need to get to work."

"I didn't mean it like that." He reached for her hand as she passed, folding his fingers over her palm, and pulling her toward him, until their bodies were only inches apart. She flushed as their eyes met.

Dylan opened his mouth to say something, but nothing came out. All she could hear was the rush of blood through her ears. His eyes narrowed, darkened, as he stared down at her, the intensity of his expression sending a shiver down her spine.

For a second she thought he was going to kiss her. The truth was, in that moment, she wanted him to. She felt dazed, confused, and so full of need it made her breath catch in her throat.

And from the darkness in his gaze, he wanted it, too.

Pulling her hand from his, she stepped back, breaking whatever stupid spell was between them. "Thank you for the coffee."

He nodded, though his eyes were still narrowed. "You're welcome."

"Do you need anything else from me? Or are we done?"

He ran the tip of his tongue along his bottom lip. "I'll get you those papers over the next couple of days."

She flashed him a smile. "Thank you. I'll see you around."

"I guess you will."

$$\text{❧} \quad 4 \quad \text{❧}$$

"**O**kay, so if you're happy with the draft this should be fairly simple. I'll send you through the final documents, you both will sign then return them to me, and I'll file. In around ninety days you'll be a single man again."

"Ninety days?" Dylan frowned. "Why so long?"

They were sitting in a booth at the Winterville Tavern. His lawyer, Jeff Martin, had suggested he travel to meet with Dylan in Winterville. He'd brought his wife and children, who were currently enjoying a carriage ride through town.

"The wheels of law turn slowly, my friend." Jeff shrugged. "It may come through faster, but I don't want you to get your hopes up."

"Everley's not going to be pleased."

"What's the rush? One of you planning on getting remarried?" Jeff took a sip of his beer.

"No. We just want it finalized. And I was hoping it would be finished before I go back to Africa."

Jeff wrinkled his nose. "It won't be done by Christmas. But it will get done this time. Just don't let your dad handle the paperwork." Dylan had told him about his dad's admission. Jeff's laughter had echoed throughout the tavern.

"I won't." Dylan's voice was grim. The two of them had a loud argument last night, that ended when Charlie had stomped off to his shed, a pack of cigarettes in hand.

Jeff checked his watch. "I need to go," he said, looking around the tavern. "I still can't get over this place. It's only the start of November and it already looks like Christmas threw up in here."

Dylan shrugged. "This is Winterville. We like Christmas."

"I can't believe you grew up here. Is it like this in summer, too?"

"It's a little less in your face. But there are still some decorations and the Christmas all year around shop stays open. And just as many tourists. Plus the lake at the bottom of the mountain is open for watersports and fishing."

Jeff lifted his brows. "Maybe we should come back in the summer."

"If you push the divorce through quickly, I'm pretty sure Everley would offer you a discount," Dylan said, lifting a brow.

His friend laughed. "Is she still here in town?"

"She lives here."

"That must be weird. How was it seeing her again?"

Dylan leaned his head back, remembering that heated moment they had yesterday morning in his dad's living room. It was like time had gone backward.

Why was it that every time they were close he felt the need to touch her?

It wasn't just that she was beautiful – anybody could see that she was. There was something inevitable about the way his body responded whenever she was around. He'd forgotten how strong the pull was. It had never happened with anybody else.

Maybe it was first love syndrome. Or the fact he hadn't gotten laid in a very long time. Whatever it was, he didn't like it. He was a logical man. He preferred to behave rationally, not give in to the beast inside of him.

Jeff was looking at him, his eyebrows raised, and Dylan realized he hadn't answered his question.

"It's fine seeing her around town," he lied. Fact was, he'd been avoiding her since their meeting. Yeah, he was a grown assed man who could control himself, but he didn't like having to do it. Better not to see her at all. Which in this small town pretty much meant staying inside his dad's house.

"I guess you'll both be relieved once the divorce is done, huh?"

"For sure."

Jeff's phone started buzzing. He lifted it to check the message. "Ah, that's my wife, wondering where I am. The carriage rides are done." He wrinkled his nose. "She wants us to have an early dinner before we leave." He finished his beer and looked at Dylan. "I'll get those papers to you this week. Get them back to me as fast as you can and I'll have you divorced in no time. Then we can sort out your will, okay?"

"Okay." Dylan stood and shook his friend's hand. "Thanks for coming, man."

"I have a feeling we'll be back a lot." Jeff raised his brows. "Shame you'll be in Africa. I'd rather be having a beer than riding in a carriage."

They walked out into the town square. It was bustling with visitors, even though the first snow hadn't yet fallen. An ornate white carriage complete with a beautiful horse was rolling down the road, and Jeff waved at his wife at the stop where she and their children had just alighted. "Come over and say hi," Jeff suggested. Dylan followed him and smiled as he was introduced to Jeff's wife, Monique, and their children.

They were talking about their carriage ride when he saw Everley from the corner of his eye.

Walking with another guy.

Everley was holding a cup of coffee in one hand, her head back as she laughed at something the man said. He was tall – not quite as tall as Dylan but not far off. Handsome, too, if you were into movie star looks.

The guy had his arm around Everley's waist. Dylan gritted his teeth, hoping she wouldn't see him.

And then her eyes caught his. The smile froze on her lips as she blinked, thick lashes sweeping down. The man holding her waist looked at her curiously, then over at Dylan, his brows lifting.

"Is that her?" Jeff asked. "Everley?"

Dylan swallowed down the bitter taste in his mouth. "Yeah."

"Looks like she's definitely ready to sign those papers. Should make it easier if she's already moved on." Jeff sounded happy.

The back of Dylan's neck tingled as her gaze locked on his. For a moment, neither of them moved.

Then the guy she was with whispered something in Everley's ear, and she nodded. She glanced at Dylan again, but this time there was no smile. Just her teeth digging into her bottom lip as she lifted her hand to wave at him.

He nodded back, and turned away, giving Jeff and his wife a tight smile. "I should let you go eat some dinner."

"Thank you." Monique gave him a broad smile. "I've already fallen in love with this place."

"Daddy, can we go to the Christmas shop? I want a toy reindeer." His daughter tugged at Jeff's hand. Jeff gave a half-grimace, half-smile and let his daughter lead him away.

"Who was that?" Casey asked, as Everley pulled him in the direction of the theater. He was still looking over his shoulder at Dylan.

"Who?" Everley asked, though she knew exactly who her friend was talking about.

"The hottie with the angry stare." Casey's lips twitched, as he glanced over at Dylan again.

"Stop looking," Everley urged. "And that's Dylan Shaw."

"Dylan Shaw?" Casey's mouth dropped open. "As in…"

"My ex-husband." All right, he wasn't quite her ex. But she hadn't explained it all to Casey, even if he was her best friend at the theater. They'd known each other for years, ever since she'd been in the chorus at her first off-Broadway show. Like her, Casey could sing and dance, and was rarely out of a job, but he'd moved into directing and was loving it.

She was lucky to have persuaded him to come to the Jingle Bell Theater to help her develop their program for the next year. He'd agreed to be her co-director because it sounded fun. And it was, for the most part, except for when one of the dancers pulled a muscle, or one of their singers lost their voice.

But between Everley and Casey, they'd managed to build a great show. They'd based it on the revues her grandma had put on every year for decades, while trying to modernize it for the twenty-first century. From the way rehearsals were going, it was going to work.

"That's the man who broke your heart?" Casey's voice grew louder as he looked over his shoulder again.

Everley grimaced. "Don't shout. And he didn't break my heart. We were never right for each other."

A cold breeze lifted her hair, reminding her that winter was well and truly on its way. They'd had a flurry of snow a few days earlier, nothing that settled, but she knew from experience that by December the wintry weather would arrive with a bang.

She hoped that they wouldn't have any storms like they had last Christmas Eve. She pressed her lips together, remembering how the electricity in the town went out right as she was performing on stage with Gray Hartson, her friend and famous singer.

This year, they had a generator installed in the town that should keep all the houses warm and cozy despite the weather, but it hadn't been tested to its full capacity.

They turned the corner and Everley pushed the stage door open, the familiar musky smell of the backstage wafting around them.

"Why did you two split up anyway?" Casey asked, as they walked down the corridor. Christmas music echoed from the stage, punctuated by shouts from the dance director and the stomp of feet as the dancers practiced.

"I think they call it irreconcilable differences." Everley took a sip of her coffee.

"Did he cheat on you?"

"No!" Dylan would never do that. Not knowingly anyway.

Casey lifted his brows. "Did you cheat on him?"

She tipped her head to the side, glaring at him.

"Okay, okay." He lifted his hands to ward off her stare. "Nobody cheated on anybody. Got it. So what gives? That guy is gorgeous. And by the way he looked at you, it was like you two were still married or something."

Everley choked on her coffee. Alarmed, Casey slapped her back, and she almost dropped the cup.

"Jeez, you okay?"

"I'm fine. Fine. And for what it's worth, we split up because he thought his career was more important than mine. He wanted me to move to Atlanta and manage the home for him. And I couldn't do that." That was the short story. The long story included long, heated arguments about their future, followed by sweet making up.

Until the day they stopped making up.

"He wanted you to give up performing?"

She leaned against the wall, remembering the passionate discussions they'd had. "He thought it was just a hobby for me." And it had hurt. Performing on stage had always been her dream, he knew that.

"Oh. Wow." Casey's eyes widened. "He's a doctor, right?"

"You have an excellent memory. And yeah, he specializes in HIV and AIDS treatment and prevention. Spends most of his time working in Africa. The rest is in Atlanta."

"I guess that's a pretty important job."

She nodded. "It is. And he's passionate about it."

"Was he passionate about you, too?"

She looked down, a smile playing at her lips. "Yeah, he was." Their arguments were explosive, but their making up had been dynamic. Until they both realized they couldn't go on like that. "But we were so young. And we both thought the world revolved around us. And I really thought he knew how much performing meant to me. That he respected my needs as much as I wanted to fulfil his."

Casey's eyes were sad. "I guess irreconcilable differences definitely covers it. You couldn't have a career and stay married."

"Not the way he wanted our marriage to be."

"Do you regret it?"

She tipped her head to the side. "What?"

"Splitting up with him? Do you ever wonder what it would have been like if you'd made a different decision?"

"No. I know we made the right decision. I love my career. I love my life. And the way we were going, we would have ended up breaking each other."

Casey looked wistful. "You two would have made beautiful children."

She shook her head. "Shut up." She didn't tell him that Alaska had already said that to her. What was it about her friends and children anyway?

"I'm telling you, the world would have thanked you for it. Imagine with his gorgeous brooding eyes and your bone structure. You could have had one doctor and one performer."

"I was only twenty-one when we separated. Children were the last thing on my mind."

"How about now? Would you like them now?"

"What is this?" She grinned at him. "Some kind of inquisition? I think I need something stronger than coffee if we're going to delve into my psyche."

"I was only asking, because David and I are talking about starting a family." David was Casey's husband. A playwright, he was the calm to Casey's exuberance. Everley loved them both madly.

"You are? That's wonderful."

"Yeah, but there aren't a lot of people who combine a career and children in this game." Casey shrugged. "Is that why you've never had any?"

"I'm only just thirty. There's plenty of time." Or she hoped there was. Because, yes, one day she'd love to have a family. But not when she was trying to re-establish the Jingle Bell Theater.

"Well, in the meantime we'll definitely want you to be godmother."

Her heart clenched. "That is so sweet." She hugged Casey tightly. "Thank you."

He kissed her forehead. "You're a good person, Everley. You deserve to be happy. And one day you'll find a guy who appreciates you for everything you are."

Their divorce papers arrived by courier two days later. They'd taken a day longer than Jeff had thought – thanks to an emergency court appearance he'd had to make on behalf of one of his clients – but at least they were here now. And the countdown to being truly divorced could begin.

It was only when Dylan went to call Everley that he realized he didn't have her cellphone number. And it wasn't exactly the kind of thing he wanted to push through the door of her little cottage without a word. So he grabbed the envelope and pulled on his coat, stepping out into the cold November air.

His dad's house was only a five minute walk from the Jingle Bell Theater, but he'd studiously avoided it ever since the weekend. There was no reason for him to see Everley, no matter how much he thought about her.

Because he did think about her. He always had.

The failure of their marriage had been his fault. And so had the failure of their divorce. This time he was going to make sure everything went smoothly. It was the least he could do.

"Dylan!"

He looked up to see Dolores standing in the doorway of the Cold Fingers Café.

He smiled. She was such a mainstay of Winterville. He'd grown up with her.

"Come in and let me make you a coffee. It's cold out there today."

He walked over to her, kissing her plump cheek. "Can I take a raincheck? I have somewhere I need to be."

"Of course. The coffee will always be brewing for you." Dolores patted his arm. "I want to hear all about Africa. Your dad tells us what he can, and shows us photos, but he's a man of few words."

"Thank you for taking care of him while I'm away."

"Phht. He won't let anybody take care of him." She leaned in closer. "You know he's still smoking, don't you? Thinks he's so sneaky, hiding in the garage, but we all see the smoke."

Dylan raised an eyebrow. "Yeah, I found his stash."

"He's a foolish old man. Gonna smoke himself to death. Have you talked to him about it?" Dolores looked hopeful.

"I have once. But I'll do it again."

She patted his arm. "You're a good boy." Her eyes alighted on the envelope he was holding. "Oh, are you going to the post office?"

"No, it's something I need to hand deliver." He hadn't told anybody else about the divorce – or lack of it – and he'd made Charlie promise to keep silent, too. He got the impression that Everley didn't want everybody gossiping about her, and he'd like to keep it that way.

"Well, make sure you come back and see me soon." Dolores gave him a wink.

"I will."

The front of the Jingle Bell Theater had a banner displayed across it. Coming Soon – The Christmas Revue.

He pushed on the front door, surprised when it wasn't locked.

There was music coming from the auditorium. As Dylan walked through the doors, he saw a troop of dancers on the stage, their bodies clad in leotards and tights as they followed the directions shouted out from the front row.

After a few minutes of watching the dancing, he felt somebody come to stand next to him.

"It's Dylan, right?"

He turned to see the same guy Everley had been with a few days ago in the street. "Yeah, that's right." It was weird how a shot of jealousy rushed through him. He tried to push it away, disliking how it made him feel.

Except she was the one who called it cheating. He frowned. This was so messed up.

The all-American gave him a cheesy grin. "It's great to meet you. I'm Casey. Do you need help with something?"

"I was just looking for Everley."

"She's in the office making some calls. I can show you the way. I'm heading there myself."

"I know the way."

"Oh. Okay." Casey smiled again.

"I spent a lot of time with Everley in this theater." Dylan had no idea why he said that. Was he staking a claim?

"Oh, that's right." Casey was following him down the hallway, like an overeager puppy on the heels of its master. It was annoying. "You and Everley were married for a while, right?"

"Yeah." It annoyed him that Casey knew that. And it annoyed him even more that he was annoyed. Damn, he needed to give her these papers and get out of here.

"She's a beautiful woman, isn't she?"

His jaw tightened, and Dylan turned to look at Casey. "Yes, my wife is beautiful."

The smile melted from Casey's lips, and it made Dylan feel better.

"You mean your ex-wife, right?"

"I mean what I mean. Excuse me." He ignored Casey's open-mouth stare and rapped on the door, and Everley's warm voice answered.

"Come in."

He pushed the door open and Everley blinked when she saw the two of them standing in the doorway. Casey's shoulder was brushing his.

"I was just showing Dylan to your office," Casey said, smiling at Everley.

"I didn't need you to show me. I knew where it was."

"Whatever." Casey shrugged. "Anyway, I'm heading home. I'll see you later, right, sweetcheeks?"

Everley looked from Dylan to Casey, her expression wary. "Yeah you will."

Dylan's jaw was almost popping. "Can we talk in private please?"

"It's okay, I'm going. I'll leave you two to your discussions." Casey shot Everley an interested glance. "Unless you'd rather I stay?"

There was a hopeful note in his voice.

"It's fine. Thank you anyway." She stood and kissed Casey's cheek before he left.

Dylan closed the door behind him, and walked over to Everley's desk. She was wearing a pair of tight jeans and a cream cashmere sweater that clung to every curve. Her golden hair was down, tumbling around her shoulders.

"I have our divorce papers," he murmured, passing the envelope to her. "I've signed my parts. I thought you might want to show them to your lawyer before you sign yours. If you could get that done quickly, I'd appreciate it. The whole thing is going to take much longer than planned."

Everley blinked. "How long?"

"My lawyer says it might be a while. A few months at least."

Her mouth dropped open. "Why would it take that long? It's clear cut. We've been separated for eight years, after all."

He shrugged. "He says that's just how the law works."

She sat on the edge of her desk, the envelope clutched in her hands. "Months," she whispered.

"I'm sorry if it's going to piss your boyfriend off."

"My boyfriend?" Three tiny lines formed in her brow.

"Mr. All-American clean cut guy." He inclined his head at the door.

"Casey?" She blinked. "Is that who you're talking about?"

"I assume you only have one boyfriend."

She straightened her back, lifting her chin. "Why would I have more than one boyfriend?"

He lifted his hands. "Hey, your love life is your business. Who am I to judge?"

She pushed herself off the desk and walked toward him, her expression furious. "Damn right it's my business." She poked him in the chest. "And this is all your fault. We should have been divorced years ago. So don't come in here and make cheap jabs about my relationships, buddy."

He could almost taste her fury. Warm blood rushed through his veins. Her green eyes were blazing, her lips pressed together in anger, her chest almost pressed against his as she stared up at him.

"Technically, it's completely my business," he said softly, knowing exactly how contrary he was being. "You're still my wife."

"Only on paper."

Yeah, he knew that. He also knew he was being an asshole, but he couldn't help it. The green eyed monster was raging.

"You don't own me," she said through gritted teeth. "Nobody does." Her chest was rising and falling rhythmically.

"I know that." Too damn well.

She ran the tip of her tongue along her bottom lip, and it took every ounce of control he had not to drop his head and kiss her. The anger was melting from her expression, replaced by confusion. She blinked, her thick eyelashes sweeping down, and he knew that she felt this, too.

This aching desire that he'd never felt for anybody else, no matter how much he tried. She brought out every emotion in him, even the ones he tried to ignore. And she brought out the beast, too. The one who wanted to possess her, no matter how much of a modern man he was.

The one who whispered in his ear that Everley Winter was his. And he'd fight anybody else who tried to touch her.

Her breath was ragged, but she still didn't pull her gaze from his. He could see the fiery flint in her eyes, the set of her jaw, and it turned him on even more. What the hell was wrong with him?

He wasn't an animal. He wasn't.

"I need to go," he said, taking a step back. It did nothing to break the electric atmosphere between them.

She nodded, unsmiling. "I'll get these papers back to you as soon as I can."

"I expect you'll be too busy with your boyfriend to look at them tonight."

"Go to hell," she snarled.

His smile was sardonic. "I already went there eight years ago. Shame you couldn't join me."

"Are we talking about our break up, or going to Africa?"

He raised an eyebrow. "Maybe both."

"It was a hell of your own making," she said softly.

"Don't you think I know that?" He had to curl his hand into a fist not to touch her. His fingers ached to feel the silkiness of her hair, the softness of her skin, the warmth of her lips. "Don't you think I pay for it every day?"

"I don't think about you at all."

"Liar," he whispered, dropping his head to breathe her in. She lifted her head at the same time, and her mouth was a breath away from his. "Do you look at your boyfriend like that?" he asked her.

"Like what?"

"Like you want to do dirty things."

"I don't want to do dirty things with you. I want to kill you."

He laughed. "Sure you do."

"Do you know how aggravating you are?" She shook her head. "No wonder we got divorced."

"We didn't. Remember?" He trailed a finger over her cheek. She didn't pull away, and it made his blood heat up. "You're still my wife."

"You keep saying that."

"Because it's true."

"I think you like it," she whispered.

A half smile pulled at his lips. "Do you?"

"Yeah. You like driving me crazy."

He pressed his lips to her ear. "I always knew the exact way to drive you crazy. Remember our wedding night in Vegas?"

She swallowed hard. "I vaguely recall it."

"Do you remember we were so loud somebody called security?"

Her lips twitched. "I remember you tripping over your shorts as you tried to run to the door and get dressed at the same time."

He couldn't help it. He laughed, because that memory was so fresh in his mind. He'd banged his head against the door, and almost blacked out. The security guard had to force his way in, only to find him laying on the floor half-naked, with Evie wrapped in nothing but a sheet, asking him who the President of the United States was.

This was stupid. He shouldn't feel jealous. He should feel pleased she'd moved on. And the truth was, he was so proud of her for making the life she'd always wanted.

"Sorry." He gave her the softest of smiles. "I don't know why we always end up arguing."

"Maybe it's our brains' way of reminding us why we broke up."

He exhaled heavily. "Something like that." His gaze met hers. "Thank you for being so understanding about this. I appreciate it."

"It's not your fault your dad thinks he's hosting a real life version of *The Dating Game*."

He chuckled. "He knows the show has been canceled now."

"He meant well. I like Charlie."

"Yeah, well he likes you, too." Warmth flashed in his eyes. "A little too much."

"As long as he doesn't get his hands on these papers, we'll be good." She was smiling now, and damn if it wasn't glorious. "Thank you for getting this taken care of. I appreciate it."

"It was my fault it wasn't done in the first place."

"It was both of our faults."

"Yeah, but I was the older one. I knew better than to leave it to my dad." He tapped his fingers on the wall next to him. "I'm going to be around town a few more weeks. We're bound to bump into each other again. I know it sounds weird, but I'd really like it if we were friends."

Her eyes met his. "I'd like that, too."

"Okay then." Friends it was. And that was a good thing. Maybe if his body got the memo, he could stop thinking about how her mouth tasted, and remembering how luscious her curves were when he used to run his hands down her body.

"I need to go check on rehearsals," she said, reaching for the door. "Shall I walk you out?"

"Sure." He glanced at the brown envelope on her desk, then pulled his eyes away. "Let's go."

"You can stop laughing now," Everley protested, as Casey shook his head, his face red with amusement. His husband, David, was pouring three glasses of wine, his hand shaking as he listened to Everley recounting her interaction with Dylan.

"I can't believe he thinks you two are an item," David said, biting down a grin. "Surely he knows you have better taste in men than that."

"Hey, I resent that." Casey pouted. "And anyway, I'm more interested in the fact that you're still married to the guy. How the heck did *that* happen?"

"I'm still annoyed that he told you. How many other people in town has he told?" Everley sighed.

"He told me because he was trying to be the gorilla with the big chest."

"From the way you described him, he *is* the gorilla with the big chest," David pointed out. "I need to meet this guy."

"Is it really going to take months to get divorced?" Casey asked, ignoring his husband.

"Yeah. After he left and I watched the dance, I Googled

it. Even worse, three months is a minimum, the courts are really backed up right now."

"It doesn't really matter, does it?" David asked, passing her a glass of wine. "It's not going to change your life. Unless you and Casey really decide to get married."

"Sorry, honey. I'm taken." Casey winked at her. "No matter what your gorgeous husband thinks about us."

David grinned at Everley. "You could have fun driving your husband mad."

"Can we stop calling him my husband?" Everley asked. "His name is Dylan. And I'm not planning on having *any* fun with him."

"I guess double dating is out then."

"Dating is out full stop. Until I get divorced."

Casey blinked. "What do you mean?"

"I mean, I won't be dating anybody until I'm officially divorced. Until then, I guess I'll stay celibate. It's only a few months."

"That's stupid," David said. "Plenty of people date while they're waiting for their divorce to be finalized."

"Not this person. I want that paper in my hand first."

David and Casey shared a look. "No sex for three months?"

"That's harsh," David agreed. "Do you think you can do it?"

"Of course I can. I've gone for longer." Everley shook her head. And then the memory of Dylan's hot stare washed over her. The way he whispered in her ear, his warm breath sending shivers down her spine. She'd wanted him then, the same way she'd wanted him when they were younger. Her breasts had felt full and tingly, and her thigh muscles pulled tight. And if he'd kissed her?

She would have dragged him to her desk.

"I don't think I could do it," Casey said.

"It's a good thing you don't have to." David kissed his jaw.

"Can you guys stop the PDA?" Everley shifted in her seat. Her body felt all tingly. Like there was an itch deep inside of her that couldn't be scratched.

"Oh my God, you want to sleep with your husband." Casey grinned, shooting a look at David.

"I do not." Everley shook her head. "It's just that denial thing. I always want what I can't have."

"Which is hot, dirty sex with Dylan." David smiled smugly.

Everley swallowed a mouthful of wine. "I don't want to have sex with him. I'm just feeling... I don't know... a little weird."

"I wish I could help." Casey blew her a kiss. "But it'd be like a fish trying to ride a bike."

She laughed, because it was all stupid. Of course she didn't really want to have sex with Dylan. Not even if every muscle in her body clenched whenever he was near. And she'd never been the type to get over a guy by getting under somebody else.

She'd just have to wait it out. Get officially divorced and forget about Dylan all over again. Then maybe she could date, and sate this ache she had.

She took a big mouthful of wine, swallowing it quickly.

"That's a woman who really needs to get laid," Casey whispered to David.

"I know."

"Can we talk about something else? Tell me about the adoption process." That was why she was here, after all. To celebrate their plans, and learn all about the process, and be one of the supporters they'd need to write a statement about why they'd make perfect parents.

"Sure, let's talk about babies," David said. "They have *nothing* to do with sex at all."

Dylan checked himself in the hallway mirror. His tie was perfectly knotted, his suit jacket unbuttoned but still flawlessly cut to fit his broad, muscled body. And he felt good, too.

Now he just had to get this donation for the medical center they were planning to build and everything would be fine.

He was the lead doctor on the application to the Carson Foundation, a family-run charitable organization that donated to projects overseas. The Carson family lived in West Virginia, and since he'd be in the state, he'd been selected to meet with them to discuss the project.

His dad looked up from his phone as Dylan walked into the kitchen. He gave a low whistle. "Looking good."

"Thanks." Dylan gave him a tight smile. "I should be back by this evening."

"Drive carefully. It's cold out there."

"If I break down I know who to call."

His dad was right, it *was* cold outside. Dylan unlocked his car right as he heard his name being called.

Everley was crossing the street, holding her coat closed around her sweet body, an envelope clutched in her hands. "I've signed everything I needed," she told him, holding the envelope out. "I thought you'd want it back as soon as possible."

"Did you get legal advice that quickly?"

She shook her head. "I read through it and everything's fine. There's nothing in there I'm worried about."

He took the envelope and looked at her. Her cheeks were pink from the icy air, her hair pulled back into a messy bun. A few tendrils had escaped and were curling around her cheeks.

"I'm sorry about yesterday." He lifted a brow. "I shouldn't have said anything about the divorce to your boyfriend."

Everley blinked, as though surprised at his change in attitude. "It's okay," she said softly. "I think we both said things we didn't mean to. Maybe it's the pressure of divorce." Her smile told him she was making a joke.

"Can you apologize to Casey for me, too? I was an ass."

She blew out a mouthful of air. "Yeah, about that..." She looked away, her lips twisting. "Casey isn't my boyfriend."

"He's not?" Dylan frowned.

She shook her head. "No, we're just friends."

He tried to take her admission in. He'd been so sure Casey and Everley had something going on. "Are you sure he feels that way? He seems into you."

"I'm certain. And so is his husband."

Dylan ran his finger along his jaw. "In that case, please apologize to him for me being such a dick."

"He thinks it's funny. And so does David. That's his husband."

She looked at him carefully, as though she was only now noticing his clothes. "You look fancy. Are you going somewhere special?"

"I have a meeting with the Carson Foundation. They're hopefully going to be giving us a big donation for a new medical center. We're meeting to discuss the project."

"Oh wow." Her smile was genuine. "I hope it goes well."

"Me, too."

"If you're around this evening, you should come to the Tavern. It's Gabe's last night in town so we're all meeting up for a drink."

"I'd like that." He smiled softly at her.

She relaxed, as though she'd been holding her breath. "That's great. We'll be there at seven, but come when you can. Casey and David will be there, too."

"That'll give me a chance to apologize in person."

"If you want to. But you don't have to grovel. As I said, they're chill. You'll like them."

"I'm sure I will." He checked his watch. "I have to go." Weird how he didn't want to. If he didn't have this meeting, he'd have suggested taking her for a celebratory coffee.

Though it felt weird to celebrate a divorce. Or at least, the start of one.

"I'll see you tonight then." She flashed him a smile.

"Yeah. See you tonight."

❧   7   ❧

Warren Carson, the head of the Carson Foundation, lived in a sprawling mansion a two hour drive from Winterville. Dylan pressed the intercom outside the impressive cast iron gates and gave his name, putting his foot on the accelerator as the electronic motor slowly pulled them open.

It took another minute to make his way up the driveway, through a wooded glade, before he arrived at the house itself. In front of the gray stone steps was an elegant fountain, water cascading into the surrounding pool from a mermaid, rising up from the surface. Dylan climbed out of his car and made his way to the front door, pressing the bell with a confident hand.

The butler answered, nodding when Dylan gave his name.

"Mr. and Mrs. Carson are in the day room. Please follow me."

Dylan had read up on the Carsons. They were from old money, but they'd increased it ten times over thanks to some clever investments in technology firms. They'd created the Carson Foundation as a way of giving back, and hand picked humanitarian causes to donate to.

As soon as he walked into the day room – which was bigger than the entire floor space of his dad's house – Warren Carson stood and smiled, walking over to shake Dylan's hand.

Like his wife, he was in his early sixties, but he looked much younger. His hair was still brown, and his body full of vigor, though the laugh lines around his eyes softened his face.

"It's good to meet you in person," Warren said, releasing his grip. "This is my wife, Grace."

"It's a pleasure to meet you," Dylan said, shaking her hand, too.

"You look so young," Grace said, smiling widely at him. "Are you really a doctor?"

"Of course he is. You read his resume." Warren shook his head.

Grace laughed. "Well, you know what they say about policemen and doctors. They get younger every year."

"Or *we* get older," Warren said pointedly.

"Would you like a drink?" Grace asked Dylan. "We have coffee or tea?"

"Coffee would be great. Thank you."

She rang the bell for the butler, quietly asking him to bring some coffee through.

"Please take a seat." Grace said to Dylan, gesturing at the cream sofas overlooking a huge picture window. Dylan sat down, glancing at their perfectly manicured lawn, stretching out as far as he could see.

"How long are you in the country?" Warren asked him.

"Until Christmas. I'm spending a little time with my father." Dylan stretched his legs out. His muscles felt cramped from the drive.

"That's lovely." Grace smiled warmly. "And is your wife with you?"

"My wife?" A wave of panic washed over him.

"You're married, right? That's what the application said." Grace smiled at him.

Damn, he hadn't wanted to lie when he'd completed the application, but he'd never imagined they'd notice his marital status. He swallowed hard, and forced a smile onto his face.

"Um, yeah, Evie.. I mean my wife...is back in Winterville. She spends most of her time there."

"That must be difficult, being separated from her," Grace said, her voice full of sympathy.

"She likes to be with her family. Her grandmother built the town." The pulse in his neck started to throb.

"Her grandmother was Candy Winter?" Grace asked, tipping her head to the side. The butler silently walked in and slid a tray onto the coffee table. Grace nodded at him, and he passed out the cups.

"Yes." Dylan nodded, trying to decide how to tell them they were getting a divorce without looking like an asshole. "She runs the theater her grandmother built."

"We've been there," Grace said, looking delighted at his confession. "A few years ago. Candy was kind enough to let us go backstage and spend some time with her. She was such a wonderful woman. What's your wife's name?"

"Everley."

"That's a pretty name. I'd love to meet her. We are such fans of the arts." Grace took a sip of her coffee. "Do you think we could arrange that? If she's anything like her grandmother, I'm sure I'd adore her."

"Ah, she's pretty busy at the moment. She's directing the rehearsals for their Christmas show. It opens in December." He shifted in his seat.

"Maybe we could come to visit." Her face lit up at the thought. "Winterville is such a beautiful town." She looked at her husband. "What do you think? We had fun last time we were there."

Warren put his hand on his wife's. "Maybe we should talk about Dylan's project first. That's why he's here, after all."

"Oh, of course. I'm sorry." She looked at Dylan. "I get a little caught up on an idea sometimes. Let's arrange a visit later."

"It's fine." Dylan cleared his throat.

"Tell us about your work in Africa," Warren said, his expression warm. "What's the situation like there right now?"

"We're working with a lot of refugees right now. Around forty thousand came into Sudan as a result of conflict in the Tigray region."

"What kind of issues are they facing?" Grace asked, leaning forward. Her face was full of sympathy.

"Most people arrived with nothing, other than the clothes on their backs. There were issues with their digestive health, exhaustion, and of course the usual medical issues you encounter in an overpopulated refugee camp. Sanitation issues, tropical diseases, childhood illnesses."

"And you specialize in HIV and AIDS treatment and prevention?"

Dylan nodded. "That's the area I concentrate on, but when there's a huge influx of people we do whatever we need in order to make people better. We're all multitaskers." And they lost a lot of patients, too. Every single one was like a stab to the chest.

"How do you think the money from the foundation will help?"

"You'll see from the application that we'd like to rebuild the medical center. What we have is extremely basic, and it won't last long term. As with all of our projects, our aim is to improve things by training local staff, and when they're ready we leave them in a stable situation. We have the staff, but they need a permanent base."

"I watched the videos you sent us," Grace said quietly. "Some of your patients are very young."

Dylan nodded. "It's a volatile situation. But there's some improvement. Your money would help a lot of people if you're willing to give it."

"Mr. Carson?" The butler's quiet voice cut through the discussion. "Lunch is ready if you'd like to come through."

Warren raised his brows at Dylan. "Let's continue this discussion in the dining room."

Dylan nodded. "Sounds good to me."

The Winterville Tavern was already busy when Everley walked through the door. She could see her sister and cousins standing at the bar, laughing with Kelly, the bartender, and the tables were full of their friends. Somebody had put money in the jukebox, and The Foo Fighters were blasting out.

"Over here!" Casey shouted. He and David were in a booth along with three of the theater dancers. She walked over to hug them all.

"Can I get you a drink?" David asked.

"It's fine. I'll go grab one from the bar in a minute." Everley flashed him a smile. She looked around the crowded tables. There was no sign of Dylan. "Can I get you guys anything?" she asked.

"We're good." Casey bit down a grin. "Are you looking for somebody?"

"No. Just wondering who's here."

"Sure." He winked. "And he's not here. I already looked in every booth."

"I have no idea who you're talking about." Everley shook her head, amused. "I'm going to the bar now."

Gabe had already ordered her a drink by the time she arrived at the bar. She kissed her sister's cheek, then hugged North before ruffling Gabe's hair. "I can't believe you're leaving tomorrow," she said, her lips curling down.

"I'll be back for Christmas," he reminded her. "It's not that long."

"But who will I call when I wake up early in the morning?"

"Holly will be back in a few weeks. I'm pretty sure she'll deal with your freak outs better than I do anyway." Gabe gave her a grin. "Anyway, you can still call me. I just don't promise to answer."

"My voicemails can be vicious," she warned him.

He winked. "I bet they can."

Everley looked around the bar again. "Um, I invited Dylan tonight. I hope that's okay."

"Yeah, I know." Gabe gave her an interested look. "He called me half an hour ago. Said he was running late. Should be here in the next half hour or so."

"Oh. Okay." Her heart did a little flip against her ribcage. "I guess I'll mingle then. Did he say if his meeting went okay?"

"What meeting?"

"He had a meeting with some potential donors."

"I have no idea. I just got a message from him." Somebody called Gabe's name, and he turned his head to talk to them. Everley pulled her lip between her teeth, wondering if Dylan was okay.

The jukebox clicked and the Goo Goo Dolls came on, singing about Iris. Everley lifted her bottle to her lips, looking around at the crowd of people. She knew almost everybody here, and it made her heart feel warm. North was talking to one of his workers from the Christmas Tree farm, and Alaska had slid into the booth with Casey and David, laughing with them about something.

Gabe had invited the cast and staff from the theater, too. She knew a few of the dancers were interested in him, but thank goodness he hadn't gone there.

She valued her cast way too much for that.

Her eyes slid to the door as it opened, a shaft of light hitting the spit and sawdust floor. Dylan was standing there, his tie loosened and the top button of his shirt undone. The moonlight illuminated his broad form and her stomach did a little flip.

His eyes immediately fell on hers, and a smile pulled at the corner of his lips. He made a beeline to where she was standing, leaning his arm on the bar as he tipped his head to kiss her cheek.

"Hey."

"Hi." Her skin heated at his touch. "Gabe said you'd be a little late."

"I came straight from my meeting. There was a crash on the highway, caused a backup."

Her eyes widened. "Are you okay?"

"I'm fine."

He looked tired, though. She could see that now that he was closer up. "It was a long day, huh?"

He lifted a brow. "Something like that." The bartender walked over and he ordered a whiskey.

"Oh my. A really hard day, I'm guessing." Everley grimaced. Dylan rarely drank anything stronger than beer. "Did you get the donation you need?"

He shifted his feet and picked up his tumbler of amber liquid. "I'm not sure. I think I might have messed things up."

She blinked. "Why? Surely they can see you're a great cause."

He lifted the glass to his lips, his neck undulating as he

swallowed a mouthful of whiskey. His eyes closed momentarily, then they opened again, his gaze catching hers.

"I made a mistake on the form."

"What kind of mistake?"

There were worry lines forming on his brow. She itched to smooth them away.

"I said we were married."

Her mouth dropped open. "What?" She wasn't sure what else to say.

He ran his fingers across his jaw. "Yeah. There was a space for marital status. I put that I was married. I assumed it was a formality, but they kept asking me about you."

She leaned forward. "What did you say?"

He glanced down at her lips. "I said that you lived here and we spent time together when we could."

"You did?"

"Uhuh." He nodded. "And then they asked if they could come visit."

She grimaced. "How did they take it when you told them we were getting a divorce?" She could imagine how excruciating it was.

"They didn't." He took another mouthful of whiskey. "Because I didn't tell them. I'm going to have to call them tomorrow and come clean about the whole thing."

"Do you think it'll be okay?" she asked him.

"I have no idea. It's not the best start, admitting I'm a liar. I should have told them at the time, but I froze. I wasn't ready with an answer that seemed acceptable." He put his empty glass on the bar, nodding when the barman lifted the bottle. "If we don't get this donation, it's my fault."

"Then why don't we just pretend we're still together?" she suggested. "I am still your wife, after all. You wouldn't be telling lies."

His eyes were wary as he glanced at her. "I couldn't ask you to do that. This is my problem and I need to solve it."

She tipped her head to the side. "You want the funding, don't you?"

"Yes."

"And if I join you for a few hours you'll get it?"

"Possibly. But all they have to do is talk to the people in town and they'll know the truth."

He was right. She put her finger on her bottom lip, thinking. "Then we don't leave them alone for a second. We'll invite them to lunch at my place, then take them on a tour of the town. We could even take them to the theater. Then we'll wave them goodbye and everything will be fine."

His brows knitted. "Why would you do that for me?"

Because I loved you once. So much. "Because we're friends," she said brightly. "Aren't we?"

"Yeah. We're friends." His voice was soft, full of an emotion she couldn't quite pinpoint.

"And I'm an actress. So you don't have to worry about them not believing us."

"That's not what I'm worried about."

"What *are* you worried about?"

"I don't know." He ran his thumb across his jaw. "It just feels strange. I'd only just found out we were still married when I'd completed that application. Next week we'll make believe we made it to happily ever after."

Everley blinked. "Well it's a good thing we're both good at pretending."

"You think I'm good at pretending?"

"Your face is always hard to read. That'll help."

"Are you sure this could work?" he asked, his voice skeptical.

"I'm certain." She nodded. "We've got this, Dylan."

A hint of a smile pulled at his lips. "I'll owe you big time."

She grinned back at him. "In that case, I want to keep the house and the children *and* the dog."

He laughed. "It's a deal." He reached out, cupping her jaw with his warm palm. "Thank you. I really appreciate it."

She winked. "I'm your wife. It's what I do."

❧ 8 ❧

She'd never been the best sleeper, but this was getting stupid. She'd drifted in and out of fitful dreams all night. Dreams that featured Dylan Shaw's piercing hazel eyes, narrowed with desire as he looked at her. In her latest one he was bare from the waist up, his chest glistening with sweat as he hovered over her body, his tongue slowly moistening his bottom lip.

"You're my wife," he was saying, his voice thick and graveled. "Mine. This time you won't forget it."

His fingers were strong and talented as he stroked her inexplicably bare legs. His gaze held her eyes for a moment longer before he dipped his head and scraped his stubbled jaw along her tender thighs, his warm breath hitting her *right there*, making her gasp with delight.

She tried to buck her hips, but his strong hold stopped her, keeping her exactly where he wanted her as he slowly kissed the part of her that needed him the most. Dylan had always loved teasing her, coaxing her to the peak of pleasure and keeping her there until she thought she was going mad.

He liked being in control, liked watching her shatter into tiny pieces in response to his touch.

Liked giving her pleasure as much as he enjoyed receiving it.

She'd never had a better lover. Nobody had even come close. She'd forgotten how much he could heat her blood with one stare, how he could steal her breath with one brush of his fingertips.

When she woke, she was covered with a sheen of perspiration. She was breathless, and not just because she'd been hovering at the edge of desperate pleasure for long, long minutes, but because she was remembering how desperately in love with him she was back then.

Exhaling heavily, she squeezed her eyes shut, but the aching need didn't abate. It only reminded her how alone she was.

She ached for a masculine, heavy touch. Warm hands, calloused fingertips. Someone to whisper sweet nothings and tell her how much she meant to him. A man with strong, hot lips that knew exactly how to kiss her into oblivion.

She wanted her husband. And she couldn't have him.

A cold shower and a strong Americano later, the memory of the dream still clung to her as she walked to the theater. They were in final rehearsals now, as the show was set to open in three weeks, and there was a sense of nervous expectation in the auditorium when she stepped inside.

"We've been waiting for you. We need to run through the final dance. Can you go and get your costume on?" Casey hugged her, a grin on his face.

She finished her coffee, because god knew she needed it. "Sure."

"You okay?" Casey frowned, as he stepped back and took her in.

"I'm fine. Why?"

"Because you seem more manic than usual." He shrugged. "And you just swallowed half an Americano in one go."

"I didn't sleep well last night. I need the caffeine."

His face wrinkled in sympathy. "Nerves for the big visit?" She'd told him about her agreement with Dylan. He thought it was hilarious.

"Shut up about that."

"I can't. I keep picturing you and Dylan having to kiss each other and I want to make it into a stage show."

She shook her head. "I'm glad my life is providing you with entertainment."

Casey grinned. "It really does. Don't ever stop."

He helped her into the red sparkly costume, lined with white fur. It had been her Grandma's. Candy Winter had always worn it for her lead role during her annual Christmas revue here at the theater, until she'd become too old to perform anything more than the final song. It felt like a homage to wear the outfit.

"Can I ask you a question?" Casey asked, pulling at the hem.

"I have a feeling you're going to anyway."

He looked up at her, amusement pulling at his lips. "Can you honestly say you feel nothing for him?"

An image of her dream flashed into her mind. "Nothing at all. We're just friends."

"So why did you just blush?"

"I'm not blushing."

"Sure you are." Casey zipped up her costume and passed her the shoes. "You like him. And who can blame you? He's hot."

She twisted her hair and pinned it into a simple bun. They'd have hair and makeup artists for the shows, but they couldn't afford them for every rehearsal. "Finding somebody attractive doesn't make for a good relationship." She of all people should know.

Casey smiled smugly. "So you do find him hot."

"Does it matter?" She sighed. "I could think he was the hottest guy on Earth and it still wouldn't change anything. We're completely unsuitable for each other. We always were. If he saw me in this outfit he'd probably roll his eyes and lecture me that the cost of the fabric would pay for a month of vaccinations in Africa. He thinks I'm frivolous and that what I do doesn't make a difference."

And if her dreams could get that message, she'd be very grateful.

"He doesn't know what he's talking about. We make a difference. We bring joy. We make people forget their troubles for a few hours and they leave the theater smiling. Don't let anybody tell you we're not important, because we are."

She nodded, emotion making her throat feel tight. "I know."

Casey slid his hand through hers, squeezing her palm. Placing his other hand on her shoulder, he turned her until they were both facing the oversized mirror on the dressing room wall.

"Sure, you're beautiful on the outside," Casey whispered, not letting go of her. "But more importantly, you shine from the inside out. You have talent, Everley. You make people smile. You make this world a better place by being in it. So don't let anybody – not even him – dull your shine. We need you."

His gaze caught her reflection, and she smiled at him. "Thank you," she whispered.

"Now, let's go do this final number," he said. "Put all this angst into your performance. Dance like he's watching and you've got something to prove. You're gonna knock it out of the park."

It was later that afternoon and she still hadn't shrugged off the memory of her dream. They'd practiced again and again, until she was exhausted from singing and dancing and being thrown into the air, but she could still feel a wistfulness deep inside her.

After the dancers left, she'd told Casey she'd close up the theater for the evening, and he'd happily headed home for dinner with David, while she slowly removed her costume and carefully hung it on the rack. She wore a black leotard beneath it, the tight fabric skimming over her every curve.

She'd lost a little weight since they'd started rehearsals. It was natural – her job was extremely athletic and nerves always dulled her appetite. She'd have to watch it, though, because she needed to keep her energy up. Maybe she'd cook a huge pot of pasta that evening, and portion it out so she'd have enough for the week.

It would be boring, but then meals for one weren't exactly fun. That's why she spent so much time with Alaska and Holly, or with North and his brothers – whenever they were home – eating steaks cooked on the grill.

But this time of year was busy for them all. Alaska was short staffed at the Winterville Inn and was covering the front desk, and North was preparing the Christmas Tree Farm for the festive rush that would start in a week or two. Her other guy cousin, Kris, was working in London, Gabe had left for training, and Holly and Josh would be on their extended honeymoon for a few more weeks.

And she really didn't want to go home and sit there alone.

Instead, she walked back to the wings, and flicked through the audio tracks, cueing up the final song for her to practice once more. There were a few steps she hadn't been happy with during rehearsal, and although her muscles ached like hell, she wanted to get them right.

The music came on, the notes filling the auditorium, and she took her place at the center of the stage. She let the sound fill her, become part of her, as her blood pumped to the beat of the drums, her muscles contracting sensuously as she began to dance.

She couldn't remember the last time she'd felt this sensual. And it translated into her dance, her body connecting with the slow beat as she moved across the floor. By the time the music came to an end she was breathless, her heart pounding against her ribcage in an attempt to get oxygen to her muscles. But it hadn't stopped the intense need pulsing inside her, or the memory of that dream.

Slowly, she caught her breath, opening her eyes to look out at the gloom of the auditorium. And that's when she saw them. Hazel eyes, speckled with green. A jawline darkened by a day's growth of beard.

The man she hadn't been able to stop fantasizing about all day.

He'd been watching her dance for the last five minutes. The way she moved her body was entrancing.

He'd forgotten how talented she was. Or maybe he'd pushed it out of his mind in an attempt to protect himself. Because when he was a little more than a kid he'd been an idiot and asked her to choose between him and her career.

Seeing her now, she'd made the right decision. She was captivating in every way. He'd spent years studying the human body, learning the physiology of muscles and bones. But she was living it. Pushing her body until she was breathless, moving sinuously as she tested her limits, arching her back until her hair almost brushed the floor.

Once upon a time, she'd tested her limits with him. And he'd pushed her until she broke the barrier of being a good girl and ladylike. They'd lay sweaty and exhausted, skin touching skin, not knowing where he ended and she began.

Everley was a body in constant motion. A ball of energy that rivalled the brightest of stars. And for a brief time she'd been his.

But now she was *hers*. And she was glorious.

The music faded and she stopped dancing, closing her eyes as her chest rapidly rose and fell, her plump lips parted as she panted for breath.

He couldn't move if he tried.

Slowly, her lids lifted and she blinked out into the gloom, her eyes adjusting until she saw him watching her. He was standing on the steps leading to the stage, wearing jeans and a sweater, his coat thrown on a chair he'd passed.

"Hi." Her lips softly curled, as though she was pleased to see him. He liked that way too much.

"I tried calling you, but you didn't pick up."

"My phone's in the office. We've been rehearsing all day." She rolled her neck, to loosen a knot. "Is everything okay?"

"I spoke to Warren Carson earlier. He and Grace are free to visit on Tuesday." His eyes flickered to hers. "Are you sure you want to do this?"

She pulled on her hair tie before retwisting it into a bun. "Of course. I said I would."

He exhaled. "Okay. I guess we need to make some plans. I suggested that we have lunch at your place." He frowned. "Or our place. At least, that's what I told them."

"You don't have to look so down about it. My place is nice. Small, but pretty." She circled her shoulders, then bent to the left. "Ow."

"You okay?" he asked her, frowning.

"There's a knot in my back. I need to take a hot shower."

"Let me take a look." He closed the distance between them. Up close, she smelled sweet, of some shower gel, mixed with clean perspiration. "Bend over," he murmured, his hands gentle as he touched her hips. She did as he instructed. Her leotard was clinging to her body, leaving little to the imagination. He took a deep breath to push away the desire.

"Tell me where it hurts." Slowly, he moved his fingers up her sides, his thumbs pressing into her skin.

"Just there." Her breath caught as he brushed right beneath her shoulder blade. A thick lock of blonde hair escaped from her bun, and he twirled it around his fingers, tucking it back into the elastic.

Her neck was exposed, shining with perspiration. He slid his finger down her skin, and he heard her breath catch. Following the line of her spine, he traced down to where she'd gasped, pushing his thumb into the knotted muscle to loosen it.

Her breath came faster, and she braced her hands against her thighs to steady herself. "Oh my, that's good," she said, and her breathy voice sent blood rushing to his thighs.

"'It's your rhomboid muscle," he murmured, feeling the tightness in her back release. "You should ice and stretch it tonight."

"I blame the dance director. She keeps making me do these crazy moves."

He slid his hands down, until his palms were cupping her hips. "Roll your shoulders," he instructed.

She lifted her shoulders back, and sighed softly. "That's better."

He was still holding her, her back pressed against his front. Everley seemed in no rush to pull away from his touch. Which was good, because he wasn't in a rush either. She felt too good pressed against him. He glanced down at her long, smooth neck and wondered what she'd do if he pressed his mouth against her skin.

As though she could read his mind, she lifted her head, turning it until she could look up at him, her head resting against his chest. "I had a dream about you last night," she said, her voice a whisper.

"You did?"

"Yeah." There was the strangest look on her face.

"What was I doing?"

She blushed, pulling her gaze from his.

A smile tugged at his lips. "What?" he demanded.

She squeezed her eyes shut, and at that moment he *knew*. It hadn't been any old dream, it had been *that* kind of dream.

"What was I doing to you?" He was hard as steel. He could feel the softness of her behind pressed against his thighs. He wondered if she could feel him, too.

"Touching me," she breathed.

He had to dig his fingers into her hips to stop himself from moving them over her stomach and pulling her closer. "How was I touching you?"

"Like you used to. When we were together." She exhaled raggedly. "This is all your fault. Now I'm all messed up and I can't do anything about it."

"What do you mean, do something about it?"

"I can't see anyone else while I'm married to you."

"We're getting divorced. You can see whoever you'd like."

"Not until I get the papers. I can't date until then."

"Who says?" Why was he asking her that? It was like playing with a scab. Painful, yet addictive.

"I do." She still hadn't moved from his tight grasp. He wasn't sure his fingers would release her even if he wanted to.

He dipped his head to breathe her in, his lips a breath away from her neck. "This is the twenty-first century, Everley." He circled his fingers against her hips. She undulated her body in response. "You can do what you want."

"I'm not a cheater."

"We talked about this," he murmured. "It's not cheating if we're separated." He pressed his palms against her stomach, fingers splayed. She leaned back against him, her head still tipped against his shoulder. He could see the soft swell of her breasts, the valley between them, and it took an act of will not to move his palms up her body.

He could take her ache away. He remembered all the ways he could make her gasp, cry out, scream.

Every time she called out his name it would burn him. Make him hers. He'd get lost in her.

She tipped her head back further, her eyes meeting his. There was a clarity to her stare that he understood all too well.

She knew that he could make her feel better. And then they'd both be lost. Because physical attraction hadn't been enough when they were kids. And now? It still wasn't enough. Because if he buried himself inside her just once, he wasn't sure he could let her go again.

He moved her in his arms, turning her and cupping her face with his palms. Brushing his lips against her heated brow, he dropped his head against her hair. "I'm sorry," he murmured.

And he was. Not just because she was burning for the kind of human touch he should have been the one to give her. But because he'd let her down when they were kids and he was letting her down now.

He thought he'd stopped hurting her years ago. And it was killing him to see her ache again.

"It's not your fault."

"Yeah, it is."

A half smile formed on her lips. "Okay, it's completely

your fault." She stepped back, as though the intensity of his touch was too much for her. "I should go. It's getting late."

"Let me walk you home."

She shook her head, as though that was the last thing she wanted. It felt like a jab to his chest. "I'm heading to the Inn to see Alaska. She might have time for dinner."

"I'll call Warren and Grace tonight, confirm their visit."

She nodded. "I'll make sure everything in the house is ready."

"I could come help."

Her eyes widened. "No, it's okay. I've got this." It was like she didn't want him alone with her in her cottage. He could guess why, but it still rankled him. "I'll ask the chef at the Inn to do the catering. And there's this new cleaning service in Marshall's Gap that are looking for clients, so I'll have them tidy the place up the day before."

"I'll pay, of course."

"It needs a clean anyway."

"I'll pay," he said it firmer. She pulled her lip between her teeth and nodded.

"Okay. If you insist."

❧ 9 ❧

"**W**ow, this is clean," Casey said, his eyes wide as he took in her sparkling cottage. "I should get them to come do our house."

"I resent that." David frowned. "I do the cleaning."

"And I'm eternally grateful for that." Casey kissed his cheek. "The same way you're grateful for my cooking."

David turned and gave Everley a pained look. "Scratch that. We should definitely get a cleaner."

Everley laughed, because their bickering always cheered her up. "I can't believe I didn't get them in before. I've set up a regular cleaning schedule. I feel free."

"So you're really going through with this?" Casey asked. He still looked unhappy about the whole thing.

"Yep. One night of pretending to be Mrs. Shaw and then I'm back to final rehearsals."

David looked around her living room. His brows were pinched, like he was thinking deeply.

"Everything okay?" she asked him.

"There's something missing."

"What?" she asked, frowning. "Did the cleaners miss a spot? Where is it?"

"No," David said, shaking his head. "It's not the cleaning, it's the husband. There's no sign of him here. No photos of him, no shoes annoying you in the hallway, no jackets slung on the kitchen stools after you've told him to put them in the closet over and over."

Casey slowly nodded. "He's right. It doesn't look like a guy lives here at all."

"Because Dylan doesn't live here." Everley gave them a strange look. "So why would he leave his things here?"

"Because you're about to pretend to be married," David said. "And one step inside is all it takes to know you aren't."

"Hey, have you even got a second toothbrush in your bathroom?" Casey asked.

"No." Horror washed over her. "Oh God, why didn't I think of this?"

"Dylan didn't either," Casey pointed out. "Maybe you guys are worse at lying than you thought." He rubbed his chin with his thumb. "What time are the Carsons arriving tomorrow?"

"They're coming for lunch. They should be here by one."

"Then we have no time to waste." Casey's voice was firm. "Call Dylan and tell him to pack a suitcase. He needs to bring it over in the next hour."

"He's not staying here." Everley frowned. She wasn't sure she could cope with that.

"I know. But we need some of his things. We can put them around the house."

David nodded. "He's right. We need to do this tonight. Have you two agreed on how you're going to answer awkward questions?"

"What kind of awkward questions?" Everley wasn't sure she could take much more. This was supposed to be easy. A favor for a friend. Why hadn't she thought about all the implications.

"Do you two intend on living apart forever? Will Dylan eventually come home or will you join him in Africa?" Casey asked.

"Do you and Dylan plan on having a family?" David said, lifting a brow. "How is that going to work if you're apart?"

Everley opened her mouth and shut it again.

It seemed like they were just getting started. "Tell us about Dylan's work in Africa, Everley," Casey said, putting his hands on his hips.

"He treats AIDS." She swallowed hard.

"Of course he does. But how has the refugee situation impacted that?"

"There's a refugee situation?" She felt so stupid. She should know this.

"Okay, let's ask Dylan some questions instead," Casey turned to talk to an imaginary Dylan. "You must be so proud of your wife. What did you think of her performance in *Cabaret*?"

"What role did she play again?" David interjected.

Casey tipped his head to the side. "I have no idea," he said, pretending to be Dylan. "Because as far as I've known we've been divorced for eight years."

"Well that's okay. Here's a check for hundreds of thousands of dollars." David held his hand out to his husband. "We *love* liars at the Carson Foundation."

"You can stop now." Everley sighed. "You're right, okay? We haven't thought this through."

"Go grab your phone and get Dylan over here now," Casey said, offering her a sympathetic smile. "We have some work to do."

"What are you doing?" his dad asked, as Dylan threw clothes into the suitcase that lay open on his bed. Everley had called ten minutes earlier, her voice nervous as she explained the dilemma. He wanted to kick himself for not thinking this through, because of course Casey and his husband were right.

It would be obvious they were lying from the moment Warren and Grace walked through Everley's door. Hell, he'd never even been inside the place. He wouldn't know where the bathroom was or the bedroom, and he certainly didn't know where she kept things in the kitchen.

They had twelve hours to learn everything they missed over the last eight years about each other. And it wasn't anywhere near enough time.

"I'm taking some things over to Everley's," he told his dad.

"Are you two a thing now?" Charlie blinked. "I didn't know."

"We're not a thing. She's just helping me out with a problem." He quickly explained his situation with the Carsons.

His dad frowned and shook his head. "Are you toying with her emotions, son?"

Dylan sighed. "No, I'm not. She offered to do this, and I accepted gratefully. This money is going to make a huge difference to our work. Without it, people will die. So I figure telling a few white lies for an afternoon won't hurt anybody. And it'll do a lot of good."

"I don't like it. Your mother and I didn't bring you up to be a liar."

Dylan stopped packing and turned to look at his dad. "Mom was the original liar. We both know that."

Charlie inhaled sharply. "That was the drugs. Not her."

"Same difference." Dylan turned back to his suitcase. He didn't want to talk about his mom. Especially not with his dad. They had an unspoken agreement not to talk about emotions.

"Everley's a good woman. She loved you a lot. Don't hurt her."

"I'm not planning on hurting her." It was the last thing he wanted to do. And yet his dad's words hit a nerve. She'd been like a bundle of nervous desire in his arms the other day in the theater. Like a pile of kindling, all he had to do was light a flame and she'd burn up.

And he'd be consumed right along with her.

Was he really doing the right thing? Sure, he could pretend all he wanted that it was just a white lie, but it really didn't matter. An untruth was an untruth, and he'd be profiting from it. Or at least his work would.

Maybe he should call it off. Come clean to the Carsons and throw himself at their mercy. He should have done that all along. Told them the truth about his situation with Everley, before he was in too deep. At least that would have been honest.

And right now, he felt like the most dishonest person in Winterville.

"No way. If you tell them and lose the money then people will suffer. What you do is important." Casey was staring right at Dylan. He'd arrived at Everley's cottage ten minutes earlier, a suitcase in his hand. But from the moment he'd walked in the door he was on edge. He'd told Everley they should call it off rather than be the liars they were.

"He's right," David said, nodding. "I have friends who've lost loved ones from AIDS. It's a terrible disease. You have a chance to make things better in the long run. You should take it."

"I'm sorry to hear that," Dylan said, his voice low.

David nodded. "I grew up in New York. The memory of

the AIDS epidemic in the eighties and nineties is a huge scar on our collective memory. And it kills me to know that there are so many people still going through that today."

"I'm sorry." Dylan's voice was soft.

"I just want you to get that donation," David told him.

"Me, too."

"You *will* get the donation." Everley smiled at him. "We just need to be convincing for a day," she said. "Let's go ahead and do it. By tomorrow night this will all be in the past."

"Are you sure?"

"I'm sure. So let's start unpacking."

For the next two hours, Casey and David drilled them with questions. As they answered, she showed Dylan where everything was – from glasses to serve drinks to spare toilet paper in case they ran out. Dylan had brought over some photographs he'd found hidden in Charlie's drawer – ones of him and Everley laughing in his dad's backyard, of them at one of her plays, of her watching his med school graduation. They slid them into frames, replacing the old pictures in them.

Dylan blinked when he saw a photograph of their wedding in Vegas on the shelf over the fireplace. "Where did you find that?" he asked her.

She shrugged. "In the Inn's attic last year. I didn't know what to do with it, so it's been in my drawer."

"It's like she knew she was going to need it," Casey said, beaming. "Hey, why don't you take Dylan to the backyard and show him where you've been working on the rose beds?" he suggested. "And while you're there, Dylan can ask you what your dream role would be."

"I know that one." Dylan smirked at her. "Momma Rose in *Gypsy*. She's just waiting to be old enough."

"Is that true?" Casey asked, looking at her, surprised. "I didn't know that."

It was weird how warm she felt at the fact that Dylan remembered. Her eyes caught his. "Yeah, it's true."

"I picture you more as Louise." Casey shrugged. Louise was the quiet, pretty girl who grew up to become Gypsy Rose Lee.

Everley smiled, pleased that Dylan remembered. "Momma Rose is such a great role. She's so passionate, and has the best songs."

Casey grinned. "You just gotta age a little first."

She fluffed her hair. "It's happening naturally."

The air was ice cold as she and Dylan stepped outside into the garden. The moon shone brightly down on Everley's yard, illuminating the snowy mountain peaks in the distance. "There's not much to see right now," she admitted to Dylan. "I cut back the roses in the fall so they will be ready to start growing as soon as the snow melts." She lifted her brows. "Plus it's dark. I figure Casey just wants to get us outside so he can finish manning up my living room."

"I didn't know you grew flowers." The moonlight on his face made him look wistful. The sharp lines of his cheeks were enhanced by the gloom.

"Why would you? I only started when I moved into this place."

"When was that again?"

She smiled. "Five years ago. At first it was my hideaway between shows in New York. But now I'm here permanently. North helped me with the garden. You know how good he is with plants."

Dylan ran his tongue along his bottom lip. "Do you ever think..." He stopped short. "It doesn't matter."

"Think what?" she asked, intrigued.

He raked the hair back from his brow with his fingers, tipping his head to look at her. "That this could have been our place."

Her breath caught. "I try not to think about that."

"What happened to us?" he murmured.

She wasn't sure if he was talking to her or to himself. Their eyes met, and she stayed silent, her throat tight as he looked down at her. There was a darkness in his gaze that had nothing to do with the night air. He looked confused, as though she held all the answers.

"We were too young. And we wanted different things."

"I wanted you."

And she'd wanted him, too. So much. "You wanted to save lives."

"I wanted you to come with me." The intensity of his stare took her breath away.

"You wanted me to give up my career. I couldn't do that."

"I wanted you to love me."

His words forced all the air from her lungs. She opened her mouth to tell him she had loved him so much. So desperately. But they'd made the decisions they had. They couldn't take them back.

"That was years ago now." She managed to inhale. "We're older now. Wiser."

"Why did you never marry again?"

Because nobody measured up to you. "I was busy with my career."

"But you've had boyfriends, right?" There was an edge to his voice.

"A few."

"Don't you want children? A lot of people I know are settling down and starting families."

She blinked. "Are you asking for tomorrow?"

"If you like."

"Then yes, we'd like children." She kept her voice steady. "Wouldn't we? When the time is right and you're able to spend more time in Winterville."

Dylan's lips parted and a sigh escaped. "Yeah. We'd like children."

"Two?" she suggested. "A little boy and a girl."

"Will they be dancers or doctors?"

This conversation was such sweet pain. "They'll be whatever they want to be. We'll love them and take care of them and give them all the confidence they need to be whatever they desire."

"And on Friday nights we'll get a babysitter and I'll take you out for dates. We'll pull up on the side of the mountain road and make out like teenagers, because when we're at home those kids always catch us."

"You'll have a pickup truck. I'll wear a pretty dress."

"We'll open the windows and the cold air will rush in as we drive. I'll put my hand on your bare thigh and you'll know it's on."

She swallowed. "I'll know *what's* on?"

He smirked, and it sent a shot of desire straight to her thighs. It hurt how much she wanted that. Not just his touch, but the dream.

And that's all it was. An impossible, enticing dream.

"We're getting good at this pretending," she said, looking at the moon. It was like a dinner plate in the sky.

"Real good." His voice was thick. "You think they'll believe us?"

"I do." Hell, *she* almost believed it. He painted such a perfect picture it almost felt real.

The corner of his lip quirked. "That's good."

"It is. That's why we're doing it, right? To get your funding."

He blinked. "Exactly."

"We should go inside. Before Casey calls a decorator and throws out all my furniture."

Dylan laughed. "Okay. Lead the way."

She noticed that he waited for a moment before following her inside, as though he needed the distance between them. When they walked into the living room, he leaned on the door jamb, watching as she snatched a cushion from Casey's hand.

"What?" Casey asked. "It's ugly."

"Alaska embroidered it for me. Don't you call my sister's work ugly."

David laughed. "It has character."

"That's another word for ugly," Casey told her.

"I should go," Dylan said, his eyes not quite meeting hers. "We have a big day tomorrow and we both need some sleep."

Everley nodded. "That's a good idea."

"Good night, Dylan," David called out.

"Thank you for your help. I appreciate it." Dylan flashed them a smile. Everley put the cushion back on the sofa, walking to the door to let him out.

"I can see myself out," Dylan said, reaching over her to unlatch the door. She could feel his chest press against her back. Brushing his lips against her cheek, he pulled the door open and stepped outside, giving her one final look before walking down the path.

She closed the door gently, and turned to see Casey and David staring at her, their eyes soft with compassion.

"Oh honey," Casey said. "Don't you dare fall in love with him again."

Everley took a deep breath and forced a smile onto her lips. "I wasn't planning on it. Now get out of here. I need my beauty sleep."

❧ 10 ❧

Dylan knocked on her door an hour before the Carsons were due to arrive. Everley pulled it open, looking beautiful in a black fitted dress. "Thank God you're here."

"Is everything okay?" He kissed her cheek and looked over her shoulder. "They're not here yet, are they?"

"No, luckily. But I need you to go pick up the food. Carl was supposed to deliver but he's short staffed in the kitchen. Just go straight around the back, he'll be expecting you."

"Okay." Dylan grabbed his car keys from his suit pocket. "Anything else we need?"

"I think I have everything else."

It was only a short drive from Everley's cottage to the Winterville Inn. He steered his car around the back of the imposing white building, and headed to the back door.

The kitchen was a hive of activity. Pans were bubbling, steam was rising, and Carl, the chef, was shouting for somebody to take the ham out of the oven.

"Dylan. Hey," he said, holding his hand out. Dylan shook it with a grin. "What are you doing here?"

"Everley sent me to pick up the food she ordered." He shifted his feet.

Carl blinked. "Oh. I just gave it to North. He was driving that way and offered to drop it off. I texted Everley to let her know."

Dylan's phone was in his car so he couldn't warn Everley. "North has the food?"

"Yeah."

"And he's driving to Everley's place now?" Dylan clarified.

Carl frowned. "That's what I just said."

Dylan swallowed. "Damn."

"Did I do something wrong?" Carl asked. "I thought I was helping. She sounded all harassed when I told her I couldn't spare anybody to deliver."

"No, you did great. Honestly." There was no problem at all. It wasn't as though Everley's oldest cousin was heading to her place right now with the food she and Dylan were going to serve his prospective donors.

And though North was usually calm, he also had a protective streak. The kind that came out when his family did stupid things.

Like pretended they were still married. Or even worse, found out that they *actually were* still married.

Dylan drove back to Everley's house like his ass was on fire. North's truck was in her driveway. Sighing heavily, Dylan knocked on the door, resigning himself to whatever fate had in store for him.

Everley opened it, her eyes wide with panic. "North's here," she whispered.

"I know."

"He's asking questions. What do I tell him?"

Dylan sighed. He was tired of lying. "Leave it to me."

"What?"

"Let me talk to him. I'm going to tell him the truth. I fucked up, and you're helping me clean it up."

"But…" Her chest hitched. "What if he hurts you?" Everybody knew North had a great right hook.

"You don't need to look so worried." He put his hand on her shoulder, smiling reassuringly. "I've got this. It's going to be okay." There was no way he'd let her take the blame for this.

North was in the kitchen, staring out of the back window. Everley had made him coffee and the mug was cradled in his hands. He turned when he heard footsteps, his brow crinkling when he saw Dylan standing there.

"Hey. I didn't expect to see you here."

"Everley's helping me with something."

North's glance flickered over Dylan's shoulder. Everley must be standing behind him.

"What kind of something?" North asked.

"It's nothing," Everley said quickly.

Dylan turned and put his hand on her shoulder. She was shaking. "It's not nothing. You're doing something amazing for me. And I'm grateful." He turned back to North. "Everley and I discovered that our divorce was never finalized. Technically, we're still married."

North's mouth dropped. "What? How can that be? You two divorced years ago." He shook his head. "Is that why you're here? To talk about the divorce?"

"Not quite." Dylan flashed Everley a reassuring smile. She was staring up at him with wide eyes. "I made a mistake when I was completing a form for a donation for my work. Said I was married. The donors are coming to visit today and Everley agreed to be my happily married wife for the day."

"I didn't agree, I offered," she protested.

He looked down at her. "This is all on me," he said, his

voice thick. She parted her lips but didn't say anything, her lashes sweeping down as she blinked.

"Why the hell would you do that?" North's words cut through the moment. His face glowered.

Everley stepped back, holding her hands up. "It's just for a day."

"But why wouldn't you just tell them you're divorcing?"

"It's a long story," Dylan said.

"And one we will have to tell another time," Everley interjected, tilting her head at North. "Because you need to go. Our guests will be arriving soon."

North's jaw was tight. "We're not done talking about this. What are you doing tomorrow night?" he asked Dylan.

"Not much." Dylan shrugged.

"Meet me at the Tavern at eight. We'll talk then."

"North!" Everley rolled her eyes. "This has nothing to do with you."

North's expression softened. He walked past Dylan, their shoulders brushing. "I'm the closest you've got to an older brother. I just want to make sure you're protected."

"I'm thirty years old," she told him.

"I know you are. I only want to have a beer with your husband. And if he says no, then I'll back off. Okay?"

She sighed. "Okay."

North's eyes moved to Dylan. "We on for tomorrow night?"

Dylan didn't move an inch. "Yeah, we're on."

North didn't smile. "Good."

"I'm so happy we got to meet you," Grace Carson said, lifting her glass of water to her lips. "You're so lucky to have a talented Everley. Amazing food, an elegant home, and a wonderful career." She smiled at Dylan. "You two must hate it when you're apart."

Everley sliced into her chicken, spearing a piece on her fork. Carl had done an amazing job with lunch. Pumpkin and chilli soup, followed by chicken in a white wine sauce with sautéed potatoes and wilted greens. For dessert they would have Carl's chocolate cake that everybody in town raved about.

"It helps knowing what an important job he's doing," Everley said, smiling at Grace. "My loss is Africa's gain."

"I bet you miss eating food like this, right?" Warren said to Dylan. "I'm guessing you don't get a lot of gourmet meals in South Sudan."

"I miss everything about Everley when I'm away." Dylan's eyes met hers. Her breath caught, because his acting was way too good. "If I could, I'd kidnap her and take her back with me."

Grace laughed. "Ah, but your gain would be the theater's loss." She leaned toward Everley. "Tell me, what was it like growing up with Candy Winter for a grandmother? She was so beautiful."

"She was." Everley smiled, because her grandmother was a much safer subject.

"And you look just like her." Grace smiled warmly. "Don't you think, Dylan? She shines just like her grandmother."

"Yes, she does." Dylan didn't smile. Instead, he stared straight at Everley. She felt her cheeks flush.

"Thank you," she said softly. He put his hand over hers, his fingers sliding through.

His gaze didn't waver. "I'm just telling the truth."

Grace sighed. "Maybe we shouldn't give Dylan the donation, and make him stay here with Everley instead."

Warren chuckled. "That's not how we work."

"What Dylan does is too important for me to make him

stay with me," Everley said, aware that Dylan was still holding her hand. With his other hand, he speared a piece of chicken on his fork and lifted it to his mouth. There was a half-smile playing on his lips. "I'd never ask him to give up his medical work. There are people who need him more than I do."

He glanced at her, lifting a brow. She smiled back at him.

"But one day you'll be together, right?" Grace asked. "Do you have a long term plan for your future?"

"Everley wants children," Dylan said, winking at her. "I do, too. So we need to work out how to make it happen."

"I'm pretty sure you already know," Warren joked. "You're a doctor, aren't you?"

Everley's cheeks flushed.

"Stop it," Grace said good humoredly, slapping her husband's arm. "I'm just asking questions."

"You're being nosy." Warren gave them an apologetic glance. "Maybe we should talk about Dylan's work instead."

"That sounds like a wonderful idea." Grace put her hands together. "Have you spent a lot of time in Africa, Everley?"

She shifted in her seat. "The time has never been right. But I'm planning on visiting next year."

"You are?" Dylan tipped his head to the side, smiling at her.

"Yes." She smiled back. "I figure I owe you some visits."

"Warren! We could go at the same time," Grace said, her eyes lighting up at the idea. "That way Everley wouldn't have to travel all that way alone."

Dylan looked as cool as a cucumber. "That sounds good. Though I'm sure Warren's schedule is as filled up as Everley's."

"And maybe they'd want to spend some time alone," Warren said pointedly to his wife. Grace's eyes widened, and she covered her mouth with her hand.

"Oh. Of course. Silly me."

Everley felt sorry for Grace. She was only trying to be nice. "Dylan, why don't you tell them about your plans for the medical center." She gave him a genuine smile. "He's so bright. I could listen to him for hours."

Grace melted visibly.

"Yeah," Warren agreed. "I'd like to hear more about that."

Breathing a sigh of relief, Everley listened as Dylan started to talk about his work. She wasn't lying, she really did enjoy hearing him talk about his experiences out there. She was in awe of the difference he made in people's lives.

And maybe it made her feel a little bit better about the choices they'd made all those years ago.

The four of them walked out of the Jingle Bell Theater, where Everley had taken them on a backstage tour before they were to head home.

"We've had such a wonderful time," Grace said, wrapping her cashmere scarf around her neck. "I really don't want to leave."

Dylan shot an amused glance at Everley. She'd been a star all afternoon, taking them on a tour of the theater, and letting them watch the rehearsal of one of the show's set pieces. Then she'd grabbed four hot chocolates for them and arranged for the cast to run through three of their numbers on stage, before the tour, while telling Warren and Grace funny stories about her grandmother and the building of the town.

"How long do you have together before Dylan goes back to Africa?" Grace asked them.

"I fly back after Christmas," he told her.

"So you'll be together for Thanksgiving. Do you have something nice planned?" Grace asked.

Everley's eyes clashed with his. "Um..."

"We're just having a quiet one," Dylan said smoothly.

Everley nodded. "That's right. My cousins are busy, so we'll probably celebrate with Dylan's dad."

"Actually, Dad's going to a friend's," Dylan said, raising his brows. "Dolores asked him over."

"Oh." Everley pulled her lip between her teeth, then glanced worriedly at Grace. "I don't look like such a great wife anymore, huh? I don't even know what we're doing for Thanksgiving." Her cheeks pinked.

"Baby, you're the best wife." Dylan slid his arm around Everley's shoulders, kissing her jaw. He felt the warmth of her gasp wash over his skin. "I just forgot to tell you."

"You should come to ours," Warren said, his voice easy. "We're having a lot of guests."

"You should!" Grace smiled. "You can stay the night. That way you can have some drinks. And it'll give me a chance to repay your gracious hospitality."

"I'm not sure that will work," Dylan said, frowning. "Everley's show opens the week after Thanksgiving. She's going to be busy."

She shrugged. "We have Thanksgiving day off. As long as I'm back early the next day it should be fine."

Dylan looked at her, trying to work out if she was serious. "Baby, you'll be exhausted."

"Oh, we'll take good care of her," Grace promised. "And you will, too. You'll both go home fully rested and ready to wow everybody at the theater."

"We should do it." Everley placed her hand on Dylan's arm. "Please?"

He still couldn't decipher if she really wanted to or not. She lifted her brow, as though trying to convey a message.

Dylan ran his finger along his jaw. "If you want to," he said softly. "I never could deny you anything."

"Thank you," she said, fluttering her eyelashes at him, and a half smile pulled at his lips.

"We should head home," Warren said, looking up at the sky. "I want to get out of the mountains before it gets dark. Thank you both for your kind hospitality." He smiled at Everley. "Your town is beautiful."

"It's been a pleasure." And so much easier than she'd thought.

Dylan slipped his arm around her waist, and she felt a bolt of pleasure deep in her abdomen. "It was all Everley's hard work."

"You're a lucky man," Warren said.

Dylan kissed her brow, his lips searing her cool skin. "Yes, I am."

"How do you think it went?" Dylan asked, rolling up his shirt sleeves. He'd walked back with her to the cottage, insisting that he help her clean up. His suit jacket was carefully laid on the back of the sofa. He'd unbuttoned the top two buttons of his shirt, and she was desperately trying not to look at the dip at the base of his neck.

How could a two inch expanse of skin turn her on so much?

It had been easier when Warren and Grace were here. They were like a natural barrier to her libido. Maybe it was the fact she'd been acting, concentrating on being the perfect wife.

Dylan started to empty the dishwasher, squatting on his haunches as he removed the plates from the bottom rack. He tipped his head, looking at her for a response.

She blinked. "Yeah, I think we did. They wouldn't have asked us to go to their place for Thanksgiving if we hadn't."

"About that." He stood, stacking the plates in the rack above the sink. "We don't have to go. You've already given up too much for me. You should be concentrating on the show. I'll call them tomorrow and tell them it's too much."

"It's fine." She grabbed a towel and helped him with the glasses, polishing them to a shine. "It'll be nice to get away for a night. It'll be a chance to rest before everything goes crazy in December."

He scanned her face, his expression neutral. "You realize there's a big problem there, right?"

She frowned. "What problem?"

"They'll put us in a bedroom together. With one bed."

She stopped polishing the glass. "That's okay," she said, her voice squeaky. "It's just for a night. We can handle that, right?"

"It's not okay." He took the glass from her and placed it on the shelf. "I'm doing my best to be a gentleman here. You shouldn't have to spend a night with the husband you're divorcing."

"Are you afraid I might try to seduce you?"

His brows pinched. "Of course not."

"Because I *am* your wife. There's nothing wrong with sharing a bed with *my* husband."

He pinched the bridge of his nose with his thumb and forefinger. "Evie, you're making it really damn hard to be a good guy here."

"You never were a good guy," she said, her voice low. "Never."

His jaw twitched. "Maybe I'm trying to be one now," he growled.

Maybe it wasn't that he was trying to be good. Maybe it was that he didn't want her. And why would he? She was history for him. A loose end he needed to tie up. Sure, he was happy for her to help him out as a friend, but he didn't feel the connection like she did.

Didn't feel a burning need every time their fingers

touched. Didn't ache deep inside like she'd never ached before.

She was mortified.

She took a step back, busying herself with lining up the glasses on the shelf. "Don't worry," she said, her voice light, "I'm pretty sure your virtue will stay intact. You can sleep on the floor."

He laughed. "I remember doing that a few times before."

Yeah, but that was after one of their explosive fights. And the making up was always so delicious.

Until they stopped making up.

The need to be alone washed over her. Maybe Casey had been right all along. She was going to get hurt, despite her protests and her belief that she was just helping a friend.

She was already hurt. That was the truth of it.

"The cleaning up is done." She hung the kitchen towel on a rack. "I'm beat. I think I'm going to have a bath and veg out."

"You sure there's nothing else that I can do?" he asked.

She forced a smile on her lips. "No, it's all good. You can head on home. You need your beauty sleep. You have to meet North at the Tavern tomorrow night."

Dylan grimaced. "I'd forgotten about that." He leaned forward, brushing his warm lips against her cheek. "Thank you," he murmured. "For everything."

Everley lay back in the bath, a half-drunk glass of wine on the wooden rack in front of her, bubbles covering her from chest to toe. Soaking her body in the too-hot water was supposed to calm her down, but instead she felt more restless than ever.

If Holly wasn't on her honeymoon, she'd call her right

now and give her a huge dose of verbal diarrhea until they'd dissected every second of her time with Dylan. But there was no way she was going to spoil Holly and Josh's first vacation as newlyweds.

She thought about calling Alaska, but her sister was too much of a romantic. And what Everley needed right now was a cold dose of reality.

Reality... what was it anyway? She thought she knew, at least until Holly's wedding. It was having a job she loved, a family she was close to, and friends who were always there for her when she needed them.

It didn't include a husband that made her feel things she hadn't in years. One who clearly didn't feel the same way about her.

She was still in love with him. That was the truth.

She'd never gotten over him. She *thought* she had. She'd had other lovers, some relationships. But they paled in comparison next to Dylan. She couldn't remember ever feeling like this.

And now she'd agreed to spend the night with him. What an exquisitely painful trip that would be, having him so close yet not being able to admit her feelings for him.

She let out a ragged breath and lifted the wine glass to her lips, then put it down again. The wine tasted too bitter on her tongue. She tipped her head back and let out a strangled groan, annoyed at herself. She was a lovesick puppy, instead of the strong, confident woman she knew she could be.

Maybe she needed Dylan to leave again. After that she could be back to normal. Forget about him and the way he made her feel emotions she didn't even know she had. The way her skin heated up every time she thought of him. The way her body ached whenever he was near.

She needed to get out of this funk. Sighing, she climbed out of the bath, drying herself off and wrapping a warm towel around her body. As she was twisting her hair into a bun, her phone started to buzz, Dylan's name appearing on the screen.

"Hey," she said softly, catching a glance of herself in the mirror. Her skin was pink from the bath. "Everything okay?"

"That's what I called to ask. You were a little distracted when I left. I wondered if I'd said something to upset you."

"You didn't do anything wrong. It was me who made a fool out of myself."

"How did you do that?"

She could hear the frown in his voice. Could picture him sitting in his dad's house, his long legs spread in front of him, his thick brown hair raked back from his face. His lips were probably pressed together as he tried to work her out.

"It doesn't matter. I'm just feeling weird this evening. Ignore me, I'll be fine tomorrow."

"I don't want to ignore you, Everley. I want to know what's going on. If I said or did something wrong, tell me."

She walked into her bedroom, dropping onto the mattress. "It's not you, it's me."

He laughed gently. "I've heard that before."

She was an innately honest person, so it felt weird to be skirting around the issue. But she couldn't let him know she was still in love with him. Because seriously, what was he supposed to do with that information? She had no idea what to do with it herself.

Catching a sight of herself in the mirror, she grimaced at the heat in her face. "You're like an animal in heat," she muttered to herself.

"Who's in heat?"

"Did I just say that out loud? Please tell me I didn't."

"You didn't just tell me you were in heat." His voice was low, edgy.

Her lips twitched. "Thank God."

"But if you were..." He trailed off, and she held her breath.

"Then that's okay. We're humans, our bodies are built for contact. We think we've got control of ourselves but all those celebrity and politician sex scandals tell us that's not true. Biology always wins out."

Okay, this was definitely mortifying. She laid back on her bed, covering her face with her palm.

"Evie, you there?"

"I'm here." She squeezed her eyes shut. "Just having a minor freak out right now."

He chuckled. "It's okay. It's normal, right? We were together for a long time. Our bodies know each other. Being up close and personal, we're bound to feel things we used to feel."

She wished that was it. But it wasn't memories that were making her feel weird. It was the emotions rushing through her right now. The feelings she had for the man he'd become, not the boy he once was.

Yes, it had been pretend today, but there was a part of her that wished it was real. That he was still her husband, that the way he touched her arm when he asked her a question was because he cared about her reply. That the way he looked at her meant more than just playing a role to get his donation.

He'd left and that was a good thing. But there was part of her that wanted him to stay. To pour her a bath, to take her to bed.

To make her feel the things she hadn't in a long, long time.

She sighed. "You think it's just sexual tension?"

"It has to be. You've moved on, I've moved on. It's just our bodies."

Maybe he was right. It was just muscle memory. Not that it helped her right now, because every cell in her body felt heightened.

Needy.

"You want to know what I've been thinking about?" he asked her.

"What?"

"Remember that time we drove to the lake the summer you were nineteen. We went skinny dipping."

"I remember," she whispered.

His voice was low and sugary. "You surprised me with that little D tattoo on your hip."

It was still there. She hadn't found the will to have it removed. "You loved it."

"I was freaking hard the whole time. Desperate to be inside you. And when we got into the lake you kept swimming away from me."

"But you caught me."

"Yeah, but only because you wanted to be caught."

Her skin tingled at the memory. "I did."

"I loved the chase, Evie, but I've never seen anything hotter than when you let me catch you. I kissed you until you couldn't take it anymore. Your hair was wet, your head tipped back, and you were clinging on to me like a vice. And when I slid inside you, you were so tight and warm, I thought I was in heaven."

The memory took her breath away. Emotions rushed through her, stripping her raw. He remembered how it was between them, and it made her ache for him.

"It's never been like that again. Never." She squeezed her eyes shut, recalling how hot and needy his kisses were. How soft he'd been with her, like she was precious china in his hands.

Behind her lids, she could feel her eyes stinging. She'd felt so safe in his arms. So cherished and protected. Nobody had ever looked at her like Dylan Shaw had. Nobody had owned her the way he still did.

Nobody had made love to her the way her husband could.

And now he wasn't hers, but her body wasn't getting the message.

Nor was her heart, come to that.

A hot tear spilled from her closed lid. Her breath caught. She didn't want him to know she was crying. That she cared.

It was too much.

"I can't do this." A sob racked through her body before she could hide it. "I just can't. I'm sorry."

She hung up before he could reply, then switched her phone off for good measure. Wiping the tears from her cheeks, she curled into a ball, burying her face in the sheets.

If she'd felt mortified before, it was nothing on this. She was crying over her soon-to-be ex-husband and he'd heard her.

She rolled over and screamed into the bedclothes. This push and pull between them had to stop, before it drove her mad.

$\maltese$ I 2 $\maltese$

She wasn't asleep when the banging started, but she sure as heck wasn't completely awake either. Everley sat up in bed, frowning as she looked at the towel still wrapped around her.

Another bang. She realized it was the front door. Disoriented, she sat up, checking the display on her alarm clock. It was almost eleven. How long had she been laying here on top of her mattress? It couldn't be more than half an hour.

When she pulled the front door open, still clutching at the towel in front of her, it came as no surprise to see Dylan standing on the step, his eyes dark and narrow, his hair a mess from where he'd raked his fingers through it.

"Are you okay? I kept calling and you kept sending me to voicemail. I was scared I'd said something stupid."

"I shut my phone off and fell asleep."

He lowered his head, inspecting her face. "Have you been crying?"

"No." She grimaced, touching her face. "Okay, maybe a little."

He tugged at his hair. "Christ, Everley. You look like

you've been crying more than a little. Was it me? Did I make you cry?"

She pulled her towel tighter, aware she was naked beneath it. "I'm just feeling emotional." She sighed. "I'm sorry to scare you."

"Can I come in?"

She stepped to the side. He walked into the hallway, closing the door behind him. "I'm so sorry," he said. "I should never have gone along with this. Asking you to pretend to be my wife."

"That's not why I'm crying."

"It's not?" His brow furrowed. "Then why are you so sad?"

"I don't know. Maybe it's nerves about the show. Or relief that today went okay. And then I completely embarrassed myself in front of you."

"You didn't embarrass yourself," he said.

She widened her eyes and he shook his head, the smile melting from his face. "Evie, I'm so sorry I made you feel like this."

"You don't need to be. It's not your fault."

"Of course it is." He shook his head at her. "If I hadn't turned up and told you we are still married, you'd be fine. And I'm all too fucking aware that I hurt you all those years ago. I didn't want to hurt you again, and yet here you are, crying because of me."

Was she still crying? She wiped her cheek with the back of her hand, surprised at the moisture she felt. "What you said about your memory?"

"Yeah?"

"Do you think about it a lot?"

He shifted his feet. "Yeah, it was a pretty perfect day."

"I think about it, too."

"Evie..." He hesitated, as though measuring her up.

She sighed. "I know it's history. That we hurt each other

too much. That we wanted different things and it could never have worked. But I've never felt like I did at that moment again. Maybe some things are just too good to feel for the rest of your life." She inclined her head at the living room. "Should we sit down?"

He followed her in, sitting on the sofa next to her, leaning forward to rest his elbows on his thighs. He had his hand in his hair again, as though he was trying to find the right words to say.

"I still remember the first time I saw you," he said, his voice thick. "I don't mean the first time I laid eyes on you, but the first time I realized that you were all grown up. It was the day before North's birthday party. You and Holly were walking across the town square, drinking soda from a can. You were laughing about something and the sun caught your hair. It shone, Evie. You fucking glowed. And I couldn't move. All I could do was look at you, and in that moment I *knew* I had to have you. I couldn't think about anything else."

His eyes caught hers. She could see a desperation in there. The same need that she felt. "And then we kissed outside North's birthday party. You were wearing a deep blue dress. Your lips were soft and warm and you did this little gasp when I slid my tongue against yours. It made me so damn hard. All I could think about was making you mine." He shook his head. "I'm not just talking about sex, though of course I was desperate for that. I knew you were a virgin. I knew we'd have to take it easy. But I had to be your first."

She was crying even harder now. She thought he'd forgotten her. Forgotten their history, but the way he was telling it, she could see he'd been thinking about it a lot.

"I was yours long before we had sex," she said softly.

"And I was yours. You know what they used to call you when I talked about you at school?" he asked her.

"Nothing good, I'm sure."

"Yoko. Because I didn't want to go out with the guys and cruise the bars anymore. I wanted to stay home and call you. I wanted to work and become the best damn doctor I could be because then I'd earn enough money to take care of you. They used to joke you'd broken the band of brothers up."

She gave a half smile. "Most of your friends were assholes."

"Yeah, they were. And they were wrong, because it wasn't you who broke up the gang. It was *me*. I wanted you and I knew I had to be a better person to get you. And I wanted that. You made me want to be the best person I could. Because you've always been too good for me. Everybody knows that. And then I went and threw away the only good thing that happened in my life."

"We both threw it away," she whispered.

"You know what they say about people like us? Right person, wrong time."

She looked down at her hands. "I've heard that said. But I still don't understand why I'm so emotional now."

"What did you do after we split up all those years ago?"

She looked up at him, surprised. "I went to New York. Got a part in a play Off-Broadway."

"So you did what I did. Threw yourself into something else because you didn't want to think about all the things we'd lost."

She blinked. "I guess." She'd moved to New York almost as soon as she'd signed those papers. Staying in Winterville had been too painful. There were memories of him everywhere she turned. It had taken a long time for her to get used to coming back. To be able to spend time here without feeling like something was missing.

"Maybe you didn't give yourself time to mourn what we lost. I know I didn't. And it's coming back now, because everything is fresh again. That loss never went away. We didn't deal with it, we just pretended it didn't exist."

Her lips trembled. "You feel it, too?"

He closed his eyes, inhaling softly. "Of course I do."

When he opened them again, his gaze burned into hers. She stared back at him, knowing just how much she loved this man. It was hard to remember exactly why she'd thrown away what they had.

Why they'd both left it behind when it was the best thing in their lives.

"Evie..."

"Nobody else calls me that. Just you."

"I know. But honey, if you keep looking at me that way, I don't know what I'll do."

"What do you want to do?" she asked softly.

"I want to pull you onto my lap and kiss you until your lips are swollen and your eyes are heated. I want to slide that towel off your body and run my fingers over you until you gasp. I want to sate the need you have. Want to bury myself inside you until you're mine all over again."

His eyes were burning. She felt warm blood rush to her skin, making her flesh tingle with electricity. "You want me?"

He slid his hand into hers. "I've always wanted you. That's never changed."

A sense of elation washed through her. He felt the same way she did. Her thighs tightened at the thought of him touching her, kissing her, sliding inside of her. She wanted him to pin her to her bed, to feel the warm, hard planes of his body over hers.

Wanted him to make her his, the way he always had.

"But it doesn't matter how much I want you," he continued. "Because we both know how it will end. The same way it did before. I'll hurt you, and I don't think I'll forgive myself if I do that a second time."

A wave of frustration washed over her. "We're older now. Things are different."

"Are they? You're happy here, I know you are. My dad kept me posted, told me how well you're doing. He made sure to let me know you were perfectly fine without me."

She smiled, looking down at her towel. "Charlie's a romantic."

"He's something, that's for sure. But look at what happened before. We're in exactly the same position. I have my work, you have yours."

"And you choose your work over me." It hurt her to say it.

"No. This time I choose *you* over me. I want you to be happy, Evie. You deserve that. You deserve a great life and I can't give you that. I get so damn wrapped up trying to save people that I hurt the ones I love the most."

She blinked at the implication he loved her. But she couldn't speak, because his rejection hurt. He didn't want her enough, and that was the truth.

She couldn't compete with his need to save the world. And truth be told, she didn't want to. Because his need to make a difference was one of the things she loved about him. You didn't try to tame a man like Dylan Shaw. You sat back and watched him fly.

"You want a family," he said. "And I can't give you that, either."

There was a sadness in his gaze that matched her own. Back when they were first married, having children had been the last thing on her mind. Even now, it was just a hazy thought, a *someday* kind of plan. Sure, she was thirty, but she knew plenty of people who had children in their thirties – and their forties.

But one day she wanted a family.

He gave her a soft smile. "You know I'm right."

"It would really help if my body knew."

"I'd like to give you a hug right now, but my restraint is hanging by a thread, and you're wearing a damn towel." His eyes were dark as he scanned down her body. He swallowed hard, his throat bobbing.

"How are you going to cope when we go to the Carsons'?"

He lifted a brow. "I'll have time to prepare myself. This took me by surprise."

"Prepare yourself how?" she asked.

He arched a brow. "How do you think?"

She sighed, because the thought of him touching himself sent a wave of desire through her body. And she didn't need that. Not right now.

"What if that's not enough?" she asked him. Because she knew it wasn't for her. She wanted to touch him, wanted to feel him. This need was just too much.

"It'll have to be." His voice was grim."

"I guess we'll see, won't we?" she said, pulling her lip between her teeth. His gaze dipped, his eyes narrowing as they watched her slowly release it.

"I guess we will," he said, nodding slowly. "But the thing is, I've lasted for eight years without you, Evie. I think I can make it one more night."

❧ 13 ❧

"This is too delicious for words." Casey grinned as Everley sat with him and David in the Cold Fingers Café the next day. "We need to go through your closet and choose your sexiest clothes. If you're going to make him suffer, you need to do it in style."

David shook his head, amused. "You want her to torture the poor guy? He's already agreed to abstinence. There's no need to put him in the second circle of hell."

Casey shrugged. "All I'm saying is that he's laid a challenge down. If he thinks he can get through one night without touching her, he's crazy. Look at her." He gestured at Everley. "She's beautiful. Every straight guy I know wants her. And she's doing him a huge favor by going to this thing for Thanksgiving, so she might as well have some fun."

"I have a feeling that it's you who wants to have fun," David murmured.

"Can't we all have fun? God knows we need it." Casey tipped his head to the side.

"Who's having fun?" Alaska asked, sitting down on the

sofa next to Everley. She was holding a coffee to go. "And make it fast, I have to get back to the Inn."

"It's a long story," Everley said. "I'll tell you later."

"Everley's spending Thanksgiving night with Dylan. In the same room," Casey blurted. David elbowed him in the gut and he let out a grunt.

"What?" Alaska's eyebrows pinched as she turned to look at her sister. "Why didn't you tell me?"

"I only agreed to it yesterday. I haven't had a chance."

Alaska smiled. "I knew there was something going on between you two. Apart from being married, that is."

"Don't go and get all romantic," Everley warned her. "I'm only doing him a favor. The foundation that is donating a lot of money to his work in Africa got confused and found out that we were still married. So I'm accompanying him to their Thanksgiving party."

"So you two aren't..." Alaska trailed off.

"Physical?" Casey finished her question with glee.

"No, we're not. And we're not likely to be. We're still getting divorced. This is just to make sure Dylan gets the funding he needs. There's nothing more to it than that. You don't need to worry or fret, it's all good."

"One room and two people who have the hots for each other. Sure, nothing to worry about." Casey folded his arms over his chest.

"Shut up." David gave him a pointed look, then smiled at Alaska. "Everley's right. Casey just likes to see the drama in everything."

"Casey also wants me to not get hurt." Everley rolled her eyes at her friend. "I wish he'd make his mind up."

"Is there a possibility of you getting hurt?" Concern etched Alaska's face.

Everley threaded her fingers through Alaska's. "No, there's not. It's all good. Dylan and I are friends. And that's how it should be. He's a good man, and he deserves to get that funding. I'm just making sure he does."

"Okay." Alaska smiled. Her phone pinged and she glanced at the screen. "Damn, three of our housekeeping staff have called in sick. I need to get over to the Inn." She stood, picking up her coffee, before giving Everley a final glance. "Just be careful," she said. "Dylan and you were like Romeo and Juliet. You burned bright, but you ended in tragedy. Don't let it happen again."

"I won't." Everley winked at her. "I promise not to fall in love with my ex-husband."

"Good." Alaska nodded. "Now I should go before we end up with no staff at all. I'll catch you later."

"Game of pool?" North asked Dylan, inclining his head at the green baize covered table. They'd met at the Tavern for the talk North insisted on having.

Dylan shrugged. "Sure. Eight ball?"

North nodded. "Works for me." They walked over to the table, each taking a cue. North grabbed a coin from his pocket, curling his fingers around it. "Heads or tails?"

"Tails."

North flipped the coin, covering it with his other palm. When he removed it, George Washington was in profile, looking unimpressed at being involved in such trivial matters.

They racked up the balls, and North removed the triangle, leaning his long body over the table to tap his cue against the white ball. It smashed into the pyramid of colored balls, sending them flying across the baize.

One ball went into the center right pocket.

"Stripes it is," Dylan murmured.

"Blue ball, top left." North walked around the table,

setting his cue up once again. His lips were pursed, his right eye squinted as he slowly kissed the white ball with the tip of his cue. The blue hit the very edge of the corner pocket, then ricocheted back.

"Win some lose some." North stood back to let Dylan look at the spotted balls. There was a purple with easy access to the bottom right pocket. He called it and leaned over, steadying the cue in his hand.

"So you and Everley, huh?" North said, right as he pulled the cue back to hit the white ball. It went careening to the side, missing the purple altogether. "That's a foul," he murmured, looking almost pleased with himself.

So that was how this was going to go. Dylan stood and looked at North. "Your turn."

North picked up the white ball and replaced it on the spot.

"What do you want to know about us?" Dylan asked him.

"I want to know why you didn't get divorced."

"I left the papers with my dad. He didn't send them in like he promised to."

North raised an eyebrow. "Charlie thwarted your divorce? Why didn't you follow up? You must have noticed when the final decree didn't come through. Did your lawyer not contact you?"

"I've never been divorced before, I wasn't sure how it worked. And we were both busy. I was shuttling between Atlanta and Africa, and Everley was relocating to New York. I guess we both made some assumptions."

North tipped his head to the side, silent for a moment. Then he leaned over to take a shot, pocketing the number six. As it span down the tube and into the side of the table, he leaned back on the edge of the baize, looking at Dylan.

"You're an intelligent man. It doesn't take a lot to find out how divorce works. Hell, I've never been divorced and I know there's a final decree involved. Are you sure you weren't trying to keep Everley hanging on by a string?"

Dylan blinked. "No, I wasn't. And if you haven't been divorced maybe you don't know just how painful it is. How much you spend every day kicking yourself because if you'd said the right thing, or done something differently, maybe the love of your life would still be at your side. Yes, I should have double checked, but I was too fucking busy trying to remember how to breathe without her. Should I apologize for that?"

North exhaled heavily. "So why aren't you divorced now? Surely as soon as you found out you should have filed the papers."

"My lawyer's on it."

"Everley's signed the papers?" North sounded surprised.

"Of course she has. She wants this divorce as much as I do. In a few months the final decree will come through and it will be over."

North's brows knitted as he took another shot, this time missing the two. "So this is done now? This pretending to be a couple thing? Everley can get on with her life?"

Dylan swallowed. "Not quite."

"What's that supposed to mean."

"The couple who came to Everley's house have asked us to their Thanksgiving party. After that it'll be over."

Narrowing his eyes, North curled his fingers around the cue, his knuckles bleaching. "This is fucking stupid. You can't keep doing this. You weren't here to see Everley crumble after you left her. You didn't see her howl with pain every time your name was mentioned. You walked away and left the rest of us to pick up the pieces. And now you're toying with her all over again."

"I'm not toying with her." Dylan's voice was low. "I'd never do that to her."

"Then walk away. Leave her alone. Don't hurt her again."

"I'd never hurt her. Never." He wanted to make her smile, not cry. He hated it when she cried. Though, he'd loved it, too. The heightened emotions had always made for the best make up sex.

North shook his head. "Everyone thinks she's this strong woman who doesn't take shit from anybody. You and I know that's not true. Sure, she has this sheen of confidence. This ability to always put on a show. But inside she's as soft as hell, man. You broke her." North's eyes were heated. "And she never quite recovered from that. So I'm asking you, man to man. Friend to friend. Leave Everley alone. Don't hurt her again, because this time I don't know that she'll recover."

"I won't hurt her. I promise you that."

North tipped his head at the table, and Dylan stepped forward to take his shot. "Yellow, middle right."

It slid in easily. He followed it up with another, then missed the third. Within a few minutes, only the eight ball was left on the green baize. North called the pocket then leaned forward, before standing up to look at Dylan again.

"When do you go back to Africa?"

"After Christmas."

North nodded, his eyes narrowing as he thought things through. "I know it's impossible for you to avoid her while you're here. This town is too damn small for that. But at least make it clear to her that there's no future. Don't leave her hanging. Even if it's painful, make it a clean break this time. No marriage, no friendship, nothing. That's the only way she's ever going to get over you."

"Shouldn't Everley be the one to decide that?"

"Did she sign the papers?" North asked.

"Yeah."

"Then she's decided."

Dylan's throat tightened. Yes, she had decided. And he

had, too. But even if they both knew it was the best way to move forward, it didn't stop their divorce from hurting all over again.

And it didn't stop him from wanting her. The need felt like a constant ache deep inside him. Not only because she kept looking at him like she wanted him, too, but because there was something so perfect about his soon-to-be-ex-wife.

Her fire, her enthusiasm, her kindness. He wanted all of it. But he also knew that eight years ago he'd taken those things away from her. Put her in pain because of the decisions he'd made.

North was right. He couldn't do that to her again. Love was supposed to be unselfish. Kind. She was still his wife, and while she was, it was his job to protect her.

Even if the person he was protecting her from was himself.

Dylan climbed out of his car as Everley walked down the steps of her cottage, a purse casually slung over her shoulders and her coat in her hands. She was wearing a pair of jeans that looked like they were painted onto her legs, and a cream cashmere sweater with a wide neck, revealing her exquisitely smooth shoulder.

He took her overnight bag from her hands, carrying it to his car. Once he'd put it in his trunk, he opened the door for her, helping her inside.

Starting the car up, he was all too aware of the scent of her perfume. The citrus and floral notes filled the car, shooting desire straight through him.

It was going to be a hell of a long day.

"You look a little uncomfortable," she said lightly. He glanced at her again, keeping his expression neutral as he pulled onto the highway. She had her bottom lip pulled between her teeth. "I guess this is getting hard for you."

He could hear the laugh in her voice, damn her.

"Are you enjoying this?"

"Maybe." She ran her fingers through her golden hair,

lifting it over one shoulder. "You know, there's one way we could make everything a little easier."

"What is it?"

"We could have sex tonight."

"What the hell?" A car stopped in front of him, and he had to slam on the brakes not to rear end it. "Jesus, Everley, give a guy some notice when you're planning on propositioning him."

She grinned. "I'm serious. We should have sex tonight. This tension between us is driving me crazy. I've been thinking about what you said, that this all comes from us knowing each other's bodies so well. What if we just let the inevitable happen? It might make it easier for us both."

"That's a bad idea. A really bad idea." He gritted his teeth.

"Why?" She shifted in the passenger seat, until she was looking at him. "You told me you felt it too."

"Of course I can feel it. I told you that. But it doesn't mean I have to do anything about it. I'm more than my base urges."

"And I'm not?"

He glanced at her. "Everley, you're so much more."

Her chest hitched.

"So why not do it?" she whispered. "Give in to our needs. Wouldn't it be easier to just chase it away for one night? And maybe then we can move on with our lives."

He raked his fingers through his hair. His back was straight, his jaw stiff. "Yeah, but I promised North I wouldn't touch you."

"You what?"

"He asked me to make it clear to you that there's no future for us. He thinks I'm going to hurt you all over again."

A grin pulled at Everley's lips. "So if it wasn't for North, you'd have sex with me?"

"That's not what I said." Frustration tinged his words.

"That's exactly what you said. I told you it would be good, and you said 'yeah, but I promised North I wouldn't touch you.'"

"Is this how it's gonna be the entire drive?" Dylan asked. "Just so I can prepare myself."

"Would you rather I turn on some Christmas music and do some knitting?"

A smile pulled at his lips. "That sounds good right now."

"Okay. But let me ask you one thing. Then I'll shut up."

"One?"

She lifted her fingers to her brow. "Scout's honor."

"Okay, shoot."

"Do you want to have sex with me?"

The tic in his jaw returned. He ran his thumb over his jawline, his gaze on the road ahead. "That's a very loaded question."

"But the answer should be simple. A choice of two words. Yes or no."

His eyes flickered to hers, then back to the road. "Yes, I want to have sex with you. No, I don't think it's a good idea."

She shifted again, and he looked her way right as her sweater fell a little lower. He wanted to tie the damn thing around her neck. "Why isn't it a good idea?" she asked him.

"You said one question. We're done here." A shaft of sun pierced the clouds, making the mountaintops sparkle.

"So that's it? No more discussion."

"That's right."

"So you won't mind if I start dating other people?"

"What?" His brow crumpled. "I mean, no. It's your life. As long as it happens once I've left town."

"Really?"

He gritted his teeth. "Yes, really. I'm not stupid, I know you've dated other guys." His eyes were like flint. "But I really don't want to know about it if that's okay. And we live in a small town so if it happens while I'm here I'll know about it. So please hold off until I go back to Africa."

"What if I meet somebody at the party tonight? Is it okay for me to flirt with them?"

"No, it's not."

"Why not?"

"Because we're sharing a bedroom. And everybody thinks we're married."

"We *are* married," she pointed out.

He grimaced. "In name, yes. But either way, I don't want to be a cuckold. And you said yourself you didn't want to cheat on me."

"And you told me it wasn't cheating," she pointed out.

He let out a grunt of frustration, then hit his flat palm against the center of the wheel. "Can we talk about something else please?"

"Sure. What shall we talk about?"

"Maybe we shouldn't talk. Maybe we should stay silent the rest of the way," he growled.

Snow started to fall as they reached the bottom of the mountain pass. Nothing too heavy, just a dusting that made everything look pretty. In the distance she could see the green swirly sign of the Deja Brew Coffee Shop, and Everley pointed it out, asking Dylan if they had time to make a caffeine stop.

"Yeah, we have time. As long as we're in and out fast."

"The words every girl longs to hear," she joked. His lips twitched, but he said nothing.

The sexual tension in the car was palpable, and she knew it was her fault. She'd been honest with her suggestion. This constant back and forth was driving her crazy, and she could tell from the tic in the jaw it was doing the same to him.

It had seemed like a good idea when she'd thought of it last night. But now, not so much. Why did she have to be so impulsive?

Maybe a bitter cup of coffee would do her some good.

He pulled up outside the shop, and she jumped out.

"Can you get me an Americano?" he asked her.

"Aren't you coming in?"

He shook his head as he climbed out, grabbing his cell from his pocket. "I need to make a phone call." He inclined his head at some empty picnic seats on the other side of the parking lot. "I'll meet you there." He passed her a twenty. She looked at it and shrugged.

"Okay." He was so hot and cold she wasn't sure whether to burn or freeze. Instead, she shrugged and walked up the steps, all too aware of his stare on her back.

"Can I help you?" the barista asked when she made it to the counter. Everley blinked and gave her order, looking out of the window toward the picnic benches.

Dylan was leaning against one of them, his legs crossed in front of him, his phone against his ear. As though he could feel the heat of her stare he looked up, his dark gaze catching hers.

She swallowed at the intensity of his expression. He looked as though he was about to hit somebody. She knew those stormy eyes. His sex eyes. The way he'd always looked before he took her to bed and made the whole world disappear.

He'd always known exactly how to make her feel good. He'd played her body like a musician played an instrument. Touching softly in places, harder in others, until she vibrated with a music only he could make.

"Two Americanos," the barista called out, passing her the Styrofoam cups. "Anything else?"

"I'll take a couple of donuts, please," she said, trying to catch her breath. Maybe a sugar rush would make everything better.

Dylan pulled his gaze from Everley's, looking down at the phone he was clutching in his hands. He wasn't making a phone call. He didn't have anybody to call. He just needed the space between them before he hauled her across the hood of his car and yanked down those sweet, tight jeans.

She was temptation personified. He'd watched her walk into the coffee shop, hips swaying, hair glinting in the winter sun, and any coherent thought had flown out of his mind. She was killing him, dammit.

Because that's the effect that Everley Winter had on him. She was the most beautiful, sensual woman he'd ever known.

She could have any man she wanted.

Yeah, but she wants you.

He could remember the last time they had sex, eight years ago. By that point, they both knew it was over, but they couldn't resist the aching need they both felt. He'd slowly slid inside, grinding his pelvis against hers, his eyes soaking in every inch of her face, trying to memorize the uplift of her nose, the perfect bow of her lips. He'd already made her come twice that night, as though trying to imprint himself on her brain. Still he rocked against her, feeling some kind of power surge as she fell apart in his arms, her body gripping him tight as she let out a loud cry.

And then a tear had rolled down her face. He'd dropped his lips to her cheek, tasting the salt of her sadness with his tongue. There had been a grim satisfaction that she was as devastated as he was, but it had been chased away by the buildup of pleasure that made him forget everything except her body and his.

Her tears had brought him pleasure. How sick was that? That hard, cruel part of him had taken pleasure in the fact that she'd miss him. She deserved somebody so much better than him.

"There you are," she said, rounding the corner. "I bought you a donut as a peace offering."

"Peace offering?"

"For teasing you in the car. I'm sorry. I promise to behave the rest of the way." She passed him the Styrofoam cup along with a brown paper bag with the donut inside. He lifted the cup to his lips, hot bitter coffee coating his tongue.

"Damn, that's good."

"Deja Brew are a fairly new brand around here. They started in Washington state, I think."

"They make a good Americano."

"The donuts are great, too. Should we head back to the car? It's cold out here." She shivered.

"Sure." Taking another mouthful of coffee, they walked back across the lot. He pressed the key fob, hearing the satisfying beep as the lock released.

"Hey Everley?" he said, before she could open the passenger door."

"Yeah?"

"Thanks for the donut."

"No problem."

"Oh, and Ev?"

She blinked, as though surprised by his sudden need to talk. "If you're thanking me for the coffee, you don't need to. You paid for it."

He shook his head slowly. "It's not that."

"Then what?" She half smiled.

"I'll touch you tonight. Make you feel good." But he wouldn't do any more. He couldn't. Not if he wanted to keep some semblance of sanity.

The smile fell from her face. "What?" She frowned, as though she couldn't believe what he'd said.

"Just for one night," he told her. "I'll touch you wherever you want me to."

"But what about you? Can I touch you?"

He inhaled sharply. "Tonight's about you, not me."

"What if you want more than just touching?"

"I won't." He was lying. He already did want more. "I can control myself."

Her eyes flashed as though she could read his mind. "I've seen you out of control. I've *sent* you out of control."

His breath caught in his throat. "Don't fight with me on this. Let me make you see stars, then I'll crawl onto the floor and sleep there." His grip on his coffee cup tightened. "Or if you prefer, I'll be the perfect gentleman and keep my hands firmly off you. Your choice." He shrugged, trying to find the nonchalance that wasn't there.

Her pink lips parted, her breath turning to vapor. "Okay," she breathed. "I choose the stars."

❧ 15 ❧

"*Let me make you see stars.*"

His words reverberated around her head as they continued their drive toward the Carson's house. She could feel her heart hammering against her chest.

It was a promise and a threat. And she knew he'd follow through. When Dylan said he'd do something, he always did.

"Did I tell you that Grace emailed me an itinerary for today?" Everley said, trying to cut through the loaded atmosphere between them.

Dylan's lip quirked. "No. What's in store for us?"

"I printed it out. It's in here somewhere." She searched through her purse, pulling out a folded piece of paper. "Here we go. Arrive between 11am and 1pm for drinks and lunch." She glanced at the clock. "We'll make that easily."

"What's after lunch?"

"Charades."

"I'm sorry?" Dylan blinked.

"It's that game where you're given a book or movie or something and have to act it out silently."

"I know what it is, I just didn't realize we were spending Thanksgiving at an English manor in the year 1920."

Everley laughed. That made him smile wider. "In that case, you'll love that it's followed by afternoon tea, British style.."

"When do we find the body in the library?" he snarked. Damn, she loved his sense of humor.

"That's not on there. Maybe it's a surprise. You'll end up being the evil doctor who stands to inherit all the old woman's money."

He glanced at her. "And you'll be the beautiful woman whose expensive tastes led me to murder."

"The doctor and the showgirl. It's a mystery writer's dream come true."

"You're so much more than a showgirl."

A smile ghosted her lips. "Thank you."

"So what's after tea?"

"Let me see." She leaned forward, squinting. "There's a walk. Then dinner. And after that it's make Everley see stars time."

This time his laugh was loud. "Is everybody taking part in that?"

"Can you imagine?" She grimaced. "I'm really hoping it's not that kind of party."

"I wouldn't let them touch you anyway." He flicked the indicator, slowing down the car as he turned right through a pair of huge wrought iron gates. "Speaking of which, we're here."

She looked ahead at the mansion at the end of the driveway. Even at this distance it looked imposing. Letting out a low whistle, she brushed some lint from her jeans. "They did say casual dress, right?"

"Yeah, jeans are fine. It's all good." She could see him glance at her thighs again. "You look good, don't sweat it."

"I just want you to get this donation."

"I know you do. And I'm thankful for it." He flashed her a smile. "You'll be great. Relax. We've got this."

Expensive cars were lined in front of the house. She took them all in, glancing from Mercedes to Jaguar to Ferrari. "Now I see why they can afford to build medical centers in Africa," she joked.

"They're not all theirs." He parked and shut the engine off, then climbed out of the car and walked around to open her door.

"Is it as imposing inside as it is on the exterior?" she asked him.

"Honestly? No. You've met Grace and Warren. Their home is exactly like them. Expensive but welcoming. You'll do fine. You're used to people with full wallets."

Yeah, she was. The theater crowd was full of them. But this felt more important. It was Dylan's work, and she wanted to help him with it. And then there was this sexual tension between them. The promise of stars.

Her mind was full of it.

Taking her hand in his, Dylan led her up the stairs. He knocked on the door, and it was opened by an older man – definitely not Warren.

"Doctor and Mrs. Shaw?"

Everley blinked. How did he know that?

"Yes, it's good to see you again." Dylan nodded. "This is my wife, Everley."

"Hi." She gave him a broad smile.

"Please, come in," the butler said, pulling the huge door wide. "Do you have luggage?"

"Yeah, I'll go and get it." Dylan glanced back at the car.

"I can arrange for it to be brought up," the butler murmured.

"It's okay. I got it."

As Dylan went down the steps, she heard her name being called. Turning, she saw Grace Carson walking up the hallway, a huge smile on her face.

"You made it," she said, holding her hands out to Everley. Everley took them, and Grace squeezed. "Oh, you look as beautiful as ever. What an exquisite sweater."

"Thank you. You look amazing, too."

Grace was wearing a pair of butter soft leather jeans and a red shirt, her hair pulled into a low bun. "Thank you. Warren wasn't sure whether to laugh or cry when he saw these pants. All I know is that wherever I walk he's looking at my butt."

Dylan arrived with their cases. The butler took them from him and placed them by the stairs. "I'll arrange for them to be taken to your room." He looked at Grace. "Is there anything else you need, madam?"

"No, we're all good." Grace smiled warmly at him.

"In that case, I shall make sure that the drinks are flowing smoothly."

Grace kissed Dylan on the cheek. "Thank you for coming. Do you mind if I steal Everley for a moment. I want to take her on a tour of the house. Warren is in the library with the rest of our guests. Third door on the left. He's pouring drinks if you'd like one."

Dylan glanced at Everley, as though checking that she was okay with him leaving her.

"I'll see you in a bit," she said to Dylan, giving him what she hoped was a reassuring smile.

Grace slid her arm through Everley's, as though they were two girls out on the town. "I love that he didn't want to leave you for a minute. So protective and handsome. You're a lucky girl." Grace took her hand and led her down the hallway. "So this is our living room," she said, pushing open a door. Everley blinked, because it was already decorated for Christmas. A huge, twenty foot tree stood at the far end of the room, decked with ornaments and reindeer, lights twinkling as they walked into the room.

"It's from the Christmas tree farm in Winterville," Grace confessed. "I couldn't help myself. They came out and decorated the whole house for us. They were already fully booked in December, so they came this week."

"Was it Amber who came?"

"Yes. She's lovely, isn't she?"

Everley nodded. "I know her well. She co-owns the farm with my cousin, North."

"The hottie? He came, too. We ordered a lot of décor. Damn, he's a fine man. I could watch him carry trees all day."

Everley didn't even want to think about how much they'd charged to drive three hours to a house in the valley, then to decorate the entire place. She knew North had probably grumbled the whole way, and Amber would have tried to quietly cheer him up.

"To be fair, he's not that much of a hottie. I remember when he peed his bed every night." That was a lie, but it made Grace laugh.

"Are he and Amber a thing? They were very close."

"Oh Lord, no. Amber knows exactly what North's like. She wouldn't touch him with a ten foot pole."

"Why, what is he like?" Grace sounded intrigued.

"I don't know. I put my fingers in my ears whenever women talk about him. But I think a lot of people have taken a trip up North." Or rather, North had taken a trip up them.

"Well, I can't say I blame them. He's definitely a handsome man."

Grace took her around the rest of the house, pointing out paintings that meant a lot to her, and antiques she'd sourced during her trips around the world. She had such an easy way to her, it was impossible not to warm up to her. "I'm so glad you're here," she said to Everley, squeezing her arm as they walked down the sweeping stairway. "Sometimes these parties can feel so stale and boring. I have a feeling today is going to be the opposite."

Everley smiled. "I wasn't planning on doing a burlesque act after cocktails or anything."

"I know." Grace laughed. "But it's nice to have some young people here..." she trailed off as they reached the bottom of the stairs, and the front door clicked. As it opened, a man who looked to be in his late thirties appeared in the doorway, a thick black woolen coat covering his tall body, his sandy hair falling over his brow.

Grace let out a squeal.

"You said you weren't coming," she said, running over and flinging her arms around him. He gave a little chuckle, then caught Everley's eye over Grace's shoulder. He held her gaze for a moment longer than felt polite. She looked away, wondering if she should head to the library to join Dylan, or wait here while Grace and whoever this guy was caught up with each other.

"Everley, come here." Grace beckoned at her. "This is my son, Miller. He's supposed to be in New York right now." She kissed his cheek. "But I'm very glad he isn't."

"It's a pleasure to meet you." Everley offered her hand. "Where in New York are you supposed to be? I lived there for a while a few years ago."

He shook her hand, a smile pulling at his lips. "Soho. I was supposed to be having Thanksgiving with friends, but one of their parents got sick. And it made me worry about my own." He shrugged. "So here I am." He released Everley's hand. "What did you do in New York?"

"I mostly worked off-Broadway."

"You're an actress?" His eyes warmed with interest.

"Miller is a huge fan of the theater," Grace told her. "He's invested in a few profitable shows."

"I didn't have much of a choice, considering my name." He lifted a brow.

"Arthur Miller?" Everley asked.

"He's my favorite," Grace admitted. "*The Crucible* changed my life."

"Grace, are you two ever coming to join us?" Warren Carson called out, walking into the hallway. His face lit up when he saw his son standing there. "Miller, my boy. So good to see you. Come have a drink."

"Only if you'll join us," Miller said to Everley, offering his arm.

"I probably should. My husband is in there." She wasn't sure why she said it. As a warning maybe? She was old enough to know when a man was showing interest in her, and that was the last thing she needed right now.

Miller showed no sign of disappointment. And when she didn't take his arm, he gently pressed his strong palm against her back, leading her into the library. Heads lifted as they walked in, people calling out Miller's name with delight. The same people gave her speculative glances, as though they thought she'd arrived with Miller.

Dylan was standing in the corner of the library, at the end of a floor-to-ceiling bookshelf filled with leather bound hardbacks, a drink in his hand as he spoke to an older man and his wife. Slowly, he turned around, his eyes narrowing as he glanced over to see Miller's hand still pressing into her back.

Murmuring something to the couple he was speaking to, Dylan stalked across the library, his eyes never leaving hers. Her heart started to hammer against her ribcage because she knew that look.

"Darling," she smiled at him, keeping her voice light, "come meet Miller, Grace and Warren's son." Her eyes met his. *Don't mess this up, baby. Your donation depends on them.*

Dylan's gaze flickered from her to Miller. He offered a hand. "Dylan Shaw."

Miller had to release his hold on Everley's waist to shake it. Dylan took the opportunity to replace it with his own, pulling Everley to his side and pressing his lips to her brow. "I missed you," he murmured.

"I was only gone a few minutes."

"It was long enough."

"What is it you do, Dylan?" Miller asked. He had the kind of grace that only the uber rich seemed to have. He was good looking, too, with expensively styled dark hair and a bone structure that seemed to be the perfect combination of his parents'.

"I'm a doctor."

"We told you about him, remember?" Grace said. "The foundation is donating to the charity he works for."

"I remember." Miller nodded. "You live in Africa, right?"

"Some of the time, yes." Dylan's voice was guarded.

"How about you?" Miller asked Everley. "Do you live there, too?"

"I live in the mountains. I run a theater in Winterville."

"You should see it," Grace said. "So beautiful. Her show opens next week."

"It does?" Miller smiled. "I'd love to come watch."

"You should." Grace clapped her hands together. "I love Christmas shows. They make me feel like a little girl again, when my grandparents took me to Radio City Music Hall to see the Rockettes."

"I'm sure we could sort something out. Let me know when and I'll see if we can find you a seat." She smiled at Miller, because she remembered the reason they were here. To get the money Dylan's work needed. And if it meant schmoozing the Carsons then that's what they would do.

"I'm back in West Virginia for a few days before Christmas. Will the show still be on then?" Miller asked her.

"Yes." Everley smiled. "Give me your contact details and I'll save you a ticket." She could feel Dylan tense next to her. She wanted to slap him. He was behaving like a baby.

A stupid, mercurial baby who couldn't decide if he wanted to ignore her or fight for her.

"I'm getting a drink. Would you like one?" Miller asked Everley. "You and Mom seem to be the only two without a glass in your hands."

"I'll have a sherry, please, sweetheart," Grace said.

"What else do you have?" Everley asked.

"Come with me and see." Miller smiled at her.

"Actually, I need to talk to my wife about something," Dylan said, his voice controlled. "Maybe you could get her a gin and tonic. With lime not lemon if you have it."

"Ice?" Miller asked Everley.

"Yes, please."

He winked at her, and ambled over to the drinks cabinet. Grace and Warren were called over to speak to some friends, leaving Dylan and Everley alone by the door.

"Stop flirting with the donors." Dylan's lips pressed against her ear. She felt a shiver rush through her from the warmth of his breath.

"I'm not flirting. I'm being friendly because you want this donation." Though she was still smiling, her teeth were clenched.

"You're also supposed to be my wife. People will talk if you throw yourself at Miller Carson."

"You think I'm throwing myself at him?" she asked archly.

"Looked like it to me."

"If I wanted to flirt with him, you'd know it." She pulled her lip between her teeth. "And he'd know it, too."

"I bet he would."

"What's that supposed to mean?" She side-eyed him.

"Nothing." He had a stupid smirk on his face. She wanted to slap it off of him.

"No, come on, tell me." Her voice was dangerously low. "I'm really interested to hear your take on it. Because for a guy who turned down no-strings sex with me, you seem pretty damn interested in who else might want something from me."

He inhaled sharply. "I turned you down to protect you."

"No, you didn't. You turned me down to protect *you*."

"Don't be angry with me." He dipped his head, his lips brushing her throat. "I'm your husband. I'm supposed to get jealous."

She inhaled sharply

"Tomorrow you can be angry," he said. "For today, you're mine."

"And tonight?"

His eyes darkened. "Tonight..."

"One gin and tonic," Miller said, cutting through the atmosphere between her and Dylan. "Lime not lemon."

Still flustered, Everley took the proffered glass. "Thank you." She lifted it to her lips, swallowing a big mouthful.

"It's a pleasure. I have to go make a couple of phone calls, but maybe we could talk later." Miller smiled at her. "I bet we know a lot of the same people. It would be good to talk shop."

Dylan's fingers pressed into her waist. "That sounds lovely," she agreed, ignoring her neanderthal husband.

"Great. I'll catch you later." He glanced at Dylan, his expression easy. "You're a lucky man."

His jaw ticked. "I know."

16

A huge lunch was followed by the threatened game of Charades in the living room. Everley was in her element, having everybody in fits of laughter as she tried to act out some movie, throwing herself on the floor and holding her hands above her head. Through it all, Dylan was annoyed at himself, because he'd been so jealous of Miller Carson that he'd made a fool of himself, the same way he'd made an idiot out of himself in front of her friend Casey.

For a guy who said he wasn't interested in his soon-to-be-ex-wife, he sure was acting possessive of her.

"It must be difficult, leaving her to go to Africa every time," Miller said, passing Dylan a glass of soda water.

"It is." Maybe that's why he hadn't come home often, much to his dad's regret. Because even seeing her messed up his brain. "But she's worth it."

"I don't know, man, if she was mine I'd find her impossible to leave."

Dylan swallowed. He wasn't going to get jealous again. Because one day a man wouldn't leave her. It could be Miller or a hundred other guys, but some lucky dude was going to capture her heart. And he was the one who had to live with that.

Everley held her wrists together as though they·were being bound. Then she tipped back her head and sighed with ecstasy.

"*Fifty Shades of Grey*!" Grace shouted out.

Everley grinned. "You got it."

A smile played around Miller's lips. "She's pretty good at that."

"Acting? Yeah."

"Mom told me she's Candy Winter's granddaughter."

"That's right. We both grew up in Winterville."

"You grew up there, too?" Miller asked.

"My dad runs a garage there."

"It's a long way from Winterville to Africa," Miller said, looking almost impressed.

"It is." Dylan nodded.

"Okay," Grace called out. "For those of you who'd like some tea and cakes, we have them in the dining room. And if you want a brisk walk afterward, Warren has kindly agreed to lead a trek into the woods at the bottom of the lawns." She smiled at everybody, her face flushed from the wine. "And for those of you that prefer more idle pursuits, you're more than welcome to take a nap in your rooms."

"Hey." Everley joined them, her face glowing. "Shall we walk?" she asked Dylan.

"Yeah, a walk sounds good."

"Are you coming, too?" She looked at Miller.

"Nah. I'm going to take the nap option. I left New York early this morning, and I need to sober up before Dad starts making the evening cocktails."

"Are they stronger than the ones this morning?" Everley asked.

"You could say that." Miller grimaced. "I'd advise one at most. And never on an empty stomach."

Everley slid her hand into Dylan's like it was the most natural thing in the world. "Do you want some tea and cake?" she asked him.

"I'm still full from lunch." He'd eaten two platefuls, hungry from the drive and his stupid jealousy. "But I'll come with you."

"Good." She kissed his cheek. "I like a man who knows how to feed his woman."

The air outside was cool. Dylan was waiting for her as she walked out of the back door, her red woolen coat buttoned to the neck, and a cream beanie pulled down tightly over her ears. He looked annoyingly gorgeous as always. He was wearing a pair of jeans and a sweater, his grey pea coat molded perfectly to his body. He looked preppy and hot and suddenly the frozen air wasn't registering anymore.

"Is everybody here?" Warren said, drunken jollity thickening his voice. He looked at Everley and Dylan, then frowned, his eyes scanning the lawn as though he was expecting people to emerge from the perfectly cut grass. "Oh. Just the three of us?"

"Seems that way." Everley bit down a smile.

"Hmm. Maybe we should go inside and keep warm instead?" Warren looked hopeful.

"You should go inside," Everley agreed. "We can take a wander. Your grounds are beautiful."

Warren's eyes lit up. "Okay. If you head down to the tree-line, you should find a path that takes you down to the lake. Follow it around the edge and it will loop back and bring you here again. If you reach the mountains, you're lost."

Dylan laughed, his eyes catching Everley's. "Got it."

They both had a pretty good sense of direction. It came from spending most of their childhood outdoors. You learned to tell the direction from the light shining between the tree canopy and the growth of the green moss clinging to the bark of trees.

"Have fun, kids." Warren lifted his hand and strode back to the house like he couldn't believe his luck.

Dylan slid his gloved hand into hers, and they followed the path through the lawn, an easy silence falling between them. They hadn't spoken much during lunch – she'd been sat next to some old family friends of the Carsons, and for some excruciating reason Dylan and Miller had been placed next to each other. Maybe Grace had thought the two youngest men in the room would be good company for one another.

But every now and then she could sense his gaze on her face. And when she turned to catch his eye there would be a strange expression on his face. A sad kind of regret that pulled at her heart strings.

"About what happened in the library earlier," Dylan said, as they walked into the woods, the air markedly cooler away from the soft winter sun.

"We don't need to talk about it. It's fine."

"No, it isn't. I was an asshole and I upset you and I'm sorry." He shook his head, his hand still holding hers.

"I just didn't understand. Miller seems like a nice guy."

"He is." Dylan pressed his lips together. "He is a good guy. Maybe when we're divorced..."

"Don't say it. I'm not going to date Miller Carson."

He bit down a smile. "Good."

"I thought you liked him."

"He's okay, but not good enough for you."

A bird trilled from a tree. She looked up, but couldn't see

it on the bare branches. "Who would be good enough for me?" she asked, smiling.

"Somebody who made you happy." His expression was serious. "Somebody who treats you exactly like the queen you are. Who makes it their life's work to put a smile on your face every morning and every night?"

"You're describing somebody from a fairy tale. Reality doesn't work like that." They'd reached some rocks. Dylan gently held her waist as she clambered over them. She could hear the pants of his breath as he followed right behind.

"It should."

"You know your problem?" she asked, as they reached the other side.

"I imagine you're going to tell me." A smile played at his lips. She loved this easy, relaxed version of Dylan.

And yeah, she loved the hot, angry jealous version too.

"You think that unless you're happy all the time you think you've failed. But life isn't like that. You don't get to have the sunshine without the rain. And you spend so much time fighting those uncomfortable feelings that you only end up frustrated."

He blinked. "I do?"

"Why were you so angry with Miller in the library earlier?" she asked.

"Because I'm an asshole."

She couldn't help but laugh at his gruff reply. "That's not true. Seriously, why were you angry?"

"He has this ease with life. The same way you do. And watching the two of you, I realized that's something I can't give you. I'm not an easy kind of guy, Everley. I'm intense and I'm messy and I have all these feelings I have no idea how to express."

"You think he's always easy? You think *I* am?" She shook her head. "That's not true. He probably shouts at Baristas when they get his order wrong. Or kicks dogs because they bark too loud."

Dylan shook his head. "Sure."

"You have passion. You have ideals. You have no idea how hot that is."

His hold on her hand tightened. "Shut up."

"You know when you kissed my neck in the library? All angry and jealous and marking your territory? That was better than most of the sex I've had in my life. And I'm not kidding about that."

His gaze darkened, but he said nothing.

"And the fact you want to give me pleasure with nothing in return all night? That was hot too, until you started being an asshole about it."

"I meant every word."

"I know you did." She bit down a smile. A soft breeze rustled through the trees, the branches above them dancing. "But every time you get angry? It's not about me, it's about you. You keep fighting yourself and it drives you crazy."

"Is that what you think?"

"Yeah." She nodded. The way he was looking at her made her breathless. "You have this idea that you have to be super-human to be a good person. That you can never make mistakes. And that can never be. To err is human."

"There's nothing wrong with having ideals."

"No, there isn't. But there's also nothing wrong with having fun. Living in the moment. Giving in to what we want. Eat the damn chocolate, drink the damn wine."

"Kiss my damn wife."

Her breath caught. "Yes, kiss your wife."

He pulled his glove from his hand, lifting it to her face. "I don't want to hurt you."

"How's that going for you?" she asked softly.

A smile ghosted his lips. "Not great."

"Maybe I can worry about myself. If I think you're hurting me, I'll tell you."

His eyes scanned her face, dipping to her lips. She parted them, breathless from the needy expression on his face.

"I can't stay away from you," he murmured.

"Then don't."

He cupped her jaw with his palm, his thumb tracing the line of her bottom lip. His eyes were dark, his brows furrowed, as he pressed his thumb into her mouth. She fluttered her tongue against him, and a low growl caught in his throat.

Slowly, he pulled it out, and when it was gone she already missed the feel of him. The taste of him. He smeared the wetness of her tongue across her bottom lip, then leaned in to run his own tongue along it.

It felt bad and yet so right. As though he didn't want to just kiss her, he wanted to consume her. Taste everything she had to offer. His breath fanned against her mouth as he slowly brushed his lips against hers, his strong fingers tipping her head so his nose slotted right against hers, his other hand wrapping around her waist to pull her against him.

His kiss was slow. Deliberate. The kind of kiss that made his intentions absolutely clear. He wasn't just making her feel good, he was claiming her.

Making her his again. As if she hadn't been all along.

His tongue slid against hers, his fingers digging into her waist, his body hard in all the right places. She could feel herself melt against him, despite the ice cold breeze rustling through the trees. And she wondered again, how would she ever find anybody who made her feel like this again.

When they parted, a smile was playing at his lips. There was a kind of triumph in his eyes that matched her own. "We should walk back," he said, sliding his hand back into hers. "Before people think I'm ravishing my wife in the forest."

It was that time of the evening when everybody was mellow and the conversation was muted. Warren and a few of his friends had disappeared to the library to smoke cigars, and others had wandered to bed. Grace had put on an album of Christmas songs, and Everley bit down a smile when she heard her grandma start to sing.

She was curled up on a sofa next to Dylan. He was talking to a couple about his work in Africa. His hand was tangled in her hair, twisting the locks idly between his fingers.

It felt normal, so real. They hadn't had a chance to be alone again since their walk. When they'd got back, Warren had dragged Dylan in for a game of cards with some potential donors he wanted to introduce him to, while Everley had taken a shower and dressed for dinner. When they were all full of the beautiful ham that Grace had served, she'd served coffee in the conservatory that was lit up with thousands of sparkling fairy lights, followed by dancing to the music from a string quartet in the ballroom.

Dylan had a glass of whiskey in the hand that wasn't touching her, but she noticed he wasn't drinking it. He had one glass of wine with dinner, and that was it. He was practically sober, unlike the rest of them.

The door to the living room opened, a burst of laughter echoing through from the library. Miller walked in, his face lighting up when he saw Everley and Dylan on the sofa.

"I thought you two had gone to bed. Nearly everybody else has."

"We probably will soon." Her stomach did a flip flop at the thought. She had no idea where she stood with Dylan, but one thing was for sure, they'd be sharing a room tonight. "Have you been in the library with your dad?"

He perched on the edge of the coffee table, resting his

elbows on his thighs as he faced her. His knees were inches away from hers. "Yeah, but the cigar smoke in there was getting to me. I can't stand the things." He shook his head. "I have to inhale enough fumes when I'm in New York."

"How is New York?" Everley asked.

"Busy as ever. The traffic is always gridlocked, there are cranes everywhere. You still take your life in your hands when you go on the subway." He grinned. "Do you miss it?"

"Not really. I loved it when I was younger, but I like running my small theater. I like the control." Dylan's thumb brushed against the top of her spine. Okay, she liked control in most things.

Except for where he was concerned.

"You're not exactly ancient now." Miller tipped his head. "How old are you anyway?"

"Thirty."

"And you've been married how long?"

Dylan's fingers stuttered, then caressed her again.

"Nearly nine years."

"Jesus, you were practically a child bride." Miller lifted a brow. "I hate to think about what I was doing when I was twenty-one. It probably wasn't legal, though."

She smiled. "Sometimes you just know."

Dylan's hand dipped to her exposed back, tracing the line of her spine.

"You two being together this long is a hell of an achievement. Not many people make it anymore. And you two have more things to contend with than most. Your careers... living on different continents. It must get lonely."

"We survive. Anyway, how about you? Any potential Mrs. Carsons waiting in the wings for you to pop the question?"

He grinned. "Not right now. When you get to my age, all the good ones have been snapped up."

Dylan pressed his thigh against hers and she could feel the steel hardness of his muscles.

"The early bird gets the worm," she said lightly.

"I know that now. You two probably had the right idea. You got to grow up together. I think that can make all the difference. When you get to your thirties, finding someone gets harder. There's the pressure. And not just from society, but from your own head. When's the right time to settle down, to have kids, to start being an adult... But on the other hand, I like my life. I don't want to change it. And having a family definitely would."

"You don't have to have a family. It's not the law."

He looked over her shoulder. "Don't let my mom hear you say that." He laughed, and took another sip of his drink. "Anyway, I have something to ask you."

"Sure."

"Why are there no pictures of you and Dylan on the internet?"

Dylan glanced at her from the corner of his eye, but still carried on with the conversation he was having.

"Um, what do you mean?"

"I Googled you guys and there's nothing."

The hair on her neck stood on end. "Is that so unusual?" she asked, trying to keep her voice casual. Why the hell would he Google them?

"It's the twenty-first century. There should at least be a photo of you two on somebody's Instagram. Or Facebook or something. I mean, there's plenty of pictures of Dylan doing his work in Africa, and a lot of you in various plays. Plus with your family in Winterville. But not of the two of you together.

"I guess we're very private. And when we're together, we're not about taking selfies."

"Well you should. You're a very photogenic couple." He took his phone from his pocket. "Mind if I take one now?"

"Oh God, no. I look terrible. And my make up must have dissolved from my face."

Miller smiled at her. "You look beautiful, Everley. You always do."

"You can take it," Dylan said, breaking off his conversation to pull her against him. He pressed his lips to her hair, breathing her in. "He's right. It will be nice to have more pictures of us. I can look at them when we're apart."

He didn't sound like he was playing a role. But then, she wasn't sure she was either.

Sliding his arm around her shoulders, he smiled easily at Miller, who pressed the button on his screen with a smile playing at his lips. "I'll message it to you," he told Everley.

"You don't have my number."

"No, but my mom does. I'll get it from her."

The couple Dylan had been talking with left, promising to keep in touch about his work. There were only a few people remaining scattered around the room. "We should head to bed," Dylan murmured, as though he could feel her discomfort. "We have a long day tomorrow." He helped her up from the sofa, his fingers sliding through hers.

"What time do you have to leave?" Miller asked.

"Six."

"Ouch. I'll probably still be asleep." Standing, Miller offered Dylan his hand, then kissed Everley softly on her cheek. "But I'll see you at the show, right?"

"Right." She offered him a smile. "Thank you for making it such a lovely day."

"Good night, Everley. And good luck with opening night."

17

From the moment they walked through the door of their guest bedroom, she could feel the atmosphere change. Electricity buzzed in the air, as though even the atoms knew that Dylan had made a promise to her.

She heard the door gently click behind her, and turned to see Dylan leaning against it, a smile playing at his lips.

Her heart started to hammer against her chest. It was the first time since their walk in the grounds that they'd been completely alone together, and the first time in eight years that they were about to sleep in the same room. But that wasn't what was playing on her mind.

It was his promise. And the thought of seeing stars.

"You sure about this?" he asked, his voice gritty, as though he could read her mind.

She swallowed hard. "I'm sure."

He nodded, his dark eyes not leaving hers. "If you want to stop at any time, just say the word. I'll hold you, or sleep on the floor or leave the room. Whatever you need."

Her chest clenched, because she could tell he meant every word. "Make me see stars, Dylan."

He pushed himself away from the door and walked toward her, and she felt a shiver wrack down her spine. She could smell the citrus and pine of his cologne as he came closer, before he reached for the zipper of her dress, his fingers a heated trail along her back.

He gently lifted her hair over her right shoulder to stop it from getting stuck in the teeth, then slid his fingers down her back, pulling at the tag until the fabric gave way.

She exhaled in relief. She loved that dress, but she liked breathing more. Dylan moved his hands up her bare back, tracing her spine with his fingers, and the relief disappeared, replaced by dark, throbbing need.

"No bra?" his voice was low.

"It's integral."

He reached the top of her shoulders, then pressed his lips against the base of her neck. "Is this okay?"

"Yes." She tried to stop the ache from sounding in her voice. It was more than okay. It was perfect. Just a slide of his fingers and the merest brush of his mouth and she was jelly in his arms.

He slid his hands beneath the spaghetti straps that kept her dress from falling, moving them over her shoulders and down her arms. The bodice fell, leaving her breasts exposed. She stepped out of it, her back still toward Dylan, oh so aware she was wearing nothing except a pair of black lace panties.

"Come here." Dylan's voice was strong. In control. She turned on her toes like a ballet dancer, her nipples hardening when she saw the dark expression on his face.

"Can I touch you?"

"Please."

The corner of his lip quirked. He was still fully dressed, his tie knotted, his jacket unbuttoned. He stepped forward and traced her cheek, blazing a trail of fire down her jaw, her neck, her chest.

"Your freckle is still here," he murmured, dropping his head to kiss the single freckle above the swell of her breast. "I used to fantasize about this freckle."

"It's a strange thing to fantasize about." Her voice caught in her throat as his lips warmed her skin.

"Not when it's the gateway drug to my favorite addiction." He kissed the swell of each of her breasts, then traced them with his hands, and she had to bite down hard to stop herself from crying out with frustration. As if he could sense her desperation, his warm lips pulled at her nipple, his tongue grazing the peak before he sucked at her.

She was already so wet. Her legs started to shake as he moved to her other breast. Lips warm, teeth grazing, his insistent, tugging sending bolts of pleasure straight to her core.

His hands slid to her waist, and he kissed his way back up to her neck, walking them back until he was sitting on the edge of the mattress and she was straddling him.

He tipped her back, her spine arching to give him better access to her chest. He bit her nipple then blew on her to soothe it, and she let out a gasp. "Dylan!"

"Mmm?"

"Your suit. I'm... wet."

A deliciously dirty smile pulled at his lips. "I don't give a shit about my suit. Sit on me." He couldn't help himself from putting his hands between her thighs, his fingers grazing the lace of her panties.

"Shit, you are wet. Jesus, Everley. Let me make you feel better."

He pulled her down, until her core was against him. She could feel the hard outline of his excitement, pressing against her, sending shots of desire to the tips of her toes. Capturing her lips between his, he kissed her languorously, sliding his hand between them until his fingers reached the elastic of her panties.

"This first one is purely for comfort," he said against her lips. He pushed his hand further down, swallowing hard at the slickness of her, his fingers teasing and touching until her hips moved of their own accord.

He was too soft. Too gentle, and it had nothing to do with his need to treat her carefully. She knew he liked to tease. Liked to coax every gasp and cry from her lips until all she could say was his name. She'd never met a lover so generous yet so taking.

Her pleasure was his drug.

She was breathing heavily, her lips stuttering against his as he slid his fingers inside her, his thumb moving against her where she needed it the most. She could feel the drum of a pulse, matching the rhythm of his touch, as pleasure coiled inside her, spitting and hissing as it waited for sweet relief.

Breaking their kiss, he dipped his head to her breast, his free hand pressed into her back to stop her from falling away. He captured her nipple, sucking and biting, as lightning shot through her, the pleasure so intense it was on the edge of painful.

She let out a cry, her toes curling, her body fluttering around him, as her muscles contracted then released as he slowed his movements, coaxing the delirium from her until all she could see was white behind her eyelids.

He kissed her shoulder, her jaw, her lips. "That one was for you. The next is for me."

"I don't think I can."

"Yeah, you can. And I want to taste you." He lifted her from his lap, her body feeling boneless as he lay her back on the mattress and pulled her underwear down her legs. Then he ran his warm palms up the inside of her calves, his fingers tracing circles as they reached her thighs.

His hands stilled. She looked at him through heavy lids, and his gaze reached hers.

"It's still there."

"What is?" Her brows knitted.

"Your tattoo." He traced the 'D' she'd had tattooed on her hip all those years ago. "You didn't laser it off."

She shook her head. "I didn't want to."

"Fuck, Everley. That's…" his voice trailed off as he shook his head. He blew out a mouthful of air. "For that, you get an extra orgasm." He pressed his lips to her hip, his tongue tasting her skin. When he pulled away, he blew on it, and it made her shiver.

"You're still dressed," she rasped. "You need to be naked."

A grin pulled at his lips. "I thought you'd never ask."

With slow, deliberate actions, he slid his jacket off, placing it carefully on the chair, then pulled at his tie, rolling it in his hands before putting it on the seat.

"Are you deliberately being slow?"

"I'm giving you a chance to catch your breath." His eyes bore into hers as he unbuttoned his shirt. When she saw his chest, she almost cried. It was perfect. Warm, tanned skin, thick ridges of muscles, and a tight, flat stomach that disappeared into his pants.

"You hanging in there, Evie?"

"Just about."

He bit down a smile, pulling his socks off, then unbuckling his belt. He had a cool easy confidence that made her chest fill with joy. He knew his body, knew what he could do with it.

Knew how it affected her.

Sure, she'd met men more aesthetically beautiful. There

were no shortage of them in the business. But not one of them made her legs tremble and her breath stutter.

None of them made her feel so feminine. So aware of her own body.

He was naked, his hardness jutting out, and all she wanted to do was touch him. But instead, he pulled at her thighs, dropping to his knees on the carpet as he pulled her until her core met his face.

"I decided to eat the chocolate," he said, running his tongue along the edge of her. "Drink the wine."

Then he buried his face against her, and she couldn't hear his words anymore.

By the time he'd wrung the fourth orgasm out of her, she was begging to touch him. He was so hard he was afraid he might explode at the merest brush of her fingers. Instead, he soothed her breasts with his lips, murmured words of appreciation against her ear, and stroked her heated body as she slowly came back to earth.

He hadn't been lying about her being his drug. Her first orgasm had been like the opposite of cold turkey. A rush that he'd forgotten about, or at least pushed to the back of his mind.

But now he was remembering just how amazing her pleasure was, and he wanted more. And that damn tattoo had sent him a little bit crazy. She was still marked with his initial.

For tonight, at least, she was all his.

Her second release had come on his tongue. Her third, he'd made her wring out of herself, watching with heavy lids as her fingers slowly circled that perfect, secret part of her.

And her fourth had come as a surprise to them both. He'd been sucking and biting her breasts, just to hear her gasp again. Then he'd moved his hand down to feel how wet she was, and the touch of his fingers was enough to make her scream so loud the whole house could probably hear.

Not that he cared. He ached to hear her again.

"Kiss me. Please." She was breathless, reaching for him. He crawled over her prone body, caging her with his arms, being careful not to let his body press against hers. Their lips touched, their tongues battled, and she wrapped her arms around him, trying to bring him closer.

He hadn't accounted for biology. Or the call of her body to his. She wrapped her legs around his hips, arching her torso until they were touching, and all he could feel was the heat of her slickness against him.

Giving in to the need, he lowered himself gently, rolling his hips until his hardness was covered with her pleasure. She gasped into his lips, and rocked against him, and... *damn*... he could feel the tempting openness of her. It took every ounce of control he had not to push his way inside.

"Evie, I don't have a condom."

She blinked. "You don't?"

"No. Do you?"

A smile flicked at the corner of her lip. "No. Should we go ask Miller?"

"Definitely not."

"I thought all guys carried condoms around." She kissed the corner of his lip. "Especially doctors."

"I wasn't exactly planning on this. Unlike you." He ran his hands down her side, pressing his fingers into the globes of her behind. "So technically, you should have brought the condom."

"I'm on the pill."

His eyes flickered to hers, the tantalizing thought of being inside of her bare flitting through his mind. "I can't have sex with you bareback."

"If it helps I had a physical last month. I'm clean."

He squeezed his eyes shut, to center himself. She was so damn tempting. "So am I. But this isn't going to happen."

"Okay. We can just make out." She dipped her eyes, trying not to smile. "Naked."

"You think I can make out naked with you without wanting to fuck you?"

She shook her head. "No."

He pressed his hard lips to hers, twisting his hand into her hair and tugging it back. "You're a bad girl."

"But it feels so good, right?" She hitched her hips, and he slid against her again. He groaned, closing his eyes. A few more of those and he'd probably come on her stomach.

"Evie..."

"I'm sorry. I'll stop."

"No, don't stop. Christ, don't stop." He kissed her again, his mouth hot against hers. Her hands fluttered around him, her nails digging into his ass. And he was moving again, his hips against hers, the tip of him *right there*.

So close to heaven.

And that's when he knew. He had to have her right then and there. Fuck the condom. Fuck being sensible. Fuck always being the one who thought about consequences.

"If we do this, we're both going to hell."

"You're so dramatic." She kissed the corner of his lip. "You should be on the stage." Then she wrapped her legs tighter around him, her hips tipping until there was nowhere else for him to go.

Not that he wanted to be anywhere else but inside of her.

He pulled her thighs from around him, splaying them out on the mattress, kissing her hard as he took control. Then he was sliding inside, his breath catching at the warmth of her, the tightness, at the tingling in his spine as he made her his once more.

And when she reached her peak again, he let out a triumphant roar, feeling her clench him tight as he spilled inside her. They were nothing but pleasure, two fireworks lighting up the sky, making the world shift on its axis the same way it had when he first fell for her.

Everley Winter wasn't the kind of woman you ever got over. She burned herself too deeply into your psyche for that.

18

Exhaustion didn't even begin to cover it. In the few days since she and Dylan had come back from the Carson's house, Everley hadn't had a minute to herself. Every hour was either spent at the theater, or at home, sleeping in an attempt to catch up on the night she'd lost to seeing stars.

Not that she'd change a thing. Not even when her muscles protested every time she was lifted on the stage. And though she had to ignore Casey's amused quips every time she winced, it was still worth it.

Dylan had driven them home early in the morning on the day after Thanksgiving. The roads had been busy, thanks to the Black Friday sales, and she'd arrived late to the theater. From there on, everything that could go wrong, did go wrong. A lighting rig fell on the stage, and though nobody was on it at the time, it meant they lost a whole morning of rehearsals to having it repaired and the whole rig checked for health and safety reasons.

And then one of the dancers came down with the flu. Everley was on tenterhooks to see if anybody else caught the virus – she only had a few stand-ins available, and if she lost anyone else they'd have to change up the choreography two days before the show opened. Not something she wanted to do.

But now opening day had dawned and nobody else was sick. They'd done their final dress rehearsal the previous evening in front of a carefully selected audience of donors and it had gone smoothly. She kept crossing her fingers that tonight would be just as simple.

She arrived at the theater at eight that morning, unable to sleep despite her physical exhaustion. It was the first of December and the Christmas season was in full swing in Winterville. The decorations in the town square were complete and the tree was lit, the lights bright in the gloomy morning air. The shop windows were stuffed with ornaments and fir cones, displaying Christmas goods for sale. And a delicious smell of cinnamon wafted from The Cold Fingers Café as she passed, making her mouth water.

Normally, she would have headed in to order an Americano with steaming hot milk, but not today. She didn't like to drink coffee or milk on a show day. Later, she'd have a decaf tea with lemon, to help prepare her vocal chords for that night's show. But for now she had to stay strong.

"Good morning!" Casey called out, as he walked into her office. He had a Styrofoam cup in his hand. "It feels like a good day to put on a show."

"Don't bring that coffee near me. I'm going through detox," she muttered, holding her hands up to ward him off.

"Ah, the physical restraint of a performer." Casey removed the lid and took a deep inhale. "I'm so glad I just get to be behind the scenes nowadays. Did I tell you that David and I ate cheese last night? Lots and lots of cheese."

"Shut up." She narrowed her eyes at him. "Unless you want that cheese rammed up your—"

"Speaking of ramming things," Casey said, talking over her. "Have you seen Dylan again yet?"

She'd told him about their Thanksgiving night. Or rather, Casey had dragged it out of her.

"Of course I haven't. If I'm not here I'm in bed."

"So you've given him up like the caffeine and milk." Casey pouted. "That's sad."

"If it makes you feel any better he'll be in the audience tonight. And he's invited to the after party."

Casey smirked. "I know he is. I asked David to make sure he's on the list." David was organizing the after party, much to Everley's relief. And unlike Casey, he wouldn't get on her back about Dylan. "Tell me, do you think you two will leave together?"

She looked him right in the eye. "No."

Casey blinked. "Why not? You have all night. You won't have to get up early tomorrow. Hell, the cast won't get here until two hours before tomorrow night's show."

"Yeah, but we're the directors. We get in midday before performances."

"That still leaves you twelve hours for passion," Casey pointed out.

"Can we change the subject?" She didn't want to talk about Dylan. Or whether or not she was planning a repeat performance with him. He'd be leaving town after Christmas, and whether she slept with him again or not, there was no future there. And she was fine with that. Or she would be, once she got her heart to behave.

"Sure," Casey said, agreeably, taking another sip of his coffee. "Let's talk about how good this latte tastes right now."

The auditorium was almost full. Everley peeked around the curtain, watching as people took their seats, staring expectantly at the stage, talking to their neighbors as they waited for the show to begin.

Backstage, the cast and crew were manic. Dancers were pulling on their shoes, shouting to each other, while singers were warming up their voices, going up the scales and down again, their voices echoing through the corridors. The costume director was barking out orders to her team, who were rapidly moving clothes down the lines of their carts, while the makeup team was fixing last minute smudges.

"Five minutes," the stage manager called out.

Casey touched Everley's shoulder, giving her a nervous smile. "Did you know Gray Hartson is in the audience?"

"I invited him. He sang with me last year."

The cast began to gather around and hold hands, ready to send up a prayer. As soon as they finished, the opening dancers were being called to the wings and Casey was running back to the other side of the stage.

She took a long, cool breath in, pushing all thoughts of Dylan from her mind. She had a show to perform, and nothing else mattered right now.

By the time the interval came, all hints of her nerves had disappeared. The audience was laughing at the right time, clapping their hands in time to the music, and singing along with the songs that they knew the words to.

There had been a few mess ups. A dancer had fallen and hurt her ankle, and was icing it in the dressing room. One of the singer's mics had stopped working, and the sound engineer had to creep on stage in his dark clothes to replace it. But those were minor things, nothing like the catastrophes they'd had earlier that week.

More importantly, the audience was enjoying it. And it filled her soul with joy.

The second half passed by almost as smoothly, if you didn't think too closely about one of the singers forgetting his lines. Then it was Everley's final song, her grandmother's trademark Christmas song, that made her all the money and helped build this town. Everley was wearing her grandmother's old Santa costume, cut off at her thighs, nipped in at the waist, sparkly as hell, thanks to the thousands of sequins that had been painstakingly hand sewn to the fabric. Two gorgeous male dancers dressed as elves carried her onto the stage, as the orchestra played the intro. Before she could begin to sing the audience erupted into a rapturous applause, recognizing the song that always ended the show.

Everley knew they weren't applauding for her. They were applauding for the memory of her glamorous grandmother. The ever young, ever beautiful Candy Winter, who stole Hollywood's heart all those years ago.

This is for you, Grandma, she thought, as the dancers set her down in the center, facing the audience. She took in a deep breath and looked out at the people staring at her, then smiled as she began to sing.

It's not snowing outside,
  I have no presents to hide,
  But when you're here by my side
  It feels like Christmas, baby

They say Santa's on strike,
  And the elves took a hike,
  But I know what I like,
  That's you at Christmas, baby

. . .

Ooh, whenever you're in town
I put on my best shoes and gown
And I banish every single frown
You know it's simply true
Whenever I'm with you
Every day feels like Christmas, baby.

She came to the final line, her lungs protesting at how long she had to hold the last note. Before it had even faded, the audience was stomping and cheering, some of them jumping to their feet as tears stung at her eyes.

They'd done it. After all these weeks of planning and auditioning and rehearsals they'd managed to put on a show that people liked. The feeling of relief and elation washing over her was almost impossible to explain. It was like a drug, sending her soaring, her feet barely touching the ground.

And then she saw *him*. Standing like the others, a smile playing on his lips as his gaze met hers.

The rest of the cast joined her on the stage, as the applause continued. The orchestra started to play the first notes of *Have Yourself A Merry Little Christmas* sending the audience into a frenzy. Casey was beside her, holding her hand, kissing her on the cheek. "You did it, Everley. You went and fucking did it."

The dancers leaped across the front of the stage, and the singers joined hands, facing the audience and nodding for them to join in. Then the whole theater was singing about their troubles being out of sight.

And that's what this was all about. Helping people to forget their troubles. To let them be light and throw themselves into something that was bigger. That brought them all together.

Maybe everybody needed a little of that.

There was nothing as captivating as watching his wife on stage, using her body the way only she knew how. Dylan's own body hummed at the memory of her beneath him on Thanksgiving. Of the way her breath had caught in her throat as he pressed his lips against her thighs. She'd fallen apart in his arms five times, and that still wasn't enough.

He wasn't sure what would be.

He'd been a gentleman all week, knowing that this show was important to her. Most days he had video conferences with the doctors in the field, talking over cases, making suggestions about treatments. It was enough to distract him, but when they were over his mind was full of her again.

One night hadn't been enough. He wanted more. Wanted the taste of her permanently on his lips. Wanted to run his hands down those talented thighs and pull them against him until they were both breathless.

Wanted to make her see stars until she couldn't take any more.

As soon as the show was over, he stood from his seat on the third aisle and pushed his way through the legs of the audience, making his way to the exit on the right. He knew the way through the maze of corridors to the dressing rooms, then read the names on each one until he saw hers. He'd been in her dressing room enough to know that they were a free for all. People constantly entered and left. Refreshment staff refilled refrigerators and support staff took costumes that had been discarded to steam and rehang them. Then there were the boyfriends and friends and family who would enter to congratulate the performers.

He pushed open the door and let himself into the room that she shared with two others, his lips curling as he saw the huge bouquets of opening night flowers filling every surface, including the ones he'd sent.

He leaned against a table, lifting a card from one of the bouquets – smiling when he saw it was from Holly and Josh. Another was from Alaska, and then there was one from North, Gabe, and Kris.

He skipped over his own – he'd delivered it to the theater earlier, and he knew exactly what he'd written on the card.

Shine bright, like the star you are. D x

There was a huge bouquet of pale pink roses and ivory lilies right at the back. He didn't need to pick up the card to see who they were from. The type was big enough to read from where he was leaning.

Break a leg. Can't wait to see the show! Miller Carson x

He turned his back and ignored it, because Miller Carson wasn't here.

But he was.

As soon as she opened the dressing room door, he felt it. Their eyes clashed, and the connection between them sizzled.

He could almost taste the need for her rushing through his body.

"Congratulations," he said, his voice low. "You were amazing."

"Did you like it?" Her face glowed as she looked at him, her lips parted softly.

"I loved it. Everybody did. You heard the applause, right?"

"I did. But half the audience either lives in this town or knows me. They'd applaud if I landed on my butt."

"You know that's not true." And now he was thinking about her butt. The way it fit perfectly in his palms. "You slayed them. It was perfect. Your grandma would be proud."

He took a step forward, and her chest hitched. Her breasts were pushed together by the sequined jacket she was wearing. He wanted to trace the line of her cleavage with his mouth.

When he looked up, he could see the intensity of her stare. It made him hard knowing that she wanted him, too. He leaned closer, enough to feel the heat of her skin radiating from her, and he began to lower his lips to hers.

"Am I interrupting?" Casey asked, pushing the door open.

Dylan immediately pulled back.

A smile pulled at Everley's lips. "Dylan was just taking my temperature," she joked, and his own lips twitched.

Shaking his head, Casey met Dylan's eyes. "What's the verdict?"

Dylan's lips quirked. "She's hot," he said gruffly.

Casey started to laugh, as two singers walked in behind him, already taking their costumes off and sighing with relief.

"Ladies, let's keep the goods covered until the men leave," Everley said, frowning as the tall blonde dancer went to shimmy out of her skirt.

"It's Casey, he doesn't care," the brunette said.

"Oh, but who's this?" The blonde's voice softened as her gaze met Dylan's. "I haven't seen you before."

"This is Dylan," Everley said, sneaking a look at him. "Dylan, this is Anna and Marta."

"I saw you on stage. You were great." Dylan nodded at them both.

"What do you do, Dylan?" Anna asked. "I haven't seen you in the theater before."

"I'm a doctor. And a friend of Everley's."

"Oh." Anna's lips curled. "Just friends. That's good. Are you going to the after party? Maybe we can have a drink there."

"Actually, he's my husband," Everley said, putting her hand on Dylan's arm. His body reacted to her possessive touch. He liked it too much.

"Oh, I didn't know you were married." Anna failed to keep the disappointment from her face.

"I like to keep my private life private." Everley smiled at her, though it didn't reach her eyes.

"Did you get married recently?" Marta asked, her eyes sparking with interest.

"Actually, before you get into all that, I just came to tell you I'm going over to the Tavern with David. He wants to check that everything's ready." Casey glanced at Dylan. "Want to come? I'm sure he'd appreciate the help."

"Sure." Dylan glanced at Everley. "I'll meet you there?"

She rolled onto her tiptoes, pressing her mouth to his. "Of course." Moving her lips to his ear, she whispered low enough for only Dylan to hear, "Don't go talking to any of the dancers. They'll eat you alive."

"Don't worry. There's only one performer I want eating me."

Casey cleared his throat. "Let's go. Before David has a fit." Dylan kissed Everley and followed her friend out, a smile still ghosting his lips.

He liked her little flash of jealousy. Maybe too much.

❄ 19 ❄

Everley made every bit of effort for the after party in the Winterville Inn as she would have done after a Broadway premier in New York. Wearing a black, sleeveless satin dress that clung to her curves, she'd styled her long blonde hair into the highest of ponytails that curled in golden waves down the nape of her neck. Her eyes were smokey and dramatic, her lips nude and matte. She wanted to look sexy but professional.

The kind of woman who people took seriously, because she ran a kick ass theater and knew exactly what she wanted.

The Winterville Tavern was buzzing by the time she walked through the door. The rest of the cast had arrived at least twenty minutes before her, but they hadn't had to walk through the theater to make sure everything was okay, and thank every single person they came into contact with for their hard work, all while in six inch heels.

David tipped his head at her as soon as she walked in. Before she knew it, one of the waiters was putting a glass of champagne in her hand. She lifted it to him and blew him a kiss, then took a big mouthful, swallowing the fizzy liquid down. She felt it hit her empty stomach within seconds.

Scanning the overstuffed tavern, she sought out Dylan in the gloom. Eventually she saw him, leaning against the bar on the other side from where she was standing, deep in conversation with North.

Her eldest cousin looked relaxed in a dark blue shirt and black pants, his elbow resting on the counter as he lifted a bottle to his lips with his other hand. He said something to Dylan, who nodded and continued the conversation. She went to walk over, but a hand touched her arm, and she turned to see one of her old Broadway directors standing there.

The next few minutes were filled with congratulations and questions about the future of the theater. Every time she tried to make her way to the bar, somebody else would accost her, and she had to smile and be welcoming, because god knew she was grateful that so many people had come to support her. She'd finished talking to one of the donors when she felt a shiver wrack its way down her spine, sending her nerve endings into overdrive.

He was here. She slowly turned her head until his gaze caught hers. Her muscles tightened at the sight of him.

"Hi." She felt breathless.

"I have no words for how beautiful you look right now," he said, his eyes drinking her in.

"Maybe words are overrated."

The corners of his eyes crinkled. "Let me take you home tonight."

"Take me home?" she asked. A little rush of pleasure shot through her body. "As in walk me to the door?"

"I just want to be with you. Is there anything wrong with that?"

Her breath caught. Because she wanted that, too. In the days since Thanksgiving, she'd missed him like crazy.

"So the doctor wants the showgirl?" she asked him, teasing.

"Something like that." He reached out to trace the line of her jaw. "Say yes. Please."

"Last time it was me begging."

He lifted a brow. "I always knew that first night would never be enough. You're an addiction. I want more."

"Everley, Gray Hartson just walked through the door," Casey whispered. "I need you to introduce me to him right now." He glanced at Dylan. "You don't mind if I steal her from you, do you?"

"Be my guest."

Casey took Everley's hand in his. "Actually, what I really need you to do is stop David from flirting with him. Gray Hartson's his hall pass."

She let him pull her away from Dylan, all too aware of his stare still warming her skin. "His hall pass? He knows Gray's straight, right? He has a wife and kids."

"Yeah, that's why I'm okay with it." Casey grinned.

"Who's your hall pass?" Everley asked him, as he pulled her through the crowd to the bar where Gray and his wife were talking to North.

"Um, you don't want to know."

Everley shook her head, amused. "Now I really do want to know. Who is it?"

Casey looked at Gray and his wife again. "He's right in front of us."

She frowned. "Gray's your hall pass, too?"

"Who's he talking to?" Casey asked, shaking his head.

"He's talking to North...oh!" With wide eyes, she turned to look at her friend. "Oh please don't tell me you have a crush on my cousin."

"He's hot. What's not to crush on?"

She grimaced. "He's moody and irritable and stupidly overprotective."

Casey smirked. "As I said, *hot*." He put his arm around Everley's shoulders. "And you can't tell him that he's my hall pass."

"Why not?"

"Because if you do, I'm going to tell him that I just caught you and your soon-to-be-ex-husband staring at each other like you want to rip each other's clothes off."

Everley sighed. "Shut up."

"You're in trouble, girl," Casey said, a grin pulling at his lips. "Chemistry like that can't be ignored."

The party was finally winding down, and she wasn't sorry because she was exhausted from head to toe. The Tavern was half-empty, and Casey was telling her to hurry up and leave, because the star of the Holiday Revue needed her beauty sleep.

"You want me and David to walk you home?" he asked her, taking her empty glass out of her hand and putting it resolutely on the table.

Her eyes slid to the bar, where Dylan was leaning on the counter. Her eyes caught his and she found herself shaking her head.

"I can get myself back home," she murmured to Casey, not breaking her gaze.

"I bet you can." There was humor in Casey's voice. "Go get him, tiger."

"I'm more kitten right now. A really tired kitten."

Dylan stared right at her as she closed the gap between them, pushing himself to full height and taking her hand.

"You done here?" he asked.

She nodded. "If I don't go soon I'm going to fall to the floor and sleep right here."

The corner of his lips quirked. "Then let's get you home."

The shoes that had seemed like such a good idea earlier were cutting into the skin of her ankles. She grimaced and reached down as they walked out into the cold Winterville night, trying to loosen the straps.

"They hurting?" Dylan asked her. Before she could nod, he'd swept her into his arms, pulling her against his chest. He smelled of cologne and whiskey. She breathed in, and it made her body flutter with need.

"Everybody will see us," she said, in a feeble attempt at protesting.

"It's one in the morning. Everybody's asleep. And you need to take care of those feet, you have to dance tomorrow." He wasn't even breathless as he carried her across the square. One hand was beneath her back, the other wrapped around her thighs. She curled her own around his neck and buried her face in his shoulder, trying to get used to the steady rhythm of his feet as he made his way to her cottage.

He only had to stop once, when he put her down gently and suggested she climb on his back instead. And then he was piggybacking her home like they were teenagers, her beautiful dress pushed up to her hips and she couldn't help but laugh as he attempted to run the last hundred yards.

"You got a key?"

"It's probably open."

He shook his head as he pushed the handle and the door swung into the hallway. "Remind me to talk to you about security."

"Tomorrow?"

"Sure." He sounded easy. "Now take those shoes off and get to bed. You want a drink up there?"

"I'd love a glass of water."

"You got any Advil?"

She frowned. "Why, do you have a headache?"

Leaning forward, he placed a kiss on the tip of her nose. "It's for your muscles. You need some sleep."

"There's some in the bathroom."

He shooed her upstairs, and she slowly climbed to the second floor. Pushing open the door to her bedroom, she collapsed onto the mattress face first, her dress billowing out around her.

She hadn't moved by the time she heard Dylan's footsteps on the stairs. The door creaked as he walked into her bedroom, then she heard him put a glass onto the table beside her bed.

A moment later, she felt his warm fingers pulling at her zipper. "You need to get ready for bed," he murmured.

"Too achy." Her voice was muffled by the coverlet.

"I've got something that will help." He pulled the straps over her shoulders, then edged the dress down her body, until she was laying on her bed in just her bra and panties. She tried to roll over to look at him, but the effort was too much. Instead she dropped her head back to the sheets, then groaned as she felt his strong hands on her calves.

There was something warm and silky on his palms, as he gently massaged her lower legs, his thumbs pressing into the muscles until the knots in them released. She groaned again as he moved up, massaging the back of her thighs, before slowly moving his hands around to the front of them.

"God, that feels good."

"Got to keep you limber," he murmured, moving his hands to the base of her behind. His touch was slow, sensuous, and it was making her insides clench with delight. He knew exactly how to relax her in every way. "Let's take these off," he said, pulling at her panties. She shimmied her hips to help him, her body singing at the touch of his fingers against her hips.

"Take my bra off, too," she whispered.

He unhooked the clasps, pulling the silk from beneath her. Then she was naked, face down, her body at his mercy. He poured some more of what smelled like baby oil into his palm, then rubbed his hands together before pressing them against her behind.

His thumbs dug deep, and she arched her back, her breath catching in her throat as his fingers skimmed the achiest part of her. She pushed against him, needing so much more than a massage. "Dylan," she whispered. "Please."

"What do you need, sweetheart?"

"I ache."

"I know you do." He circled his thumbs against the crease where her ass met her legs. "But you need to sleep. Let me help you relax."

He brushed his thumbs against her thighs and she let out a groan.

"That feels good." Her mouth was muffled by the pillow.

"Here?" He brushed his thumbs against the inside of her thighs.

"Higher." His teasing was killing her.

He chuckled softly, then feathered his thumb where she needed him the most. A bolt of delicious electricity shot through to the tips of her toes, and she curled them with need. Then he was circling his thumb against her, and her hips moved to the rhythm of his touch. She could feel the desire building, thickening, making every cell in her body tingle.

Before she could beg him for more, she felt the mattress shift. He pulled her up, so her knees were against the bed and her ass was raised, kissing her softly between her legs.

All thoughts of her aches were gone, replaced by the soft,

sweet touch of this man who knew exactly how to make her see stars.

She fisted the bedsheets, her cries louder, her back arching as he took her to oblivion, telling her how beautiful she was, how good she tasted, how he would never get enough of her.

When the peak came, she didn't just see stars. She saw exploding rainbows and sparkling diamonds, her body collapsing as he released her thighs, leaving her sprawling chest down across the bed.

And when she came back to life, she twisted her body, crawling across the mattress to where he was sitting, with a big fat grin on his face. The achiness and exhaustion of a few minutes ago was gone, replaced by an electricity that sparked across her body, making her want him all over again.

"Get your clothes off and get in me," she pleaded.

"Aren't you tired?" he asked.

"I'm not that tired." She could never get enough of this man.

He laughed and kissed her. "Your wish is my command."

Everley Winter was going to be the death of him. It wasn't just the sex, amazing though it was. It was feeling her in his arms, her soft body curled against his, her breath a slow rhythm against his chest. He couldn't remember the last time he felt this content. It was like every muscle in his body had finally stopped resisting her and was relaxed instead. Welcoming the feel of her skin against his.

"You okay?" he asked, brushing the hair from her brow, and reaching for the glass he'd left on the bedside table. "You should take those Advil now. Before your muscles go on strike."

She laughed, taking the glass, then the tablets he held out. "Ah, it was worth it. But I'm not sure I can go another round."

Nor was he. "I guess we'll have to save it for another day."

She tipped her head to the side, a smile ghosting on her lips. "Another day?"

She was fast becoming his favorite addiction, again. "I figure I'll let you use my body for stress relief after work. It's the least I can do as your husband."

She pulled her lip between her teeth, as three tiny lines appeared on her brow.

"You okay?" he asked, worried he'd said the wrong thing.

"Yeah, I just don't want this to get weird. I feel like I've found my friend again. I don't want to ruin things between us." She swallowed. "I really like being with you."

"I like being with you, too." His expression was serious. He wondered if she knew exactly how much he liked it. If it was any other time, if she was any other person, he'd tell her.

But he wasn't going to keep her awake with a forensic conversation about exactly where this was going. Not when she had another show tomorrow. He cared about her too much for that. She needed sleep. Recovery. And while he was still her husband, he'd make sure she got what she needed.

And then what, dumbass? You're going to walk away?

She rolled onto her side, curling against him. He tangled his fingers into her silky hair, rubbing her neck the way he knew she liked. Her head was against his chest, and he could feel the warmth of her breath on his skin. It was slow. Rhythmic. She always had the most amazing recovery time.

He pressed his lips against the top of her head, breathing in the sweet fragrance of her shampoo. "We won't let this get weird," he told her. "I like you, I think you like me. We can work with that."

"No promises, no pain. Just being together until we're not," she murmured.

He ran his tongue over his dry lips. "Is that what you want?"

"You're leaving in less than a month. And I have this show until then. I'd like to spend time with you. But I don't want us to make plans. To pretend this is anything more than being together in the moment. I think that's where we went wrong before, each of us having this view of the future, and our views turning out to be completely different." She traced her finger idly over his chest. "But this time we're grown-ups. We know that happily ever afters are a myth. And we know that you'll be going back to Africa and I'll be staying here and soon we'll be divorced."

He pressed his lips to her temple. "You want us to be friends with benefits?"

"No, I want us to be kind to each other. To have no expectations. I want us to end this thing as friends."

"I'll always be your friend," he promised. "You're amazing, you know that?"

"I'm a pain in the ass. I know *that*."

He laughed, then leaned down to kiss her softly. "You're not a pain in the ass. You're a woman who knows what she wants. Who has so much energy that sometimes she has no idea how to switch it off."

"You're helping," she murmured, as he stroked her back again.

"Good. That's all I want to do. Help." He kept stroking, loving how she relaxed against him. He wondered if it would always have felt like this, if they hadn't separated. If he'd still want her every day. If the touch of her skin against his would still feel like a miracle if they hadn't been apart.

If she'd always be able to calm him the way he calmed her.

But this was just a moment.

A friendship. Something worth protecting.

And when it came time to leave, he'd do it better this time.

Because this time, he wouldn't be breaking her heart.

20

Dylan could hear his dad's coughing before he even walked into the Cold Start Garage. He hadn't seen much of him in the week since Everley's opening night. His dad was at work during the day – and Dylan was working, too – and in the evening he'd walk to the theater and wait for Everley to finish, before taking her home.

"Hey," he called out, blowing out a mouthful of air as he walked into the garage.

His dad coughed again, rolling out from beneath a truck. "You're home."

"Yeah. And you sound bad."

"Just a cold. It's winter, it happens." He coughed again, rolling off the creeper and pulling a handkerchief from his overall pocket. He spat, and Dylan grimaced because what he coughed up looked bad.

"You should be at home. Call the doctor and get some antibiotics."

"If I called the doctor every time I got a cold I'd be a poor man by now. He doesn't need to be bothered by me."

Dylan sighed, raking his hand through his hair. "Dad,

that stuff is yellow. That means it's infected. Which means you have an illness that needs to be treated. This is the twenty-first century. We have medications for this stuff. And for Christ's sake, stop smoking. You're going to kill yourself."

"But I don't have time to make a doctor's appointment. I don't have time to stay at home. I have a business to run, and that's what I'm doing." He coughed again, his face red. "Now get out of here."

"You're sixty-four years old. You should retire."

"Yeah, tell that to my bank balance."

Damn, his old man was aggravating. "I've told you before, I can help you. I can pay your rent, help you sell this place. You don't need to be working anymore."

His dad stood, his handkerchief still in his hand. "And then what do I do? Sit in the coffee shop and do crosswords like Frank? Wander aimlessly around town looking for a bit of gossip? I'm a single man, Dylan. I live alone. If I didn't have work, what would I have?"

"You have me."

His dad spluttered. "You're a grown man. Your job isn't to entertain me. Not that you could, *from Africa.*"

"I could stay."

"No, you couldn't. If you didn't stay for your wife all those years ago, then don't give me some bullshit that you'd stay for me. And I wouldn't want you to, anyway. I don't need your pity, Dylan, or your crap about me giving up smoking. I'm a grown man. I'll live my life the way I want to. You don't need to fly in here like Superman and think you can make everything better."

"I'm not flying in here like anything." He tried to keep his voice even.

His dad sat down heavily in the chair next to his desk. The surface was overflowing with paperwork. "You want to know why I didn't send in those papers?" he asked, his voice low. He coughed again.

Dylan felt a tingle at the back of his neck. "My divorce papers?"

"Yeah. *Those*. It would have been easy to do. Just take them into the Post Office, ask for a stamp. Instead, I put them on the shelf over the fireplace and looked at that damn envelope every day for months. Wondering if I was doing the right thing."

"Why did you do it?" Dylan asked, his voice low.

"Because I didn't want you to end up like me. Sixty-four years old and alone."

Dylan gritted his teeth. "That wasn't your choice to make."

"Don't you think I know that? I underestimated your need to be a damn superhero. It's not just me you think you need to save, it's the damn world. But the world won't love you back, Dylan. And by the time you're my age, I'll be nothing more than worm food. And you'll still be alone."

"Thanks for that."

"What?" Charlie lifted his hands up. "It's true, isn't it? You have this belief that if you sacrifice yourself for the greater good then everything will turn out fine. That if you don't make the kind of decisions your mom did, then you'll be a good person. But tell me this, how was you leaving Everley any different than your mom leaving us?"

Dylan wasn't sure how the conversation had taken this turn. He ran his hands through his hair. "It was completely different. Mom left because she was a crackhead. I left because I'm a doctor and it's in my fucking job description to save lives."

"You left because you didn't think you deserved her love. The way your mom believed she didn't deserve ours."

Dylan's jaw twitched. "Do not compare me to Mom." His voice was thick with warning. "Don't do that."

"Why not? She ran away, you ran away. The family resemblance is clear."

"I didn't run away. I went to do my job. To help people who couldn't help themselves."

"You left because you couldn't accept that girl's love."

Dylan blinked. "That's not true."

"Sure it is. You weren't sure of her love. You had to test it. See if she'd follow you wherever you went. And she didn't, so she didn't love you. Isn't that what you thought?"

"We were kids. We made a mistake. We wanted different things and that's why we split. And if you hadn't interfered, then this would all be in the past."

"And is that what you want? For it all to be in the past?"

Dylan ran his thumb over his jaw. "It's not about what I want. It's a fact."

"So that's why you're spending every free minute you have with Everley?"

Dylan shook his head. "It's not like that."

"Then what's it like? Tell me, because it sure seems like you're spending every night with your wife to me." He started to cough again, his face getting redder. He lifted his handkerchief to his mouth, but nothing came out except a low gurgle.

"Dad?"

Charlie's body was moving, but there was no sound. Dylan ran to him, dropping to his haunches. "Cough, Dad. Cough."

No sound came. He made his dad lean forward, then hit him on the back five times, until something dislodged.

His dad inhaled raggedly. Dylan lifted his head. "We need to get you to the doctor," he said softly.

"I don't like the doctor."

"I know." He pressed his palms against his dad's cheeks, feeling heat there.

"*You* can write me a script."

"I can't. It's unethical. And your doctor needs to know about this. To start monitoring you."

"I'll go as soon as I've finished this truck."

"You're not getting under that truck again. What if you choke? What if you bang your head?"

"Morris needs that truck for his deliveries tomorrow."

"Okay." Dylan stood, looking at the beat up Ford in the center of the garage. "Do you have a spare pair of overalls?"

His dad frowned. "Why?"

"If I repair the truck, then you have to go to the doctor. *Today*."

"You can't fix the truck." His dad was looking better now. The water in his eyes had dried up.

"Sure I can. I spent enough time here as a teenager. I'll get under the truck and you can give me directions."

"You'll ruin your precious hands."

Dylan shook his head. "Shut up and tell me where your overalls are."

"In the store room." He inclined his still red face at the door on the other side of the garage. Dylan nodded and walked over, his jaw still tight.

"Thank you," his dad said.

A smile ghosted across Dylan's mouth. "Anytime."

Everley knocked on Holly and Josh's door. Her cousin and her husband had arrived back from their extended honeymoon earlier that day, and had invited her to join them after the show was over. She'd protested that it would be late, but Holly had shooed her off, telling her their body clocks were all over the place anyway.

Josh opened the door, and a smile pulled at his lips. He

wrapped his arms around her in a huge hug, and she grinned up at him. "Look at you, you're all tan and smug," she said, her heart full of warmth. It was hard not to love Josh when he adored her favorite cousin so much. He and Holly had met under the weirdest of circumstances. His company had bought the town, and planned to redevelop it into a ski resort, but along with the rest of their cousins, Holly and Everley had fought against him.

And somehow, in the middle of the fight, he and Holly had fallen for each other. It was one of her favorite love stories.

"Being away for a hundred years did you good," she told him.

"It was five weeks," he said, pulling her inside. "And it's the first vacation either of us have had in years."

"I can't wait to hear all about it. What was best, Europe or Barbados?"

His eyes twinkled, as though he had memories he couldn't share. "They both had their advantages. Europe was cold but romantic. Barbados was hot and... yeah."

Everley grinned. "I'm not jealous at all."

He led her through to the large living area, where Holly was sitting and chatting with North and Alaska. The three of them stood and hugged her. She felt the tiniest of pangs because two of their gang – Gabe and Kris – were missing. But Gabe would be back soon, and Kris had no choice right now but to be in London for work.

Holly was looking amazing. Her face was tanned and glowing, her dark hair pulled into a low, messy bun. Everley squeezed her tight, because, damn, she'd missed her.

They weren't just cousins, they were the closest of friends. It had been beyond difficult not having her around to talk about everything she'd been going through. But she'd made herself a promise that Holly and Josh's honeymoon would be drama free, and that included telling her cousin that she was still married to Dylan.

Josh poured her a drink and passed it to her, and she took a long sip. She'd taken a shower after the show, and changed her clothes, but she still felt buzzy and full of energy.

"So how's the show going?" Holly asked as they sat down beside the roaring fire. North and Josh were on the other side of the room, leaning over Josh's laptop and looking at something. "I'm so sorry I missed the opening night. But we have tickets for tomorrow."

"It's pretty good." She grinned. "We've had a few hiccups, but ticket sales are great. We're almost fully booked now."

"That's amazing." Holly's mouth dropped open. "Wow."

"That's not all Everley's been doing," Alaska said, her voice low. "Ask her about Dylan."

Everley grimaced, checking that North wasn't listening. Thankfully, he and Josh were too busy talking about something on the laptop.

"What happened with Dylan?" Holly asked, her expression full of curiosity. "I know he was at the wedding. Did you two talk?"

Everley bit her lip. "We're kind of still married."

"And that's not all. I hear that a certain doctor is sneaking into her house every night after the show and not leaving until the morning." Alaska looked delighted to be the source of gossip for once.

Everley shook her head. Small towns. Love them or hate them, they always knew everything about you.

Holly gazed at her, shocked. "How are you two still married? And how long have you been sleeping with him?" She leaned closer, her voice low. "Tell me everything."

She listened raptly as Everley filled her in, every now and then glancing to make sure that North and Josh were still distracted. Sure, North had to know something was going on, but he didn't need to hear the gory details.

And she had no doubt that Holly would fill Josh in later.

"So how's the sex?" Holly asked her.

"Amazing." Everley sighed. "It's like nothing else I've ever felt. He knows me, he knows my body. He's pretty much ruined me for everybody else."

"He ruined you eight years ago," Alaska said, shaking her head. "You were just in denial."

"Don't go getting too excited about things. He's still leaving after Christmas. It's only a short-term thing."

"What's a short term thing?" Josh asked, walking over to them. "I hope you're not talking about my honeymoon prow- ess," he said, pressing his lips to Holly's brow.

"They're talking about Everley and Dylan," North grumbled.

Everley's eyes shot to her eldest cousin. "You know about that?"

"I'm not stupid. I hear the gossip. I just choose to ignore it." He shook his head. "I told you and Dylan what I thought. If you two want to make mistakes, that's up to you."

"It's not a mistake. We're both good with what we have." Her words were soft. North was protective but he also had the kindest heart. She knew he worried about them all. "*I'm* good with it," she said again, her voice soft.

"Okay then." North shook his head. For a moment nobody said anything, and the silence felt way too loaded for a reunion

"Maybe we should change the subject," Holly finally said, rolling her eyes.

"Tell us about your honeymoon," Alaska said, shifting in her seat. She never did like awkward conversations. For the next few minutes they listened as Holly described their journey through Europe, then their two week stay in Barbados.

"Thank goodness you came back," Alaska said, staring at the photograph of their hotel." I was worried you'd love being away too much."

"I spent half the time finding new places to hide Holly's phone," Josh admitted, grinning at his new wife. "I can't tell you how many times she wanted to call to check that everything was okay."

"You can't talk." Holly smiled at him indulgently. "You're the one who tried to schedule a video call from the pool."

"I canceled it."

"Only because I threatened to take my top off and show everybody."

Everley bit down a laugh.

North sat down next to her on the sofa. She bumped her shoulder against his, and he bumped her back.

"You okay?" she asked him.

"I'm fine. Just trying to convince myself not to lock all three of you in the attic." There was a hint of amusement in North's voice. She kissed his rough cheek.

"You need to stop worrying about all of us and start worrying about yourself. Maybe if you were getting some horizontal time with the ladies, you'd stop worrying about our love lives."

"Oh, he gets his share," Alaska said. "We had a bachelorette party in last week. At least two of them were flirting with him."

"At least he avoids my dancers," Everley said. "Unlike Gabe."

North's brows raised. "How did we get onto my sex life?"

"I have no idea." Everley grinned. "But I prefer it to talking about mine."

North sighed. "Yeah, I do, too."

She bumped his shoulder again, and he shook his head, an indulgent expression on his face. They were good. That made her happy.

"Well, I don't care to hear about anybody's sex life, because I'm too busy with my own. But maybe we should raise a glass to being back together again," Josh suggested, holding up a bottle of champagne. North jumped up to help him, looking relieved at the change of subject.

"You look good," Holly mused, looking right at Everley. "Whatever Dylan's doing, long may it last."

"Dylan always had this effect on her," Alaska said, taking the glass that Josh passed to her. "He can calm her like nobody else does. Remember when she had that huge show at drama school and Dylan put his hand on her arm and she pretty much melted?"

"I remember." Holly nodded. "Nobody else has that effect on her."

Josh slid a glass into Alaska's hand, but Holly refused the one he offered to her. "I'm still feeling tired after the flight. If I drink I'll be asleep."

"Good point. We wouldn't want that." Josh winked, then lifted his own glass up. "To family. Those we were born with, and those we found." He smiled at them all. "And to those who aren't here with us right now."

They all knew he was talking about Gabe, Kris and their beloved Grandma.

"To family," they chorused, lifting their glasses and taking a sip.

Everley smiled as she looked around at them all. Family was everything. And it was great to be around them again.

As she slid into her car later that night, she saw that Dylan had sent a message.

I don't think I'm going to make it to your place tonight. Dad's sick. Will call you later. D xx

She frowned, turning her key to start the ignition, then pressed the Bluetooth call button, saying his name into the voice recognition. The buzz of her call blasted through the car's speakers, before she heard Dylan's low, smooth voice answer her call.

"Hey." Just the way he said it sent a shiver down her spine. Sure, she was a mature woman. One who turned into a giggling eighteen-year-old whenever she heard Dylan Shaw's voice.

"What's up with Charlie?" she asked him, backing out of Holly's drive.

"He has a cold. It's gone to his chest. He refused to go see a doctor until we finished all his repairs for the day _and_ delivered the trucks back to their owners. By the time we were done the only place open was the urgent care in Marshall's Gap. We got back an hour ago."

"You sound exhausted," she said sympathetically.

"He's an exhausting man. It's like dealing with a toddler."

Everley laughed, because she knew exactly what he meant. "He needs to give up the cigarettes."

"Believe me, I've said that to him about a hundred times today. The good news is that he's coughing too much to smoke." His voice softened. "How are you? Did you have a good time tonight?"

"I did. Holly and Josh looked fabulous. They had such a

good trip." She ran her tongue along her bottom lip. "And they know about us. I'm sorry."

There was a pause. "It's fine. My dad does, too. I guess we were stupid to think we could hide it from everyone. Winterville lives for gossip."

"So you're okay with them knowing?" she asked him.

"I'm fine with it if you are."

She turned left onto the main road, and a truck passed on the other side, honking at her.

"What's that?" Dylan asked.

"Some truck didn't like the way I turned." She could see the lights of the town ahead of her, sparkling like a Christmas scene on a fireplace. "I'll be passing by your place in five minutes. Want me to come over and read Charlie the riot act?"

"He's asleep. I'm sitting on the porch with a beer."

"In that case, I'm definitely stopping by."

"I'd like that." There was a warmth to his voice that sent a shiver down her spine.

"Yeah, I would, too."

She'd barely pulled in his driveway before he was walking toward her car, pulling open the door and helping her out. Though it was dark outside, the porch light cast a warm, yellow glow on his tanned skin. He was smiling at her, his eyes crinkled, the shadows beneath his eyes made worse by the lamplight.

"Hey." The corner of his lip quirked. "You look beautiful."

She closed the car door and leaned back against it. "You're not so bad yourself. How's your dad?"

"Still asleep. He'll be that way until morning. The doc gave him something to help."

She reached up to trace his laugh lines. "You're tired."

"Arguing with my dad does that."

She smiled. "If he's giving as good as he gets it sounds like he's not too sick."

"No, thank God. Though if he keeps smoking he will be." He put his palm over her hand, pressing it to his cheek. Everley's stomach did a little flip flop. Sure, his strong jaw was darkened by beard growth, and his eyes looked a little glassy from exhaustion, but it did nothing to diminish his beauty.

It only made her want him more.

And from the way he was staring at her, he wanted her too.

He gently pushed the hair from her face, caressing the line of her cheekbone with the pads of his fingers. He traced them across her top lip, along her jawline, as though he was trying to memorize every sculptured inch of her features.

By the time he leaned toward her she was breathless. His eyes captured hers as he pressed the sweetest of kisses to the corner of her lips, making her thighs clench and her breath catch.

Need for more tugged at her. She had to curl her hands into fists to stop herself from touching him. The car door pressed against her back and his wool covered torso and denim clad thighs pressed against her front, as he braced himself against the car and leaned closer still, capturing her mouth with his.

Kissing Dylan was like saying a prayer and having it answered at the same time. It was light and darkness, and so much desire. She couldn't stop from touching him for one moment longer, uncurling her hands and burying her fingers into his thick brown hair.

Her nails scratched at the nape of his neck and he moaned into her lips, deepening the kiss as he pressed his body to hers, leaving her in no doubt that he wanted her as much as she wanted him.

When they parted, she was breathless. A smile pulled at

his lips, crinkling his eyes, and he was still leaning into her, palm pushed against her car.

"How was your day?" he asked her.

"Busy. We had a lighting problem. It took until an hour before doors opening to solve."

"You're amazing, you know that? You take everything in your stride." He slid his fingers into her hair, caressing the skin at the nape of her neck. "But now you need to get some sleep. You look tired." He kissed her jaw, making her skin tingle. "Stay here with me tonight."

"In Charlie's house?"

He smiled against her skin. "Yeah. He's out for the count. He won't notice. And you know he loves you."

"You sure that's okay?" She looked up at him. She wanted nothing more than to curl up in his arms. Her bed would be too empty without him.

"Yeah. I promise not to do any dirty stuff."

She bit down a smile. "Dirty stuff?"

"You know what I mean."

"Maybe I want the dirty stuff," she whispered.

He leaned in closer, tucking his thumb under her chin, tilting her head until their eyes met. "You'd need to be quiet."

"Have you met me?"

Dylan grinned. "Many, many times. And you're right, you can't be quiet. I'll have to gag you."

She shivered, and he pulled her into his arms.

"We should probably go inside," he murmured. "Death from hypothermia is definitely unsexy."

She pressed her lips against his rough jaw. "Okay then. Let's go to bed."

21

"Hi Dolores."

Dylan's low voice woke her. Everley sat, eyes blinking as they became accustomed to the sharp morning light. It took her a moment to realize she was in Dylan's room at his dad's house.

"Do they know he's sick? He'll get to it as soon as he can." Dylan paused, raking his hands through his hair. "What? That's not fair. Okay, tell them I'll be there in twenty minutes. Don't let them leave. He needs that contract." His voice softened. "Thanks, Dolores. He owes you a drink when he's better."

"What's going on?" Everley asked, as he slid his jeans up his thighs.

"There are five trucks at the garage waiting to be serviced. One of my dad's big contracts with a delivery firm." He sighed. "I need to go talk to them, make them not leave for another garage."

A loud hacking cough came from Charlie's room down the hallway.

"Shit. I need to give him his medicine." Dylan looked at his watch, his brow creasing.

"I can do it." Everley laid her hand on his wrist.

Dylan's eyes caught hers. "But you have your show. You need to leave."

"Not until this afternoon. You go do what you need to. And when I need to leave I'll make sure there's somebody with him."

"Who?"

"I'll figure it out. This town loves your dad. There'll be someone who wants to sit with him."

Dylan ran his thumb along her jaw, his gaze soft and warm. "You're amazing, you know that?"

"I know." She grinned. "Now go save your dad's business."

"I owe you one." He pressed his warm lips to hers, his mouth moving softly.

"Who are you going to find to do the services on those trucks?" she asked when he broke the kiss. Charlie was the only mechanic in town. As well as Winterville's official snow remover.

"I'll probably do it myself."

"Seriously?"

"Services are fairly easy. Dad let me do them all the time when I was a kid." He pulled a t-shirt over his bare chest. "Five of them will take all day though."

"That's hot."

He shot her a confused glance. "What is?"

"That you can still service a car."

His brow furrowed. "Are you serious?"

She nodded. "I'm picturing you all oily and dirty, rolling out from beneath the truck in your jeans and a white t-shirt."

"You've been watching too much *Grease*."

She pulled the sheet around her, climbing to her knees. "You can be my Danny Zuko any time."

"Danny who? Do I know him?"

She pushed him playfully, a little thrill shooting through her when she felt the hard plane of his chest against her palm. "Get out of here. Go make those trucks better."

He kissed her again, this time curling his fingers around the back of her neck, his lips hot and demanding. When they parted, she was breathless.

"Thank you," he told her. "Every time I need help, you're there."

"That's what wives do."

He slapped her bare behind playfully. "Among other things." He glanced at his watch again. "Now I really have to go. Dad's prescriptions are in the kitchen. Just follow the doctor's instructions."

She touched her fingers to her head in salute. "Aye aye, Captain."

Twenty minutes later, she was showered and back in yesterday's clothes, carrying a tray into Charlie's room. He looked up at the sound of his door opening, surprise widening his eyes when he saw her walk in.

"Hello Charlie. I'll be your nurse for the morning."

He tried to sit up, but started coughing again. She slid the tray onto his bedside table and passed him a glass of water, helping him sit so he could sip at it.

"Well you're much better looking than my son," Charlie told her, as she sat on the side of his bed and passed him the first set of pills. "How much is he paying you?"

She grinned at him. "I had to fight for the job. You know how much the women of Winterville love to take care of their men."

He laughed, and this time he managed to stave off his cough. "Funny thing," he said. "I didn't hear you arrive this morning. It's like you were here all night."

"Are you asking me something?" She passed him the coffee she'd made him, along with some oatmeal.

"Just talking out loud. Wondering if you're taking care of me as a kindness or because you're my daughter-in-law."

"I'm taking care of you because you're my friend, Charlie." She shook her head. "Dylan told me you make a terrible patient."

"Dylan been bitching about me again?"

"Something like that."

"Where is he anyway?" He looked over her shoulder.

"He's at the garage. You had some jobs come in."

"The McKenzie Contract." Charlie blanched, then passed her his half-drunk coffee cup and tried to move his legs. "They're my biggest client. I need to get to the garage."

"You're staying exactly where you are, buddy." She pressed lightly on his shoulder. "Dylan's doing the services, and you're recovering."

"Dylan's doing the services?" His voice rose an octave.

"Yep. And don't look at me like that. He learned from you."

"He should stick to what he's good at," Charlie mumbled.

Everley shot him a look. "Don't start. He's doing you a favor. A nice thing. The least you can do is be grateful to him."

"I don't need his help. I told him that yesterday. You should have seen him trying to repair that truck. If he messes up this contract I'll go bust."

"Charlie, he's not going to mess up. This is Dylan we're talking about. The golden boy. He's good with his hands." She blushed when she said that, but luckily Charlie didn't seem to notice. "Let him do this for you. He wants to. And maybe in return you can give up those cigarettes, before they're the end of you."

"Did he ask you to say that?"

"Nope. It's all me. Seriously, Charlie, smoking kills. You know that. You need to give them up. You don't want Dylan having to take over the business, do you?"

"Hmph. No. He needs to go back to Africa. They need him there."

She pulled her lip between her teeth. "They do." Her voice was soft. "So let's make a deal. You give up on the cigarettes, and I won't tell him he needs to stay here to look after you."

Charlie's eyes met hers. "Are you sure you want him to go back?"

"It's his job, Charlie. The thing he loves doing. Now do you think you can make it to the shower without my help? Because you're smelling a little bit fresh, if you know what I mean."

"Of course I can," he grumbled, not letting her help him get out of bed. "I've got a cough, I haven't broken my legs."

She bit down a smile, because she loved this man.

It was just after noon when Everley put her head around the garage door. Alaska had turned up twenty minutes earlier, and had already gave Charlie hell about his smoking habit. She'd shooed Everley away, telling her that she already had a line about a mile long of volunteers to help look after Charlie.

It was heartwarming how the town always closed ranks when one of their own needed help.

The smell of grease and diesel permeated her nose. There was a van parked in the center, the hood up. Four others were lined up outside.

Dylan was leaning over the engine, talking to an older man, a piece of paper in his hand. He turned his head and looked at her, a slow smile pulling at his lips.

She stood for a moment, taking in his old jeans and black t-shirt, his hair pushed back from his face. His bicep muscles were taut, his skin tan, and there were some grease marks on his face.

"How's it going?" she asked him.

"Slow. Eddie just got here, thank God."

Eddie stood and tapped his hand on the front of the van. "It's looking good. You remembered a lot."

"This is Everley. I'm not sure if you ever met her. Evie, this is Eddie, an old friend of Dad's. He came over from Marshall's Gap to help me out."

"Hey Eddie." She grinned at him. "You think you can make a mechanic out of him?"

"Yeah, he's good. I'll do the hard stuff and he can do the rest. We'll get the vans out of here by the end of the night." He lifted a brow, as though he was only half joking.

Dylan walked over to her, leaning to press his lips against hers. "Eddie's a godsend," he told her. "Turns out a few things have changed on cars since I was a kid. He's going to help me get through these, then we'll divert the rest of the week's work to his garage."

"Charlie won't be happy," she murmured.

"He'd be more unhappy if his customers got a bad service."

He smelled of oil and perspiration, but it wasn't a bad smell. Just unusual for him. When he'd been in medical training she'd gotten used to the smell of antiseptic and clean. It was funny how that smell still brought back memories of fast kisses and slow touches after he'd get back from a shift at work.

"How's he doing?" Dylan asked her.

"He's grumpy, but he got some sleep this morning. Alaska came over, and he got another lecture from her. I figure whoever looks after him tonight can give him another."

"I'll look after him tonight," a female voice called out. They looked over to see Dolores standing in the doorway. She was holding a tray of coffees and pastries. "I brought you some coffee to keep you going," she said, sliding the tray onto the table, shifting some paperwork that Charlie had left there. "And tonight I'll take Charlie to mine. My son is home and he's a registered nurse. He can help take care of him."

"You can't do that," Dylan protested. "He's my dad, I'm a doctor."

"But you don't know all of his hiding places," Dolores pointed out. "There are no cigarettes at my place. I figure he can go cold turkey and recover from his chest infection all at the same time."

"She has a point," Everley said, tipping her head to the side.

"He hides them in his car footwell," Eddie mumbled. "I found them there one time."

Everley tried not to laugh, because they were all turning on Charlie now.

"That's agreed then," Dolores said, looking happy that she could have Charlie under her strict eye.

"Did I agree?" Dylan asked, looking confused.

"No, you didn't. But since the whole town knows you've been spending every night at a certain person's house," Dolores said, putting her hands on her splendid hips, "then I think you'd be happy that I'm taking him off your hands."

Dylan's warm eyes met Everley's. She could see the amusement in them.

"In that case, I'm very grateful," he said. "Thank you."

"You're welcome. Now I need to go back and finish up at the café. I have a patient to prepare for."

"How long are you planning on keeping him?" Everley asked her.

"As long as it takes," Dolores said, her eyes narrowing.

"That man needs to make some life changes." She turned on her heel and walked out of the garage, and Eddie stared after her.

"That's a formidable woman," he said, taking a pastry from the tray she'd left. "I'm not sure whether to feel sorry for your dad or be envious of him."

Everley's chest rumbled with laughter. Dylan winked and grabbed a coffee, taking a long sip. "You want a pastry?" he asked her.

"Not before a show." She inhaled heavily, the aroma of coffee overpowering the grease. Damn she missed it. "Speaking of which, I should go, too."

"I'll walk you out." Dylan said.

They stepped outside into the cold December air, their breaths turning frosty as they left the warmth of the garage. Dylan brushed his palms on his jeans, then reached for her, cupping her face with his hands and pressing his hot lips to hers.

Her toes curled as his tongue slid against hers, her back arching causing her body to press into him.

"I'm dirty," he murmured. "Or I'd be tempted to do so much more."

"Never stopped you before."

The corner of his lip quirked up. "Thank you for all you've done. I appreciate it so much."

"I wanted to help. I love Charlie, too."

His eyes softened. "I know you do." His brows knitted, as though he wanted to say more, but had no idea how to put it into words. "I'm going to be working late here tonight. Eddie's good at vehicles, but he's hopeless at paperwork. It'll take me another couple of hours in the office after he's finished the last van."

"Come to mine," she urged. "Whenever you finish. There's a key beneath the potted plant."

He shook his head. "Didn't we already talk about security measures, or do I need to lecture you again?"

"I'd prefer you showed me how angry you are," she whispered, kissing him again. "Later."

His bare arms were covered in goosebumps from the cold. And maybe from her, too.

"I need to go," she said. "Before Casey starts going crazy."

"I'll see you tonight."

"Yes you will."

"And I'll show you how much I appreciate you."

She grinned. "I'd still rather you punish me."

***

"Somebody looks like the cat that got the cream." Casey was leaning on his office desk, his phone in his hand. "Have you just seen a doctor?"

"Shut up," she said, grinning. "And I can't drink cream. I have a show to sing in."

"I drove past Dylan's dad's house last night. Saw your car there."

She caught his eye, shaking her head. "You've been living in a small town for too long. What were you doing driving past Charlie's house?"

"David and I went for dinner at the Inn. We were celebrating. We got through the first stage of the adoption process."

"You did?" A smile burst out over her face. "That's wonderful." She hugged him hard. "You guys are going to make the best parents."

"There are still more stages to go, but I'm feeling hopeful." He cocked his head to the side. "Do you think I'll make a good dad?"

"You'll make the best dad," she said, her heart feeling full.

"Any kid would be lucky to have you and David for parents."
It was the complete truth. Casey had the energy and David
was the calm, firm foundation in their partnership. "I'm kind
of jealous."

"You are?" Casey lifted his brows. "Feeling a little
broody?"

She wrinkled her nose. "Not exactly. It's just nice that you
know where your life is going. If you're lucky, by this time
next year you'll have a family to celebrate Christmas with.
And before you say it, I know you and David are already a
family, but this is more."

"Yeah, it is." Casey's voice was soft. "It's a lot to take in."

She winked at him. "You've got this."

"How about you?" he asked. "How are things with you and
Dylan?"

A smile pulled at her lips. "They're good. Really good."
She told him about Charlie and his illness, and that Dylan
would be staying at her place again that night.

"And you're okay with him leaving again?"

Her heart gave a little tug. "I have to be. He has his job, I
have mine. And we promised each other we wouldn't make it
weird. This time we're not going to bitch at each other, we're
going to enjoy the moment."

David tipped his head to the side. "Is that enough?"

She swallowed. "Yeah, of course it is. I was fine without
him for all these years. I'll be fine again."

"Oh honey." His voice was soft. "You're falling for him,
aren't you?"

"Of course I am. I wouldn't be spending every night with
him if I wasn't. But that's okay, because this time I know how
things will end up. I'm not afraid of being on my own again.
We'll part as friends, not as enemies."

Casey let out a sigh. "Why can't he just stay here? That
would make things so much easier."

"He has a vocation. A need to make the world better. I guess he finds it hard to do that in a little town in the mountains."

"Yeah, well Winterville is part of the world, too. He could make this place better," Casey grumbled.

"Will you stop looking like somebody stole your last cookie?" Everley asked him. "I'm fine. More than fine, I'm happy. I'm a big girl and I know what I'm doing. Let me enjoy this time with him."

"Okay, but when you're in the pits of despair after he's gone, don't expect me to mop up your tears."

She smiled at him. "Liar. You'll be the first one in line with the Kleenex."

"I know. But that's only because I love you."

22

Time was passing too fast. It was hard to believe that the show had been running for two weeks already. The cast and crew had settled into a good rhythm, with only the slightest blips that she and Casey had to deal with.

It had finally begun to snow regularly in Winterville, with the white flakes blanketing the ground, making everywhere look festive and pretty. The Inn was full of visitors enjoying the delights that the town had to offer, spending their days on sleigh rides and shopping in the elegant gift shops, then their evenings in the full audience at the Jingle Bell Theater.

Charlie was slowly on the mend, thanks to Dolores' tough love. Dylan had been spending the evenings with him, before walking back to Everley's to meet her after work. Casey had grumbled that she was walking home alone again, and had insisted on installing the Find My Friends app on her phone. She'd laughed, because he obviously hadn't gotten used to small town life as much as she'd thought. There was still a little New York in him.

She slipped her key into the door, the light of the overhead lamp illuminating the pale flakes as they drifted to the ground.

She always loved this time of year. Sure, Winterville in the spring and summer was pretty, with its green canopy of trees and grasses that waved in the gentle breeze. But this town was made for winter. For the snow topped mountains that framed the view and the blanket of white that greeted tourists as they arrived in the town. And on nights like this, when the lights twinkled on the giant fir in the square, it was breathtaking.

She stepped inside her cottage, smiling when she saw Dylan in the kitchen, laying on his back in front of her kitchen sink, arms stretched out as he twisted a pipe with a wrench.

He'd taken to doing little things every day for her while she was out at the theater. He'd serviced her car, oiled all the squeaky hinges in her house, and rehung the rail in her closet where her clothes had been weighing it down. And of course her path and driveway were cleared of snow every day, so she didn't break her neck when she got home.

The dripping tap in her kitchen must have been the next thing on his list. She watched silently as he tightened the join on the pipe, his t-shirt lifting to reveal a small slither of muscled stomach, then he tapped it twice and sat up, eyes widening when he saw her standing there.

A slow smile pulled at his lips. "I didn't hear you."

"I'm like a ninja. Or Santa."

He put the wrench down on the counter and walked over to her, kissing her softly on the lips. "You showered," he murmured.

"I did."

"I guess I need to as well. Do me a favor and turn on the faucet first. I want to see if I've fixed the drip."

"You didn't need to do that." She liked it, though. Too much probably. Walking over, she twisted the faucet and water poured out. When she turned it off there wasn't a single drip.

When she turned to look at him, he was smiling at her. She couldn't help smiling back. "Thank you."

"It's a pleasure. Now I'm going to take a shower." He winked and pulled his t-shirt off, shoving it straight into the washing machine. She really tried not to ogle him, though it was almost impossible. He was just too beautiful not to look at. Broad shoulders, muscled chest, ridged abdomen.

And he was hers. For now at least.

Grabbing a glass of water, she pulled the refrigerator open to see what she could eat.

"I've made pasta," he shouted out. "You just need to warm it up."

Damn, she could get used to this. Except she shouldn't she knew that she shouldn't. A little part of her wondered if his need to make everything perfect in the house came from the knowledge he'd be leaving soon. That made her feel sad. Pushing down that thought, she walked out of the kitchen and made her way to the bathroom, steam billowing out of the door when she pushed it open.

Shucking off her clothes into a pile next to his, she pulled open the shower door and stepped inside. The cubicle was small, he had to step back to give her enough space to pull the door closed behind her. Then she wrapped her arms around his neck and pressed her brow against his shoulder.

"You just took a shower," he murmured, as the spray cannoned down on them both.

"I know. I wanted another." She kissed his shoulder, tasting water covering his skin. "Tell me about your day."

"It was fine. I had a meeting this afternoon. Plans for the

project are going ahead. Then I popped in to see my dad, then came back here and mended the faucet. How was the show."

She slid her arms around his back. She could never get enough of touching him. "It went well." He'd been to see it at least five times. "The audience seemed happy."

He ran his hand down her back, tracing her spine with his fingertips. "How about you, are you happy?"

She looked up, her eyes shining. "I really am."

His voice was gruff. "Me, too."

Dropping his brow to hers, he looked deep into her eyes. She wondered if he could see the emotions swirling behind them. She'd been stupid to think if they had sex it would get rid of this tension between them. Instead she just wanted him more every day.

Wanted to come home to him mending the faucet. Wanted to know he'd be waiting for her.

Wanted to feel his skin against hers like this every night.

He slid his hands over her behind, then hitched her up until her face was level with his. He kissed her softly, then turned around, pressing her back against the tiled wall, pressing his hard body against hers.

She tugged at his hair, their kisses getting harder, deeper, until they were moaning against each other's lips. With one hand still holding her, he slid the other between them, touching her where she needed him, his fingers circling and caressing until she couldn't help but call out his name.

And when he was inside her, everything felt right. He was holding her close, whispering how good she felt, how much he needed her, how he never wanted to let her go. He was the perfect mixture of gentle and rough. And as she reached the peak again, he swallowed her pleasure with his mouth, his own desire making his thrusts unsteady and yet so damn perfect.

She could never get enough of this man. She never wanted to.

Even though she knew one day soon he'd walk out that door and wouldn't look back.

"Has Charlie moved back to his place yet?" Everley asked later that night, when they were tangled in bed together. After their shower they'd eaten the pasta he'd made and watched a detective show to wind down, her body curled against his on her cream leather sofa. When she'd finally felt sleepy, he'd taken her to bed, and she'd curled into him the way he liked it.

And now her head was against his chest, her hand resting on his hip, as he softly stroked her hair and they talked in hushed voices.

"He's moving back in tomorrow. I think he's reluctant though. He's gotten used to being at Dolores'. All those home cooked meals and 'Charlie, don't you move from the couch' are getting to him."

Everley smiled against his chest. "Do you think there something going on between them? They're always as thick as thieves."

Dylan ran his thumb over her bottom lip. It was swollen from their kisses. "If there is, he hasn't told me."

"Would you be upset if they got together?" She lifted her head to catch his eye. He blinked, looking thoughtful.

"No, I'd be pleased. And probably relieved that he had somebody to look after him. Somebody he could look after, too."

"He's been single for a long time."

Dylan nodded. "Yeah, he has. Too long probably. He's kind of set in his ways."

"Is he still in love with your mom?"

His brow creased. "How could he be in love with her? She's dead."

"I know, but maybe he's still in love with the idea of her. Her memory." Everley held her breath, because Dylan never spoke much about his mom. When they were younger, asking him questions about his mother was like throwing her head against a brick wall. Pointless and painful.

She knew his mom's death had hurt him, even though it had happened years after she'd abandoned him with his dad. Dying from her drug addiction all alone in a dirty squat house in the city had been a terrible way to go.

"I think he's scarred by her memory," he finally said, his fingers tangling in her silky hair. "I guess we all are."

Her breath caught, because it was the first time he'd mentioned her effect on him. "Do you think of her a lot?"

"Not really. I can barely remember what she looks like without seeing a picture. Can't remember the sound of her voice at all."

"I hope Charlie comes to terms with the loss one day. Before somebody else snaps Dolores up."

"I wouldn't hold your breath," he murmured.

It was as though he was talking about himself, too, and that made her heart ache.

It was too simplistic to say that he chose to save lives because he couldn't save his mom's. But there was a driving force behind him that not many people had. She knew it was there, because she had it, too. For different reasons.

"Speaking of parents, how are yours? Are they coming to the show?" he asked softly.

She lifted a brow, because her relationship with her own parents wasn't exactly something to be proud of. "I offered to send them tickets, but Dad's recovering from a bout of bronchitis. Mom doesn't want him to come up where the air is cold."

Her parents lived in Florida. Had for years. Her dad, the middle child of Candy Winter, had always hated this town. And when he'd inherited it, along with his brother and sister, he'd sold it to the highest bidder.

It was Everley and her cousins who'd saved it – especially Holly whose business acumen was their secret weapon. And though her father had still received payment for the town, there was a bitterness between them that Everley wasn't sure would ever disappear.

As though he sensed her melancholy, Dylan pressed his lips against her temple, running his finger down her spine. "If it makes you feel any better, my dad would adopt you in a heartbeat."

"He kind of did, by not sending in those divorce papers."

Dylan smiled against her brow. "I guess he did. Either way, I'm almost certain he prefers you to me."

"That's good, because I prefer him to you, too," she teased.

Dylan chuckled. "Is that right?"

"Yep. He's rocking that silver fox look. I pretty much married you to get closer to him."

"You always did like older men." He lifted a brow. "I just never knew how much older."

"I've only liked one older man." She traced her finger over the ridges of his stomach. "You."

He captured her wrist in his palm. "Let's keep it that way."

She opened her mouth to ask him what that meant, thinking of the time limit they had. But then she closed it, because she was the one who'd made him promise not to talk about the future. To just enjoy the moments between them for what they were.

It was what she wanted, after all. And she'd promised Casey she wouldn't expect anything more.

Even if there was a part of her that wanted it all.

23

"**A**re you sure they don't mind me coming?" Dylan asked two days later, as they climbed out of his car and walked to North's low-level lodge.

The rooftops were blanketed with snow. North had cleared his driveway, but a light dusting had already peppered over the blacktop, making it glint in the moonlight.

Everley shook her head. "Of course they don't mind you coming. Gabe wants you here." He'd arrived the previous night, but Everley hadn't had a chance to see him yet. She was almost vibrating with excitement.

"At least one of your cousins doesn't plan on hitting me."

"You and North were always friends," she pointed out.

"Until I started sleeping with you."

She slid her hand into his. She was looking more beautiful than ever, her face glowing in the winter sun. It was her first day off since the show had premiered, and he'd thought she might want to sleep. But he should have known better. Everley Winter never slept when she could be doing something.

Not that he minded, when that included *doing* him.

She pressed the doorbell, and within seconds the door was pulled open. Letting out a squeal, Everley launched herself at her cousin, Gabe, who caught her right before she could bowl him over, his laughter echoing all around them.

"Jesus, you're like a damn missile," he said, hugging his cousin. "The Department of Defense should bottle whatever you've got."

When she jumped to the ground, Gabe held his hand out to Dylan, who shook it.

"Come in," he said, stepping to the side so they could both walk into the hallway, and Dylan closed the door behind them.

Loud chatter echoed from the room at the back of the house. As they walked up the hallway, Dylan could see it was a huge living and kitchen area, overlooking the farm and the mountains beyond. North was leaning on a massive island, a beer in one hand, the other gesturing as he spoke to Holly and Josh.

Alaska was sitting next to a woman that Dylan recognized but couldn't remember the name of. A moment later she was introduced as Amber – North's business partner, a beautiful thirty-something brunette, who was grinning over at North.

"There's something between those two," Everley whispered in his ear. "But neither of them will admit it."

He bit down a smile, because according to Everley there was something between most unmarried people in Winterville that they wouldn't admit to. Case in point – his dad and Dolores.

North nodded at them both, grabbing a beer for Dylan and a glass of water for Everley, who'd decided to drive them here. Everley walked over to hug Holly and Josh, then joined her sister and Amber whose faces lit up as she approached.

"Good to see you," Gabe told Dylan.

"Likewise."

Gabe's eyes flickered to Everley and back to Dylan's. He waited for her cousin to say something, but instead he looked at North. "You need any help with dinner?"

"I got it under control," North said.

"And I'm helping," Amber said, smiling as she joined North behind the kitchen island. "Because we all know that North can't cook potatoes for shit."

Dylan laughed and Amber shrugged at him. "Just trying to keep it real."

"You go ahead," he said, lifting his glass.

"It's so nice to have you here," Amber told him. "With you and Josh, us outsiders are slowly building up to outnumber the cousins."

"Hey, there are only three of you," Gabe pointed out. "There are six of us."

"Yeah, but Kris isn't here, and it's only a matter of time before somebody snaps Alaska up." Amber lifted a brow at Gabe. "And you'll have to succumb and get a girl eventually."

"None of them will have me." Gabe didn't sound at all upset about that. "They know I'm an animal."

"A cuddly animal," Amber teased. "A teddy bear."

Gabe winked at her. "You keep on believing that."

"How long until dinner?" Gabe asked his brother.

"About half an hour. Why, you hungry?"

"Gabe's always hungry," Alaska teased. "Remember the year he stole all the candy canes from the tree at the Inn?"

"I remember the stench of vomit coming from our bathroom, yeah." North grimaced.

"I'm not hungry," Gabe protested, holding his hands up. "I just wanted to run something by you all before we eat."

North frowned. "What kind of something."

Gabe looked over at Holly. No, not Holly, Josh. The other man gave him an imperceptible nod. Gabe cleared his voice.

"Maybe we should all sit together, so I'm not shouting across the room."

It took a long moment for everyone to shuffle their way to North's luxurious sofas. There weren't enough seats, so Dylan found himself wedged into the side, with Everley sitting happily on his knee.

Gabe looked uncharacteristically nervous. He inhaled deeply, then looked at them all. "So here's the thing. I'm retiring."

"From competing?" North asked, his voice low.

"Yeah. My injury hasn't healed completely, and I need to accept it probably never will. I can still compete, but I won't win, and there's no point in delaying the inevitable."

"Oh, Gabe." Everley sighed. "I'm so sorry."

He gave her a small smile. "It's okay. It's been a long time coming. Most of my contemporaries are already retired."

"So what will you do?" North asked. "Become a trainer?"

"You know there's always a job for you at the theater," Everley said, her voice warm.

"And at the Inn," Alaska added.

"Hey," North protested. "If he's doing anything, he's working with me. I could do with a right hand man."

"And what am I?" Amber asked.

"You're not my right hand woman. You're my boss." North's voice turned soft.

Gabe shook his head. "I'm not working with any of you. I already have a plan." He looked over at Josh again. "Or rather, *we* do."

"What?" Holly asked, whipping her head around to look at her husband. "Do you know something about this?"

"It's Gabe's story to tell," Josh murmured. "I just helped him think things through."

North looked like somebody had slapped his face.

"Can I just talk, then you guys can ask me all the questions you want?" Gabe sounded frustrated. "And for the record, I asked Josh for help because he's a neutral party. I wanted his thoughts before I got you guys shouting at me."

"Go ahead." North still looked like he'd been sucking lemons.

"Okay. So I know I could come work for any one of you, and I really appreciate that. But I don't want to work for my cousins or brother. I don't want to have a job that's given to me because we share blood. I want something for myself."

North went to open his mouth, but then shut it quickly.

"So I'm going to open up a ski resort."

There was silence for a moment. Everley turned to look at Dylan, her brows knitted. She clearly had no idea this was coming.

"But I thought we didn't want a resort here," Holly said, confused. "That's why we fought Josh when he bought the town." She turned to her husband. "Is that why you kept it a secret, because you knew we wouldn't like it?"

"Honey, just listen, okay?" Josh said softly, placing his hand on hers. "Gabe hasn't finished."

"Thank you." Gabe shook his head. "Okay, so the resort won't be in Winterville. It's going to be a few miles out. We'll start with building the slopes and have it be an outdoor center for skiing, snowboarding, and other winter activities from November to March. Then in the summer, we'll turn the lake into a water sports zone. It'll provide year round employment, and boost the income to Winterville, because more people will want to stay here."

"We're already fully booked," Alaska pointed out.

"We always wanted to expand," Josh told her. "We have the land to build a lot more cabins. And to expand the Inn itself. Gabe's plan will help fund it."

Holly was listening carefully, her brow pinched. "But who's going to fund the resort?" she asked Gabe. "We're in the black here, but just barely. We haven't got the funds for a capital investment."

"I already have some partners. And a couple of firms interested in the investment."

"Are they good investors?" Holly asked him.

"You might have heard of one of them. Cam Hartson, the ex-NFL player."

Dylan blinked in recognition. Even he knew that name.

"Isn't that Gray Hartson's brother?" Everley asked

"Yeah, that's right." Gabe nodded. "I've met Cam a few times in passing at fundraisers, but the last time I saw him we got to talking. He'd retired and was giving me some advice. I told him about my idea and he's interested in being part of it. He and his family only live a few hours away."

"You've never done anything like this before," Holly said, pulling her lip between her teeth. "Do you really think this could work?"

"I know I haven't. And I'm the first one to put my hands up and say I need help. Which is where Josh comes in. I'd like to steal him from you."

Holly started to laugh.

"Not like that. I want him to be part of the resort from the start. To be the CEO."

Holly touched her husband's face. "Is that what you want?"

"You and I need to talk it through first," Josh said to her. "But either way Gabe can do this. If I don't go work with him, I know people who can." Josh was staring into his wife's eyes. "And I know we have other stuff going on and that's important to me, too. I wouldn't make this decision without discussing it with you first, sweetheart."

"It's a great opportunity," she said softly. "And I know you're getting bored helping me."

He kissed her cheek. "I'll never get bored of helping you."

Everley gave the softest of sighs. "You two need to stop this. You're making me go all gooey."

Holly and Josh exchanged a glance. "In that case, we should probably tell you something else," Holly said, biting down a smile.

"What kind of something?" North sounded warier than ever.

"We just confirmed it when we got back from our honeymoon." Holly slid her hand into Josh's. "I'm pregnant. We're going to have a baby."

"Oh my God!" Everley jumped off Dylan's lap. Her face was glowing with happiness. She ran over to Holly and Josh, hugging them both. "No wonder you ate so much on your honeymoon. I can't believe this. So much good news all at once. We get Gabe back, and we get a baby cousin, too."

Dylan felt his stomach tense at her excitement. Another reminder of how much Everley loved babies; how much he couldn't give her. He tried to smile as Alaska and North were hugging Holly, Josh and Gabe, all of them laughing and talking as Amber sat down next to Dylan.

"Okay, now we're definitely outnumbered," she told him. "There's nothing for it, you're going to have to stay around a little bit longer."

Dylan had been quiet all the way home. In fact, he'd been quiet most of the night. She'd put it down to the fact that her cousins were noisy, but now Everley wasn't so sure.

"Wasn't that a great night?" she asked, leaning her head against Dylan's shoulder as they walked up to her front door. "I'm so happy Gabe's coming home for good. And that he'll have something to give him direction."

Dylan took her key from her hand and slid it into the

lock. She felt happy but exhausted, and he slid his hand around her waist. "I'm glad he's coming home," he said. "I know you missed him."

"And then there's the baby." Everly sighed, as they walked inside her cottage and Dylan closed the door behind them. He helped her shuck off her coat, and hung it up, taking his own off and hanging it on the next empty hook. "Did you see North's face? He hates being taken by surprise, and tonight was full of them. Holly and Josh are going to make the best parents. And then there's David and Casey adopting soon. I can't wait. Do you think Holly will have a boy or a girl?"

Dylan's lips twitched. "I'm a hundred percent positive it will be one of those," he said, deadpan.

Everley laughed. "Thank you, Doctor Shaw." She blew him a kiss. "I'm not sure what I'd want if I was Holly. Maybe a little boy that looks just like Josh."

"You want a baby that looks like Josh?" Dylan raised a brow.

"Stop twisting my words." She laughed. "You know what I mean."

He walked into her kitchen and pulled a bottle of water from her refrigerator. "Want one?" he asked her.

"Yes please."

"Why don't you go take a bath? I'll close up down here."

"You could join me," she suggested, her lips curling.

"Maybe. I have some emails to reply to. And I need to work on a paper."

Everley blinked. "You've been quiet all evening. Are you okay?"

He wrapped his arms around her, pulling her against him. "I'm fine. It was nice to see you so happy tonight."

"You looked like you were enjoying yourself, too."

"Yeah, I did." He sounded hesitant. It made her hackles rise.

"There's definitely something wrong. What is it?"

"I guess I got a little wistful." He ran his hands through her hair. "Watching you so happy about Holly and Josh. Knowing that once upon a time that could have been us."

"Holly will make a good mom," she murmured. "And I'll be a kick ass auntie."

"If it wasn't for me, maybe you'd be a mom by now, too."

"What?"

"Maybe if we'd never gotten married you would have found somebody who wanted exactly what you did. You would have settled down, had a family. I don't know."

She frowned. "You think I don't have a family because of you?"

Her tone made him blink. He looked suddenly wary. "I don't...."

"I haven't spent the last eight years pining for you like some kind of Miss Haversham," she told him. "It's like you think the only reason I don't have kids is because I wanted them to be little Dylan Shaws with cocky smiles and no sense of responsibility."

"You think I have no sense of responsibility?"

She shook her head. "Sorry, I should have said a misplaced sense of responsibility."

"What's that supposed to mean?"

She exhaled heavily, not liking the direction of their conversation. "It means that you try to save the world, while letting those who love you down. Yes, all of this could have been ours. *Yours*. But you didn't want it. You had a world to save, you couldn't just hang around in Winterville and spend time with the people you loved. Not when you could be saving all the people in Africa because you couldn't save your mom."

"You have it all wrong." His voice was low.

"Do I? Because I wasn't the one who implied that you

were so amazing that you ruined people's lives just by leaving them."

"That's not what I said." He gritted his teeth, running his fingers through his hair. "I was trying to apologize for messing up your life."

"Do you really think I haven't had a family because of you?" Her voice rose up, because that hurt.

He swallowed, his eyes not quite catching hers. "I have a feeling there's no right answer to that."

"I've had boyfriends. I've dated. If I'd found the right guy I definitely would have had kids with him."

Dylan's jaw twitched. "Okay."

"And when we're divorced, I'll try again. Because I do believe in love, Dylan. I believe in happily ever after. And I want a family."

His eyes were dark, capturing hers. Damn, she loved this man. So much it hurt.

But she wasn't going to let him break her. Not again.

"The thought of seeing you pregnant, and the baby not being mine, kills me."

Her bottom lip trembled. "It kills me, too."

"I have no idea how to give you what you want." He pulled his gaze from hers, turning to look away. His hand tugged at his hair. "I wasn't lying when I told you how good it is to see you happy. That's all I want for you. And I know I'm not the man to give you that."

"Why not?" Her chest felt achy and tight.

He tipped his head back and inhaled sharply, his beautiful eyes closing. She could see him in profile. Straight, strong nose, sharp jaw, lips that knew exactly what they could do to her.

When he brought his head down, she could see how distraught he was. His eyes wouldn't stay still. "Because I'm messed up, Evie. And the only way to deal with my brokenness is to run away. To be with strangers. Make them better. God knows that otherwise I just leave devastation in my wake."

Her eyes stung. Not because of his words, but because it was the first time he'd acknowledged what a mess he was. He made every part of her ache, this man who was beautifully broken. The man who healed others, because he couldn't heal himself.

"Do you think if I could make you happy, I'd walk away?" he asked, his voice full of grit. "Do you think I'd turn my back on the one good thing that's ever happened in my life? You were the fucking love of my life, Evie. You still are. And that's the reason why I can't stay with you."

Hot tears spilled over her cheeks. It was like he'd taken off every piece of armor, exposed his most secret, vulnerable thoughts. And it was painful, not only for her, but for him, too. She knew how much it took for him to admit he wasn't perfect.

That he was afraid. That the tough, masculine shell he showed to others had a crack.

And somehow she'd squeezed under it. A sob caught in her throat at how alone he looked right now, his body straight and hard, but his eyes shining and soft.

"Don't cry," he said, shaking his head. "Please don't cry, baby."

She couldn't help it. She stifled another sob, wiping the tears from her cheeks with the back of her hand.

His expression softened as he walked toward her, reaching out to cup her wet cheeks. "I promised myself I'd never make you cry again."

"You can't control other people's reactions," she whispered. He was so overwhelming. The citrus and wood smell of his cologne wrapped itself around her, his height blocking out the light from the living room lamp. And his touch. So gentle, yet so weirdly reassuring. The doctor's bedside manner turning into something altogether more sensual.

"I can control them by walking away."

"You think I didn't cry for you when you left?"

His breath caught. "I hoped you stopped quickly when you realized I wasn't worth crying over."

She reached up to touch his face. His jaw was rough from a day's growth. "I wish you could see yourself the way I do," she told him, rolling onto her toes to press her lips against his. "And I wish you understood that emotions aren't something to run away from. They're the things that guide us. Let us know what to do next."

"I grew up listening to my parents argue. Listening to my mom make my dad cry. I promised myself I'd never be that person."

"And you're not. But you're not a robot, either. People argue, Dylan. People cry. That's what life is all about. Smiling one moment, sobbing the next. We don't get to have the sunshine without the rain."

He dropped his head until his brow was pressed against hers. Tears were still rolling down her cheeks, more controlled now. Still, he brushed them away with his thumb, then pushed the pad against his tongue, a low noise rumbling from his throat.

It was weirdly erotic. She pressed her body to his, feeling the hard, thick ridge of him. Was he feeling it, too?

"Don't cry anymore, please?" he said roughly.

"I won't cry tonight." She didn't need to. She felt stronger already.

"Okay." He nodded as though it was a deal.

For a moment all she could hear was the harsh rhythm of his breath and the drum of her pulse in her ears. His eyes bored into hers, making her skin tingle. Then he brushed his lips so softly against hers, she wasn't sure it was even a kiss.

"I'm sorry," he whispered.

"So am I." And she was. She didn't want to talk about things that hurt either one of them. They didn't have time for that. "It's late," she said softly. "Let's go to bed."

He nodded, saying nothing, then took her hand in his. He lifted it to his lips, placing the sweetest kiss on her palm but his eyes were dark and needy. "Okay. Let's go."

❦ 24 ❦

"I can't believe you're going to be a mommy," Everley said, sliding a coffee in front of Holly. "Or that you're going to have to drink decaf for nine months. How on earth will you survive? I'm finding it hard enough to drink this herbal tea crap until the show is over."

Holly laughed, lifting the cup to her lips. "Thank God Dolores knows how to make a good decaf. And I'll just have to get more sleep. Josh is already insisting on taking over all the housework and cooking. I'm pretty much living the life of luxury right now."

"Is he excited?" Everley asked her. "I didn't get to talk to him much last night."

"He's over the moon. Already talking about when we can try for a second." Holly rolled her eyes. "Though if he keeps any more secrets from me, he probably won't get a chance."

"Are you pissed at him for not telling you about Gabe's plan?"

"Hell yes. I don't care if he promised to keep it quiet, I'm his wife. Next time he keeps a secret, I'm chopping his balls off."

"At least that'll solve the question about a second baby." Everley smirked.

"Anyway, enough about me. You and Dylan looked awful cozy last night." Holly's brows lifted. "How's it going with you two?"

"We're friends."

"Shut up."

"Friends who can't keep their hands off each other," Everley conceded, a smile flitting across her lips.

"And you're also husband and wife," Holly pointed out, lifting her coffee to her lips.

"That's being taken care of. We've already signed the papers. We should be divorced within a few months."

Holly tilted her head to the side. "I don't understand. You two looked so good together at North's place. You looked happy, he looked happy. Why are you still getting divorced?"

"We're happy because there's no pressure. Not like when he wanted me to follow him for his career, and I wanted him to follow me for mine. We always worked great in the present. It was the future that was our undoing."

"So when he leaves that's it. You're done?"

Everley pressed her lips together, looking over Holly's shoulder at the café beyond. Every table was full, and there was a line for orders out of the door. Dolores had lit the fire and put on Christmas music. "Yeah."

"And Dylan? He's okay with walking away? He looks like he really cares for you."

"He says I'm the love of his life."

Holly blinked. "Seriously?"

Everley filled her in on the discussion she'd had with Dylan the previous night.

"That's so sad," Holly said, her voice soft. "You two should be together."

Everley met her cousin's gaze. "Maybe we're grown up enough to realize that happily ever afters don't always exist."

"And you're okay with that?"

"I don't really have a choice. And I'm okay with just living for now. For taking what we can. For saying goodbye properly this time, without the hurt and pain."

"You're going to feel the pain," Holly said, sounding certain.

"No, not this time. I'm going to love him and let him go. Sure, I'll be sad for a few days, but maybe he's doing me a favor. He can't give me what I want, and I can't give him what he needs, so we're setting each other free."

"What is it you want?" Holly asked her.

Everley shrugged. "What *you* have."

"Decaf coffee?" Holly grimaced.

Everley laughed. "Well, maybe not *that*. But I want somebody who is there for me. Somebody who supports me the way I support them. I want a family one day, and I want somebody to share that with. And Dylan's adamant that can't be him."

"He's an idiot."

"Maybe he's just a realist. We both are."

"You sound so strong," Holly said, shaking her head. "How can you let the love of your life leave you twice? Doesn't it hurt you to lay in his arms and know there's an expiration date?"

"Nope. Because I don't think about it. He says he wants me to be happy and he's not the guy to do it. I'll trust him on that."

"You're crazy, you know that?"

"I do. You've told me enough times." Everley winked at her. "Now stop with that sad look. Unless it's about the decaf, because then you can totally be sad."

Dylan walked through the town square, heading for the theater. It was about five minutes before the final curtain was due to fall.

He walked past huge tree in the center. There was a blanket of snow on the ground, save for the roads where his dad had plowed.

Dylan had plowed a few times, too. His dad was back working mornings at the garage, but he was too tired to plow as well, so Dylan had stepped in. It was the kind of mindless task that calmed him. Let him be alone with his thoughts.

Not that his thoughts were always calm. They were mostly of Everley.

In less than two weeks he'd be heading back to Africa, with a hefty influx of cash thanks to the Carsons. And he'd be saying goodbye to Everley Winter for good. Because he knew that was the only way.

She wanted a family. And he knew better than anybody that he wasn't the man to give that to her. Every child deserved a parent who always put them first. Who was there when they laughed for the first time, when they walked, when they talked.

A parent who knew what the hell they were doing. And he definitely wasn't that.

He crossed the road to where the Jingle Bell Theater stood, the echoes of music and laughter spilling out into the cold streets, his mind still full of her. The night before when he'd told her she was the love of his life he hadn't been lying. And because he loved her, he needed to let her go so she could be happy.

And it killed him that he wasn't the one who could make her happy. It killed him more that whenever she cried they always ended up in bed. That somehow her tears aroused him, like some kind of asshole who got off on making girls upset. It had happened again that night they argued. But he was determined not to make her cry again.

He pushed open the stage door, following the familiar maze of corridors to Everley's dressing room. A group of performers greeted him by name – he was becoming a familiar face around here, thanks to his inability to keep away from her.

"Hey, a few of us are going out tonight. You and Everley should come," one of the dancers said.

"Thanks," he said, nodding politely, knowing full well they wouldn't be going out. They could barely keep their hands off each other. Maybe it was the knowledge that their time together was running out that made them so hot for each other. Whatever it was, tonight definitely didn't involve other people.

He could hear the final number start up. Everley would be carried in by two male dancers right now. He'd feel jealous, except one of them was married and the other was definitely not interested in Everley.

Oh, and the fact he wasn't supposed to feel jealous. There was that, too.

Her dressing room was empty. The two other dancers she shared it with were in the finale, too, and would be here at the same time as Everley. Dylan leaned against the wall, his eyes alighting on a bunch of flowers at the center of her vanity. The card was open next to it, as though she'd barely had time to open it before rushing off to the show.

I can't wait to see you perform next week. Miller xx

. . .

Dylan's mouth felt dry. Sure, he wasn't supposed to feel jealous, yet here he was doing it all over again. He was the one who'd said he was guilty that she hadn't made a family. And she'd been honest with him, telling him that when he was gone, she'd date again. Hopefully to find somebody she could settle down with.

That one day she'd be pregnant with another man's child.

But not Miller Carson. Dear God, please not him.

He clenched his teeth, trying to push the image of Miller and Everley out of it. Of their glowing faces as they both cupped her swollen stomach.

Bile rushed into his mouth. He swallowed it down, closing his eyes for a moment. He couldn't stand the thought of her being with anybody else. He loved her too much.

Then find a way to make it work.

The voice in his head sounded so sure. As though it was that easy. As though he hadn't tried to make their marriage work all those years ago.

"Hey." A deep voice pulled him out of his thoughts. He looked up to see Casey walk into the dressing room, a big smile on his face. "You look like you were a million miles away."

"Hi." Dylan shot him a smile. "How's it going?"

"Pretty good."

"Everley tells me your adoption application is going well," Dylan said.

"Yeah, it's going well." Casey grinned. "David thinks we'll pass through pretty soon. We could have a child by early next year."

"That's amazing." Dylan's smile was genuine.

"How about you? You still going back to Africa?"

"That's the plan." Dylan's voice was light.

"Everley's going to miss you."

"Yeah. I'm going to miss her, too." His throat felt tight. "She's not somebody you leave behind easily."

Casey smiled. "She loves you. You know that, right?"

His throat tightened. "Yeah, I know."

"And you? Do you love her?"

He didn't need to think about his answer. "Yeah. I'm in love with her."

"Then what the fuck are you doing, man? Why are you going back to Africa when she's here? Why the hell aren't you fighting for her?"

"Because she deserves better than me."

"Bullshit. If you think you're not good enough for her, then *make* yourself good enough. You don't walk away from something you want. That's just crazy."

Dylan met Casey's stare. His brows were knitted, as though he couldn't understand what was going through Dylan's mind. Maybe Dylan wasn't sure either.

Could he make himself good enough? The thought was tantalizing. He wanted to, that was for sure. Wanted to be the man that a woman like Everley deserved. Wanted to be the one to make her smile, make her laugh.

Get her pregnant.

But what if he couldn't? What if he ended up hurting her all over again? Gabe and North wouldn't have to kill him if he did, he'd do it himself.

The dressing room door opened and Everley walked in, her lips curling as she saw Dylan and Casey standing there.

"Thanks for the advice," Dylan murmured to Casey.

"Worth thinking about," Casey murmured back, before giving Everley a bear hug.

Yeah, it was. And it was beyond time for Dylan to do something about this situation. Because Everley wasn't the sort of woman you turned your back on twice.

❀ 25 ❀

"You're not asleep," Everley murmured sleepily that night, curling against Dylan's warm body. He was staring up at the ceiling, his eyes wide and thoughtful. He brought his gaze to hers and stroked her hair softly.

"I was just thinking about something."

"What?" she asked, curiosity pulling at her. She was usually the one who couldn't sleep.

"Doctors Overseas has a couple of therapists on call. I was thinking about arranging a video conference with them."

"Therapists? As in counselors?"

"Yeah." He tipped his head to the side. "Does that make me sound troubled?"

"No. I think it's a great idea. Would you talk to them about your mom?" She rested her chin on his chest. His skin was warm and unyielding.

"Among other things, yeah."

"Then go for it. I'm a huge fan of therapy. I've done some myself over the years."

"You have? I didn't know that."

"Why would you? It was after you left. I had this great

223

therapist in New York. My grandma recommended her, actually."

"How long did you go for?"

"A few months. It was good to have somebody neutral to talk to. It really helped me come to terms with my relationship with my parents. Or lack of."

"They don't deserve you," he murmured, feathering his fingers down her neck.

"Yeah, that's the conclusion I came to as well. It isn't my fault that our relationship is pretty much nonexistent. Therapy helped me accept that. For it to be a fact rather than something that hurt me." She traced a circle on his chest with her finger. "Hopefully you'll be able to get to that place about your mom, too."

He lifted her hand to his lips, placing a kiss on her palm. "I want to be a better person. This is the first step."

"You're already a good person. One of the best I know."

"I'm not so good that I didn't feel jealous when I saw Miller Carson's flowers tonight," he said, his voice gruff.

"You saw those?"

"Yeah. And they pissed me off."

She bit down a smile. "They're nothing. I sent him a bottle of champagne to thank him for something, and he sent those back in return."

"You sent him champagne?" Dylan blinked.

"Yes, and you can stop looking all angry about it. He's arranged for some journalists to come watch the show, and I wanted to show him some gratitude. If we get more publicity, it could help put us on the map. I want to build up our spring and summer program, and to do that I need to attract some good actors and singers who have probably never heard of this place. Miller's helping me with that." She placed her palm over his pectoral muscle, resting her chin on top of it. "Are you really jealous of him?"

"Yeah," Dylan grunted. "Really damn jealous."

Her lips curled. "That's kind of sweet. But you have nothing to worry about. Miller is a friend, and a new one at that. More of an acquaintance, really."

He lifted a brow. "What are the journalists going to do? Write up the performance?"

"Something like that. They want to interview me, too. They're entertainment journalists, but if I can get a word in for the town, too, I'm going to do it."

"Of course you will." He smiled fondly at her. "You always get what you want."

"Not always." She swallowed.

"Have you thought about what to say if they ask about our marriage?" His words were soft.

"I figure I'll deflect the question. There's no point in letting people know about the divorce until it's done, right?"

"Right," he murmured, that thoughtful look in his eyes again.

"Speaking of which, have you got an update from Jeff recently?"

"About the divorce?" He still sounded strange. "No. I called him a couple of days ago but his PA said he was in court. He'll call back."

"Did I tell you I sent him and his family tickets to the show?"

He smiled. "I should have guessed you would. You have this knack of making connections with everybody you meet."

"Do I? I'm not sure if that's a compliment or not."

"It's definitely a compliment, baby. It's one of the things I fell for about you."

"You know what made me fall for you?" she asked, a wicked smile curling at her lips.

"I'm almost afraid to ask."

"Your thick, hard, throbbing..."

He'd grabbed her and turned her over before she could finish her words, pressing her back onto the mattress as he hovered above her. "This?" he asked, his voice thick, as he slid himself against her.

"Yeah, that." She gasped as he hit the part of her that felt everything, sending delicious shots of pleasure to her toes.

He slid inside her, her breath catching in her throat as she felt the fullness of him. Their gazes connected as he began to move, her body rocking in time with his.

It wasn't just his body that had made her fall for him. It was his soul. And yeah, he was a little broken, but so was she.

But when he moved inside her, they made each other whole.

"So, why don't we start with what you hope to achieve from today?"

Dylan crossed his legs, leaning back on the kitchen chair as he looked at the laptop screen. Thankfully, his dad was at the garage. He had no idea what Charlie's reaction would be to him having a therapy session, but it wasn't something he planned on telling him right now.

"I want to be a better person," he managed, shifting uncomfortably.

Laura – the therapist – nodded. "That's quite a big aim. Maybe we can break it down a bit. Why do you think you aren't a good person?"

Dylan swallowed. "I don't know. I've hurt some people I didn't want to hurt."

"Do you have somebody specific in mind?"

"Yeah, I do." He blinked. "Her name's Everley. She's my ex, no my wife." He grimaced. "It's complicated."

Laura didn't bat an eyelash. "How did you hurt her?"

Everley's words came back to him in a rush. "I pushed away her love, then ran away." He sighed at the memory. Saying it made him feel sick.

Laura nodded slowly. "Okay, so maybe we can talk about how that happened. How long were you married?"

"Less than a year. But also for nine years."

She listened as he explained his marriage to Everley – and the subsequent non-divorce. Not once did she look shocked or surprised. Just understanding.

"You still have feelings for each other."

"Yeah."

"And you'd like to have a relationship with Everley?"

"Yeah, I would."

"What's stopping you?"

"I go back to Africa soon." Dylan pressed his lips together. The thought of leaving Everley behind made his stomach twist.

"Plenty of people in the organization are married. And there are other positions you could apply for. Ones based in the US." Laura shrugged. "Or you could leave and take up a position in a local hospital. Is that really what's holding you back?"

He blew out a lungful of air. This was harder than he thought it would be. There was part of him that wanted to push all of this away and not think about it anymore. "I guess I'm scared of hurting her again."

"How do you think you'll hurt her?"

"I don't know. I mess things up a lot. If we're going to do this thing, I want to guarantee I won't make her cry again. Unless I can do that, I need to let her get on with her life." He raked his hand through his hair, his stomach still churning.

"Do you think that's a realistic plan?" Laura asked gently. "Nobody can guarantee they won't cry. And relationships have ups and downs. I could even argue that a healthy relationship involves accepting there will be conflict, and that resolving the conflict can sometimes lead to tears."

"I can't make her cry again," Dylan said, shaking his head.

"What is it about her tears that scares you?"

He blinked. "I don't know."

"Maybe you do. There's something there. This fear of her crying. What do you think it is about it that makes you panic?"

Dylan crossed his arms, frowning. "I don't panic. I just don't want to make the girl I love feel sad."

Laura looked at him for a moment. Even though she was only on a screen he felt uncomfortable.

"Okay, so maybe we can hone in on this," Laura suggested, her voice gentle. "Tell me how you react when she cries."

"I feel bad. I want to make her stop." He gritted his teeth. Maybe this session was a bad idea.

"And physically? What does your body do when Everley has tears?"

He shifted his gaze away, heat suffusing his body. "I don't know…"

"You look like you do. And any reaction is okay. I'm not judging, I'm only trying to help. Whatever you say here is between us, Dylan."

"I get aroused." Saying it out loud made him want to throw up. "That's what I fucking do. I get turned on by her tears, and that makes me a monster. And that's why I need to be better."

His face burned with embarrassment. He wanted to hide it in his hands. Fuck, he was messed up. He couldn't bring himself to look at his therapist right now.

"Dylan? Are you okay?"

His jaw ticked. "I'm hanging in here."

"Do you think you could look at me?"

Gritting his teeth, he lifted his eyes to hers. Again there was no judgement. It almost made him feel worse. "I'm looking."

"Let's break this down a little further. What is it about her tears that makes you react like that?"

"I don't know." He shook his head. "But I don't like it."

"I took a look at your notes earlier. Your mom left when you were a young child. Is that right?"

His eyes narrowed. "Let's not make this about my mom."

"I promise I'm not. I'm just trying to get some context. How old were you when she died?"

"I was ten. My dad got a visit from the police. They were still married but we hadn't seen her in years." Dylan's jaw twitched.

"And she died of a drug overdose?" Laura asked.

"Yeah."

"How long had she been an addict?"

Dylan ran his thumb along his jaw. "Since she was a teenager. She got it under control for a while when she was pregnant with me, but then she got worse once I was born."

"Do you remember her being affectionate toward you?"

He shrugged. "I don't remember anything about her at all. Not really."

"How about your dad? Was he affectionate?"

Dylan frowned. It was hard to remember. "I think so. I've always known he cares."

"Okay. And from your notes, I see your mom was your primary caregiver as an infant and toddler?"

"That's right." He nodded. "My dad was trying to build his business up. He owns a repair garage."

Laura held his gaze for a long minute. He could see compassion there, and it made him feel like a freak.

"What is it?" he asked her.

She smiled gently. "I don't think you get aroused by tears

because you're a monster. I think you get aroused by them because they show that somebody cares about you."

"What?"

"We're humans, Dylan. We seek connection from the earliest age. And from what you've told me about your mom, you didn't get that connection. You probably developed what we call a fearful avoidant attachment style. You desperately want to have a normal relationship, but that child inside of you fears being rejected again. So you test the person you're with, to see how attached they are to you. And when the person you desire cries, that's a sign to you that they care. And I think *that's* what you find arousing. That Everley loves you enough to cry for you."

"You think I get turned on because she loves me?" His voice was thick. He frowned, trying to think it through.

"I think it's a distinct possibility. It's something we could explore more if you want further sessions, but it's not abnormal for a child who doesn't receive love and affection during their formative years to push their spouses or partners to test their attachment."

"So how do I stop doing that? How do I stop getting turned on when my wife cries?" She'd gotten his attention now. There was a truth to her words. They made sense in every way. Was she right? Was he really not an asshole who got off on tears?

"You're already doing it. You acknowledged the situation and talked about the things that contributed to it. Starting with your childhood and working up from there. And when you're ready, you'll talk with Everley about it. That way you can deal with the situation together."

"She deserves better than me."

"Does she?" Laura lifted a brow. "Because from what you've said, Everley sounds like a strong, determined woman. If she loves you, then there's a reason for that. I think you have a lot of fine attributes. You're a good man. You work to make this world a better place. And you take care of those you love, even if sometimes that care is misguided." She smiled softly. "At the beginning of this session you told me you wanted to be a better person. I think your real task is to understand that you're already that person. Now you need to go find your wife and make her understand how much you care about her."

He nodded slowly. That was all he wanted. For Everley to be his. To take care of her, to keep her safe. To make her happy. "Okay."

She glanced at her watch. "I think this is probably a good place to leave it. Unless you have any questions?"

No, he didn't have any questions. But he was beginning to find answers. And for the first time in forever, they gave him hope.

❧ 26 ❧

Something was going on. Everley sensed it when she walked into her dressing room. Her first clue was that Dylan wasn't there, leaning on her vanity the way he had for the past few nights. Ever since their argument it was like he couldn't bear to be parted from her for longer than necessary. He'd either meet her here, or message her to tell her he was heading to her place, and she hadn't received either.

When he was here, he'd help her take off her costume, the tension between them building as his fingers brushed against her skin. Sure, they were surrounded by people when she changed into her jeans and sweater, but there was a promise in his eyes that was so sensual.

And then they'd walk back to her cottage, their restraint hanging by a thread until they made it through the door and were all over each other. One thing was for sure, the physical aspect of their relationship was only getting better.

There was a card on her vanity, propped against the mirror. Her name was written across it in Dylan's familiar scrawl. She picked it up, a smile playing on her lips, as she slid her finger beneath the flap, easing it open.

Meet me by the Christmas Tree. Dress warm. D xx

Her smile widened. She loved surprises. Especially ones involving him. It took her all of five minutes to remove her costume and hang it up haphazardly, then slide her legs into her jeans. Once she'd put her cream cashmere sweater on, she leaned into the mirror, checking her hair and her makeup. Satisfied that she looked okay, she grabbed her coat and a scarf, sliding her denim-clad legs into knee length leather boots.

"No Dylan tonight?" Marta asked.

"I'm meeting him somewhere." Everley kissed her cheek. "Gotta go."

The air was biting as she stepped out of the stage door, the wind curling around her in an unwelcome embrace. Snowflakes danced in the air, hitting the ground at an angle as the white blanket accumulated against the side of the theater. She walked around to the front of the building, where the audience was still spilling out of the open doors, some of them waving and shouting at her as she made her way past.

And then she saw him.

In the center of the square, leaning against the wooden chassis of a white painted open carriage, two horses attached at the front. He was wearing jeans and scuffed boots, a dark woolen pea coat with a grey sweater peeking from underneath. His hair was her favorite kind of mess, falling over his brow, framing his beautiful face. The same face that was giving her the sexiest of once-overs.

"What's this?" she asked breathlessly, as he walked toward her, holding his hands out. She took them, and he pulled her against him, his hand pressing into her back.

"Date night," he said gruffly. "Every married couple needs them to keep the relationship fresh."

She lifted a brow. "We wouldn't want the relationship to be stale, would we?"

He shook his head. "That's why I paid the babysitter double. We have all night together."

"What will we do?" She beamed at him, loving his playfulness.

"I'm thinking at some point I'll probably drop to my knees and eat my wife like she's my breakfast, lunch, and dinner. But first, let's go on a carriage ride."

Everley pulled her bottom lip between her teeth. "You keep calling me your wife."

"That's because you are."

"For now," she pointed out, as he helped her climb up into the carriage.

He leaped up beside her, taking one of the red blankets stored beneath the seat, and tucking it carefully around her legs. Then he slid his hand inside her coat, cupping her waist as he leaned in to kiss her cheek. "Well, Mrs. Shaw-for-now, are you ready to take a ride?"

She laughed. "Always."

He turned to the driver. "Let's go."

The driver lifted the reins and called out to the horses, who began to pull away, the carriage wheels creaking as they began to roll. Snow was still gently falling, catching on the fleece of the blanket that covered her lap, and peppering Dylan's hair.

"I've never been on a carriage ride," she told him as they reached the road that bordered the square.

"Never?" He frowned. "But you've lived here most of your life."

"I know. I guess it's always one of those things that I wanted to do but never got around to."

He winked. "Well tonight I'm planning on bringing all your fantasies to life."

"*All* of them?"

He pressed his lips to her chin. They were warm and soft. "Every single one, baby."

"But then what will we do?" she asked, teasing.

"Then you can dedicate the rest of your life to pleasing me." He grinned.

"You mean the rest of the month. Until you leave."

He lifted a brow. "I said what I meant, Everley."

She shifted to look at him. "What's going on? You seem different."

"Why does something need to be going on? I'm taking my wife on a trip, that's all. Stop worrying and enjoy yourself."

"Oh, I'm enjoying myself," she told him, grinning. "I really am."

He looped his arm around her shoulders, pulling her closer against him. She could smell the citrus notes of his cologne, feel the warmth of his breath as he rested his lips against her brow. The sound of the horses' hooves hitting the road kept up a constant rhythm as the driver steered them out of the town square, pointing toward the Winterville Inn. It was lit up against the dark backdrop of the sky, its towers and turrets beckoning them.

But instead of turning into the sweeping driveway, the driver took the next turn, taking the carriage down a single track path that made the chassis rise and fall in rhythm to the clop of the hooves. It was only when they came to a stop that she realized where they were going.

"You rented a cabin?"

"I thought about us eating outdoors, but decided I liked my balls attached to my body." He grinned and climbed down from the carriage, then reached up to help her out. His hands were curled around her waist, and as he lowered her to the ground he pulled her against him, pressing his lips to hers.

"Do you remember our honeymoon?" he asked.

"When we holed up in a Vegas hotel room and stayed naked for three days?"

He grinned. "Yeah. This is kind of like that, except colder and we're older."

"You rhymed."

"I'm a poet and I didn't know it."

There was definitely something different about him. She wished she could put her finger on it. The smile didn't leave her face as he took her hand and led her into the cabin. Twinkling lights were strung across the roofline, and from the inside she could hear the sound of Christmas music. "Did you do all this yourself?"

"Of course." There was a fire roaring in the grate. A table was set up in the center of the cabin, and next to it was one of the Inn's waiters, wearing a full dinner suit and bow tie. As he saw them enter, he walked forward, taking Everley's coat and hanging it on the hook by the door.

"Champagne?" he asked her.

"Yes please." She looked at Dylan, trying to figure him out.

The waiter pulled a dark green bottle from the ice bucket and filled two flutes, passing them to Everley and Dylan. "Your dinner is ready when you are," he told them. "It's on the electric warmer. If you unplug everything and leave it on the porch I'll collect it all later."

"Thank you, Derek," Everley murmured.

"Anytime, Miss."

"Missus," Dylan corrected softly, and Everley bit down a smile. He was playful *and* possessive. It sent delicious shivers down her spine.

"Is there anything else you need?" Derek asked them, not affected at all by Dylan's correction.

"No, that's it. Thank you for keeping the fire burning."

"It's a pleasure, Dr. Shaw." Derek nodded at Everley. "Good night Mrs. Shaw."

She swore she could feel Dylan's smirk without even looking at him.

After Derek left, and Dylan closed the door behind him, she turned, still holding the champagne in her hand, her eyes catching his.

He had always left her breathless, but the expression on his face pushed all the oxygen from her lungs. He was staring at her with dark, needy eyes. His lips were parted, his jaw strong. Her chest hitched in an attempt to draw in air.

"Would you like to eat?" he asked, his voice low.

"Depends what else is up for offer."

His eyes raked down her body, taking in her curves. "Dinner first. Pleasure later."

"Spoilsport."

"You've used up God knows how many calories on stage. I need you strong for what I have planned."

"Then let's eat."

He smirked and lifted the lids from the plates, taking them from the warmer and carrying them over to the table.

"Winterville Chicken Pot Pie," she murmured.

"It was always your favorite."

"It still is." It touched her that he remembered. "I can never be bothered to make one, but I always order it when I eat at the Inn."

Dylan helped her into her chair, then topped up their glasses, before walking around to the seat opposite her. A low rumble echoed from her stomach, and he grinned. "Bet you're glad I'm making you eat first."

She hadn't realized how hungry she was until she slid the first delicious forkful of pie between her lips. She closed her eyes, letting out a groan as the food slipped into her needy stomach, the taste of chicken and herbs filling her senses.

"Jesus, you look just like that when you swallow me," Dylan murmured. "Who knew I was at the same level as a chicken pot pie."

She grinned. "You last longer than this pot pie will."

"Glad to hear it. You've eaten half of it in less than a minute."

She managed the other half just as quickly, then followed it with the beans and mashed potatoes, all covered in a delicious gravy. When she finished, she put her silverware neatly on her empty plate and looked up at Dylan.

He was still grinning at her. His plate was hardly touched. "You know what I like about you?" he asked.

"That I can swallow a whole plate of food without chewing?"

"Well yeah. But apart from that?"

She leaned forward. "Tell me."

"Every. Damn. Thing."

His words made her chest tighten. "You do?"

"Yeah. Look at you," he said, lifting his brows. "You're beautiful. You're talented. You're one of the most generous people I've ever met. And you eat like a goddamned animal. You're the full package."

"You're being very sweet." She pulled her bottom lip between her teeth. "Are you going to tell me what this is about?"

His eyes captured hers. "I want you."

"That's good. Because I want you, too."

"I don't think you understand. I don't want this to end. I want you to be with me. However we do it, whatever it takes. I can't walk away from you again."

She opened her mouth, then closed it. His words had completely taken her by surprise.

"I know we said we wouldn't talk about the future. I know I promised you that. But I can't leave town without you knowing how I feel about you. I'm in love with you, Everley. I always have been. You're the light to my darkness, baby. You're the first thing I think of in the morning and the only person I want to be with at night. And if I'm coming on too strong, I understand, but I don't want you to be in any doubt that I want to be with you."

Her throat felt tight. Dry. "But how will it work? You live in Africa, I live here."

"I have no idea. But I want us to try to work something out."

"Would you expect me to follow you again?"

"Hell no." He shook his head. "I was such an idiot putting all that pressure on you. I've seen you on stage, I know you belong there. I'd never want to take that away from you. This is on me to manage. To find a way. Not you."

"But your work is important. It's what drives you."

"*You're* important." His voice was so sure. "That's what I didn't realize back then."

Her eyes stung, because she could see from his face that he meant every word. "You're important to me, too."

He closed his eyes, breathing out heavily. As though he'd needed to hear those words from her.

"But I can't take you away from your work. The same way you can't take me away from mine. I couldn't bear to see you stuck here in this town, resenting me because I stopped you from following your heart and doing the one thing that's always driven you."

"I could never resent you. It would be my choice."

"You think you could walk away from the thing you love?"

He ran his tongue along his bottom lip. "I walked away from you once."

"I know. And it hurt us both. But we survived." Barely, though. "We're not those kids we once were. We're adults and we need to make adult decisions. If we go forward with this, I need you to be certain it's what you want. Because if I give my heart to you, I can't let you break it again."

"I won't. I promise you that." He reached for her hand. "And I'll work things out. I'll talk to my team and see if there's something I can do to base my work here. I could consult with local doctors on difficult cases, or work with the head office in training new recruits. I have no idea, because I need to speak to them, but I'm certain there's something I can do that'll help me spend more time with you." A half smile pulled at his lips. "I want it all, Evie. I want you and I want to save the world."

She exhaled, a lightness coming over her, taking away the ache in her chest. "You think you can have it all?"

"If you'll let me." He tipped his head to the side, still half-smiling. "What do you think? Will you take a chance on me? On us?"

She nodded, her heart singing. "Yes, I will."

"Then come here." His voice was gruff. Before she could stand, he was out of his chair, pulling her up, stroking the hair from her face with his warm fingers before leaning down to press their lips together. His tongue slid against hers, his fingers steadying her jaw as he kissed her again and again until she felt giddy and high.

"Let's go to bed," he murmured.

"Sounds good to me."

"Me, too. I'm ready for dessert."

"Jesus, Dylan, that's a lot to spring on us. Talk about leaving us in a hole."

He was video conferencing with his boss in the field. The connection wasn't great, and the audio was lagging the video feed, but Dylan could still see the setting sun behind Alex's tired face. He was six hours ahead of Winterville, and the lines in his face told Dylan that he'd had a long day.

"I won't leave you in a hole," Dylan reassured him. "I just want to work out a way where I can withdraw slowly from my position in the field and work from here."

"We'd counted on you being part of the project for the next few years. At least until the medical center is built and staffed. How soon do you want to leave?" Alex asked, running his hand through his gray hair.

Dylan swallowed. "I want to leave within six months. Sooner if possible." He needed to prove to Everley that this is what he wanted. If he stayed away longer, she'd be less likely to believe him. And he couldn't stand the thought of losing her again. "I'm sorry. I know this isn't what we planned. But the injection of money from the Carson Foundation should help with funding my replacement."

"Such a damn shame," Alex murmured. "You're one of the best we have."

"I'm sorry." Dylan exhaled heavily. "I'll keep working until we find a replacement. And I'm hoping that I can still give you some remote support. We have video calls after all, and telephones."

"When the equipment works," Alex reminded him. The screen flickered as if to prove his point.

"Yeah, I know. But hopefully we can invest in some better equipment with the funding. It'll help with our long-term plan of having local medical staff do the majority of the work, and only have them turn to us for advice when needed."

"Yeah, I can see that. But I'm still worried about you, man. You're like part of the furniture here. Are you sure you're making the right decision in leaving this behind? You told me yourself that it was your calling, that there was nothing else you wanted to do but work here with us. I'm worried that you're making a rash choice and you'll regret it later. Maybe you should sleep on it for a few days. Make sure it's the right one."

"I know it's the right one."

"But why the change of heart? Is it your dad? Is he sick?"

"No, not my dad," Dylan said. "Though being closer to him will be good. It's something else. I've met the woman I want to spend the rest of my life with."

Alex blinked on the screen. "You've only been gone for a few weeks. How can you be sure?"

"I've known her most of my life." Dylan lifted a brow. "And I'm certain. I've made my decision and I'm not changing my mind. So let's talk about how we move forward with the project."

"Okay." Alex nodded. "I'm disappointed, but let's talk."

27

"Can you believe it's only two days until Christmas?" Casey asked, grinning as he walked into the dressing room. Anna and Marta squealed his name, as Everley turned on her stool and gave him a grin. "Not that you care when you're all loved up," he added, winking at her.

She'd told him about Dylan's declaration. And that they were going to try to work things out.

"I'm more worried about this interview I'm doing later," Everley told him, outlining her lips with a soft red pencil, before filling them in with a same color of lipstick. "Why did I agree to it anyway?"

"Because it's good publicity for the theater. Which is nothing but a good thing." He pressed his lips to her head. "And anyway, you love talking about yourself, you'll be fine."

"You're so rude." She shook her head, rolling her eyes at his reflection in the mirror.

"That's why you love me." He ruffled her hair and she batted him off. "Anyway, I wanted to check in with you before I head out to pick my folks up. Whose idea was it to have a friends and family day so close to Christmas?"

"Mine," Everley said dryly. "And it's a great idea." The twenty-third was the day that the staff was able to buy seats for half price, for their friends and family who were visiting from out of town. "Look how happy it's made everybody," she said, pointing at Anna and Marta.

She'd allocated her own tickets weeks ago. Dylan would be in the audience. And she'd given Miller Carson three tickets, for himself and his journalist friends. She'd given the other tickets she had to Dylan's lawyer friend Jeff and his family.

Tomorrow would be their final performance before Christmas. Instead of an evening performance they'd have a matinee, so those who traveled could make it safely back to their homes in time for Christmas Eve night.

She'd learned from her mistake the previous year when they had an unexpected snow storm on Christmas Eve, and all the guests at the theater had been snowed in for the night. So this time they'd perform early, and everybody could get home in the daylight. Tomorrow night, for those cast members who weren't spending Christmas with their loved ones, she was throwing a party at the Winterville Inn.

And Dylan would be there, too, along with Charlie and so many of their friends. She was excited just thinking of it. She'd be spending Christmas not only with her family, but with the man she loved.

She couldn't stop smiling.

"Well if you're sure, I'll head out." Casey kissed her cheek carefully, so as not to mess up the face paint she'd applied. "Break a leg. Except don't. Broken bones and Christmas don't mix."

"Don't worry, I'm planning on keeping all my bones perfectly intact." She blew him a kiss as he left, closing the door behind him. A moment later, one of the male dancers cracked the door, craning his head through the opening.

"There's somebody asking for you in the office," he told her. "They asked me to pass a message to you."

"Is it Miller Carson?"

"Yeah, that's right." He nodded.

"Could you be a sweetheart and bring him to me." She wasn't expecting to have her interview until after the show – when they'd booked a table at the tavern – but it would be rude to leave them waiting.

"Do you want us to go?" Marta asked. "Leave you alone in peace?"

Everley wrinkled her nose. "You don't have to. I don't want to throw you out of your own dressing room."

"It's fine. She's having a thing with Xavier and she wants to surprise him in case he's still getting dressed," Anna said, shooting a smile at her friend.

"Shut up. And anyway, I've never seen a guy look better naked than him." Marta pulled her friend's hand. "We'll see you on stage."

"Thank you." Everley blew them a kiss. "Hope you catch him in his shorts."

She smiled as Miller walked in, along with an older man wearing round glasses, and a younger brunette who was clad all in black.

"Hi," Everley said. She was wearing her costume, thankful that she'd gotten ready earlier than usual, but her feet were still clad in her fluffy slippers. "I'm so glad you could all make it. Did you get your tickets okay?"

"We did." Miller gave her the warmest of smiles. "I know we're meeting after the show, but I wanted to introduce you all first." He looked at the younger woman. "This is Ria Carside from the *Footlights Website*."

Everley leaned forward to shake her hand.

"And you probably know Robert Danvers from *Playbill*," Miller added, introducing his other companion.

"Of course I do. Thank you so much for coming down. I know it's a long way from New York."

"It's a pleasure. I'm staying with some family in northern Virginia for the holidays, so it's not too far out of the way." Robert shook her hand. "I knew your grandmother. You look extraordinarily like her."

"Thank you." Everley took a deep breath. "We're trying to do her proud here." She glanced at the refrigerator at the corner of the room. "Can I offer you a drink?" she asked them. "We have either water or champagne."

Robert laughed. "It's okay. We'll head to our seats. I want to get a feel for the theater."

Another rap came on the door. Everley bit down a laugh. It was getting busy even by theater standards. "I'm sorry, let me just see who that is."

When she opened the dressing room door she saw Dylan standing on the other side, and her heart did a little skip. Behind him was a family, a man in his thirties, his wife, and two young children who could barely stand still with excitement.

"Hi." Her face split into a grin. Dylan's eyes caught hers and she felt a shiver snake down her spine. How was it that even when they were surrounded by people every glance he gave her made her feel hot and needy?

"This is Jeff Martin and his wife, Monique." Dylan nodded at the couple. "And these are their children, Lila and Tom." He looked over her shoulder, his eyes narrowing momentarily as he spotted Miller leaning against her vanity. "You're busy," he murmured.

"No, it's fine. Come in." She smiled broadly at Dylan's friends. "If you don't mind me getting my finishing touches on while you're in here."

"It's okay. We'll catch you later." Dylan winked at her.

"Don't be silly, it's fine. Miller was just introducing his

friends. This is Robert Danvers and Ria Carside, the journalists I was telling you about." She gestured at the two of them standing with Miller. "And this is Dylan Shaw," she told them.

"Come on in," Miller said. "We're leaving anyway. It's good to see you again, Dylan." He shook his hand and brushed past him into the hallway, closely followed by Robert and Ria.

Keeping a smile firmly on her lips, Everley greeted Dylan's friends, showing them around her dressing room. The little girl oohed and aahed over the head pieces, and her cheeks pinked with happiness as Everley let her try out her stage lipstick, as Monique asked her questions about the theater and her grandmother. After ten minutes, the deputy stage manager shouted out that they had fifteen minutes, and Everley glanced at Dylan because she really needed to get stage ready.

"We should head out," Dylan said, kissing her cheek again. "I'll see you after the show."

"I have that meeting with Miller and the journalists, remember?"

He lifted a brow. "Oh yes. *Miller*."

"Don't be like that. He's just a friend. And he's doing me a big favor."

"As long as he's not expecting any favors in return," Dylan muttered.

Monique was pulling her children away from Everley's vanity, and she shot Everley a grateful glance. "Thank you for letting us drive you crazy," she said warmly. "These two will be talking about this for weeks."

"I hope you all enjoy the show."

Jeff was the last to leave. He beamed broadly at her. "Oh hey, it was great news, right?"

"What was?" Her brow crinkled.

"About the divorce."

Everley swallowed. "What about the divorce?"

Jeff glanced at Dylan, who was talking to Monique in the hallway. "He didn't tell you?"

"Tell me what?" Everley asked. Her chest felt weird. As though it was full of steel wool.

"That your divorce went through so quickly. How crazy is that?"

She felt the color drain from her face. "I'm sorry?" From the corner of her eye she saw Dylan look over from his conversation with Monique, his eyes wary as he looked from her to Jeff.

"Oh." Jeff swallowed hard, looking over his shoulder at Dylan. "He didn't tell you?"

Her hands started to shake. Dylan knew they were divorced and hadn't told her? The past few days they'd had together were the best of her life, and he'd been lying about them? She inhaled a short, ragged breath, willing her eyes not to tear up and sting.

"Dylan?" she asked softly. "Did you know about this?"

Jeff grimaced. "Shit."

"Jeff!" Monique shook her head. "The children are here."

"We should take them to our seats," Jeff said, sliding through the doorway to where his wife was standing. Dylan hadn't moved, though his eyes were still firmly on Everley.

"Ten minutes until beginners," the assistant stage manager shouted.

"You go sit down," Dylan said to his friends. "I'll join you in a minute."

Jeff looked relieved to be dismissed, hastily ushering his family down the hall. Without saying a word, Dylan stepped into Everley's dressing room and closed the door behind him.

She couldn't quite get her breath. It was like there was a barrier between her throat and her lungs. "Was Jeff telling the truth?" she asked, her voice low.

Dylan looked at her warily. "Yes. We're divorced.

"But I thought it would take months. That's what you told me."

"I know. But it turns out that since we had no children or joint property they pushed it through in thirty days."

"So we're not married?" She shook her head, trying to let the details sink in.

There was a tic in his jaw. "No. We're definitely divorced."

"And you've known this for how long?"

"Two days."

"Did you know before you took me to the cabin?"

He swallowed. "Yeah, I knew."

"So you lied to me?" She wasn't going to cry. She wasn't. Even if her eyes were stinging like crazy.

"I didn't lie. I was going to tell you. Just not then."

"That's lying, Dylan. You called me your wife when I'm not. You didn't give me all the details when you asked me to make a choice." Her throat felt so tight it was getting difficult to breathe. "You had information that I didn't have. I'd call that lying."

He gave a short, angry laugh. "So what, if you knew we were divorced you would have said no? Sent me back to Africa with my tail between my legs?"

"I didn't say that." Her teeth were gritted. "I'm just saying that I don't appreciate being lied to."

"Five minutes until beginners."

"Shit. I have to get ready." She shucked off her slippers and slid her feet into her high heels, leaning down to fasten the straps. When she glanced up at him, she could see his eyes were dark, focused on the top of her stockings, exposed where she was bending over.

"Don't you dare look at me right now," she hissed. "Keep your eyes averted."

"Evie..."

"Don't fucking Evie me, either." Maybe it was a good thing that the hurt had gone, now replaced by a white cold anger that made her skin buzz. "How dare you lie to me. I'm so pissed off with you. You slept with me knowing that we're divorced."

"Seriously? That's why you're pissed with me? Because I made you come three times and we didn't have a fucking paper contract? Are you going to tell me you don't sleep with guys unless you're married to them? Because I've heard the fucking opposite."

"What the hell does that mean?" Her mouth dropped open. "Are you calling me a whore?"

Dylan's jaw twitched. "No, I'm calling you a hypocrite. You had sex with me before we were married. And I'm almost certain you had sex with other guys after I left. Unless that was okay because you were married to me."

"Don't you dare." She put her hand up, palm facing him. "Don't you dare remind me that I had sex with other guys when I was married to you. That wasn't my fault. I didn't know."

"I'm just pointing out that your thinking is completely messed up."

"And I'm just pointing out that you're a damn dirty liar," she said, her voice full of anger. "So shut the hell up."

"Everley? The curtain's about to go up," the deputy stage manager called, his voice nervous. He could probably hear their argument through the door. The whole cast almost certainly could. Her face burned at the thought of it.

"I'm coming," she called, trying to keep her voice steady. Then she turned to Dylan and pointed at him with a straight, angry finger. "This discussion isn't over," she told him. "Not by a long shot."

❦ 28 ❦

We're performers, my darling. We smile through the pain to put smiles on other's faces. It's our job. It's what we do.

Everley could remember her grandmother whispering those words to her eight years ago, when she was agonizing over whether to take a role in an Off-Broadway performance soon after she and Dylan split. And her grandma had been right, she had managed to smile even though her heart was aching.

And piece by piece she'd managed to pull herself out of the pit of depression, slowly finding joy in life again. She'd faced forward, not back. Rebuilt herself and made a life that she loved.

But now she could feel the pain stabbing at her heart all over again.

He'd lied to her. Sure, you could say it was a lie by omission or a little white lie, but the fact was he had information that he hadn't shared. And it made her feel sordid. Like she didn't matter.

He was making decisions without consulting her. The

same way he did all those years ago. It made her want to be sick.

And she hated that.

As the first song began, she danced onstage, her smile plastered to her face as the voices of the cast rose to a crescendo. Thank God her body knew the steps by heart, because her brain really wasn't working properly. All she could think about was him and his lies.

When the intermission came, she stayed close to the wings, refusing to go back to her dressing room in case Dylan was there. She couldn't stand to see him right now. She stood next to the closed curtains, her jaw tight, her body tense.

"You okay?" Casey asked, joining her.

She looked up at him. "I'll survive. What are you doing back here? I thought you were sitting with your parents."

"I was, but I noticed you were a little off." He shrugged.

Her face fell. "Tell me nobody else noticed that. Was I really that bad?"

Casey's voice was soft. "It was nothing that most people would see unless they knew the show by heart, but you missed some steps and a couple of words."

"I've got some things on my mind."

"Yeah, I guessed that. And also, the gossip mill is churning backstage. People are saying you and Dylan had a fight."

"We did." Her breath stuttered. "We're divorced and he's been hiding it from me."

"What?" Casey frowned. "I thought you two were tight. He asked you for another chance, didn't he?"

"Yeah. All the while knowing we were divorced." Her eyes met her friend's. "He didn't tell me, Casey. He asked me to make a life decision without giving me all the facts."

"Would you have made a different decision if you'd known the truth?"

"That doesn't matter. What matters is that he lied to me. That he didn't trust me with the facts. And I'm so angry with him."

"I can see that." Casey gave her a half smile. "But as long as the audience can't, you're good. Now go back to your dressing room, drink some water, and retouch your makeup. You need to change your costume, too."

"What if he's there?"

"He isn't. I just walked past. Only Anna and Marta are in there. Talking about a guy in shorts." He screwed his face up. "Come on, let's go."

Casey was right, Dylan wasn't there. She did the quickest of changes, taking a long drink of water before touching up her makeup and preparing herself for the second half of the show. And though she smiled and sang and danced her heart out, she still knew it wasn't enough.

She should have performed better, she knew that. Even if it was mostly friends and family in the audience they deserved more from her. They'd come to be entertained and she couldn't help but feel that she'd short changed them.

She wasn't even going to think what Robert Danvers and Rea Carside had to think about her performance. One thing was for sure, if Casey had noticed there was something missing, then they would, too.

And it was Dylan's fault, damn him.

By the time they took their final bows, her cheeks were aching from smiling. And her chest was aching for a whole different reason. She didn't hang around to talk to the cast like she usually did. Instead, she'd thank them tomorrow when her words didn't come through gritted teeth.

When she yanked open her dressing room door, Anna and Marta were already there, pulling their dresses over their head. And Dylan was leaning against the wall, his face like thunder.

"There are people changing in here," Everley said to him, her voice dull. "Can you wait outside?"

"He's okay. He never looks anyway," Marta said. "Not like some of the letches."

"It's not okay. Please leave." Everley glared at Dylan.

"We need to talk." His voice was low.

"Not here." She glanced at Anna and Marta again. They'd stopped changing and were looking at her and Dylan with interest.

"Then when? You have that meeting with Miller and the journalists. And I need to explain why I did what I did."

She lifted her hands up. "You know what?" she growled, exasperated. "If you want to do it in front of an audience, then have at it. I'm sure Anna and Marta are as interested as I am to hear why you didn't tell me about our divorce."

Marta gaped. "You two are divorced?"

"Yep." Everley didn't take her eyes from Dylan. "So go on, tell us. We're desperate to hear."

Dylan glanced at Anna and Marta. "Could you two give us a minute?"

"Sure," Anna said.

"No you don't," Everley said through gritted teeth. "He wants an audience, he said so."

"I didn't say that," Dylan shook his head. "I just want to talk, dammit."

"We should probably go," Anna said.

Marta frowned. "But it's getting interesting."

"Ladies, if you can give us some space, I'd be really grateful." Dylan flashed them a smile and it sent an angry bolt down Everley's spine.

"It's fine. We can get changed in the other room." Anna quickly gathered her clothes, Marta following suit. When they left the dressing room, Marta gave them a final, baleful glance.

As soon as the door closed behind them, Dylan turned to her, his jaw tight. "Look, I know you're angry at me."

"Angry doesn't even cut it. Furious. Apoplectic. Unfuckingbelievably irate." She shook her head. "No, even those don't come close. Did you see me on stage? Did you see how much the rest of the cast had to carry me? Did you see me miss my damn cues and join in the singing a beat after everybody else?"

"I thought you were great."

Her face flamed. "Don't you dare say that. Do you know what you've done? I made an idiot out of myself in front of the people I wanted to impress. And it's your fault that I did. Any other night and it would have been great." Her eyes were stinging, but she wouldn't let herself cry.

Wouldn't let him see her tears. Not when he was the one who caused them.

"If you've cost me this theater, I'll never forgive you," she whispered harshly.

"So that's it? No waiting to hear my explanation? Just a whole heap of fucking blame for you missing a few chords of a song?"

"They weren't a few chords. They were the notes at the beginning of songs." Her eyes were stinging as she held in her tears. "But go ahead. Astound me. Tell me the simple explanation you have for lying to my face. I'm all damn ears."

Dylan took a deep breath, his jaw twitching. He looked as angry as she felt and she had no idea why. He was the liar. She was the victim who looked like a fool right now.

"I found out about our divorce the day I met you in the square. I'd already made up my mind about asking for a second chance, and I didn't see why I needed to tell you about it being finalized. I wanted you to make a decision without the pressure of that."

"Bullshit. If you wanted me to make a decision free of any

pressure then you'd have told me." She shook her head. "You were afraid, weren't you?"

"Of course I wasn't."

"So why did you lie?"

Dylan dragged his fingers through his messed up hair. "I didn't fucking lie. I just didn't tell you."

She threw her hands up. "It's the same thing. Lying by default. And don't tell me you forgot. You lied for a reason. I deserve to know what it is."

He opened his mouth then closed it again. "You know what, you're right. Maybe I knew if I told you then you'd go crazy like this. Maybe I just wanted a nice, easy night without the goddamned theatrics. I told you that I love you that night. I told you I want to be with you. Don't those mean anything?"

"You lied about one thing. How do I know you weren't lying about that?"

He gave a humorless laugh. "Are you serious right now?"

"Damn right I am." She took a step back, needing the space from him. "Do you want to know why I think you lied?"

The corner of his lip pulled up. "Oh, I'm certain you'll tell me."

She folded her arms across her chest, all too aware how ludicrous she must look in her red sparkly Santa dress, cut high at the thigh and pushing her breasts together. At least her face matched it right now. "I think you don't trust me. Don't trust that I love you. You did the same thing when we were younger. Pushed me away because you were scared I might leave you. Made the choice on behalf of us both. And now you're doing it again."

His mouth dropped open. "If you didn't notice, I'm the one who asked if we could give this another shot."

"And you didn't trust me to say yes if I knew we were divorced."

"Would you?"

She let out a huff. "What does that matter? You didn't give me a chance. You made decisions for me." A sudden memory of that night in the carriage flitted into her mind. "Why did you call yourself my husband when you knew you weren't?"

"When?" He frowned.

"The night in the carriage. You said you're a husband taking care of his wife."

"Because I *am* your husband, Everley. That piece of paper doesn't matter. I'm yours. I've always been yours. And you're mine."

She gritted her teeth. "I'm nobody's. I'm my own person and I make my own decisions. When people do me the favor of asking my opinion."

"We're going around in circles here. I messed up. I get it. I should have told you. But it changes nothing, Evie. I love you. I want you." His jaw tightened. "Well I do most of the time."

"What's that supposed to mean?"

"It means you're angry."

"So I'm not allowed to have emotions now? Should I be the ice king like you?" Her teeth clenched. She felt so betrayed. Like she was sweet little Everley who wasn't allowed an opinion or a brain. She'd felt the same way when he'd assumed she'd travel wherever he went when they'd got married. As though what she wanted didn't count. He'd make the decisions and she'd follow behind demurely.

But that wasn't who she was. She couldn't be. She was a grown woman with the right to make her own choices about life. And if he couldn't see that, then where did that leave them?

"I'm not an ice king. I just have control," Dylan said, his voice low.

"That's not control, that's avoidance." She shook her head. "You know what? We really are going around in circles. You have no idea what you did wrong, do you?"

"I should have told you."

"Yes, but you don't know *why* you should have told me."

He lifted an eyebrow. "It would have avoided all this."

She lifted her palm to her brow. She could feel the sheen of perspiration mixing with the heavy make-up they used. "I need to get changed. I have an interview to go to."

"Oh of course. That's much more important than us."

Her gaze whipped to him. "Don't you dare accuse me of choosing my career over you."

"You did it once. How do I know you're not doing it again?"

He was using her own words against her, and it hurt. Like a knife jabbing at her heart. And those stupid tears that she'd been pushing down started to fill her eyes, spilling over and staining her cheeks.

She lifted her hand to wipe them, knowing she was probably smearing her make up all over her skin. Dylan's eyes were dark, darting to her face and then away. "Stop with the fucking waterworks," he said, stepping back.

"You think I want to cry over you?" she asked him, wiping them again. "Because I don't. You don't deserve my tears."

"I know that." He raked his fingers through his hair, stepping back again, as though he couldn't stand the proximity between them. His eyes shifted to the door. "I have to go."

Her brows knitted. "Now?"

"Yeah." He nodded, his jaw twitching. "I need to go right now. And you need to get ready for this meeting with the journalists."

"But you wanted to talk. Here I am, *talking*." She was so confused. It was like somebody had flipped a switch. Did he really hate her crying this much? She tried to swallow down the tears, but they continued to fall. "What's wrong?" she asked, reaching out to touch his arm.

"Don't touch me," he rasped, flinching. "Please don't touch me." He circled around her as though she was radiating something poisonous, and reached for the door. Her heart was hammering against her chest because this was so damn crazy.

She wasn't going to beg. Not when he was the one who'd lied to her. If he wanted to run away and ignore her emotions then he could do exactly that. "Okay, go," she said, as he turned the handle. "Run away like you always do. I'm glad we're divorced. You're a liar, and you don't deserve to be my husband."

He yanked the door open, and her already aching heart fell to her feet. Because standing there, with shocked expressions on their faces, were Miller and the two journalists.

It was obvious from Miller's face that he'd heard enough. A pulse drummed in Dylan's neck as their eyes met, before Miller's gaze passed over Dylan's shoulder, and he knew they'd landed on Everley.

"Are you okay?" Miller asked her. Something about the way he said it sent a hot rush of blood through Dylan's veins.

"Of course she's not okay," he said, his voice raspy. "I made her cry."

"I can see that," Miller said dryly. "Do you want me to make him leave?"

"No. He was going anyway." Everley sounded small, like a child. "I'm sorry, we didn't know you were there."

"You don't need to apologize to him," Dylan was so pissed he could barely think. And he had a goddamned hard on. Yes, it was disguised by his jeans and jacket, but it was there, for fuck's sake, and it needed to go.

He needed to put some space between him and Everley. Figure out how the heck he was going to explain this to her. But then Miller pushed past him, his shoulder slamming into Dylan's, and he saw red.

"What the hell?" He twisted, grabbing Miller's jacket in his fist.

"You heard the lady, you're leaving," Miller said, his voice low.

"I'm not going anywhere. And she's not a lady, she's my wife." Slowly, his fingers released the fabric.

"Not from what I heard." Miller arched an eyebrow. "You're divorced. And I have no idea of the details, but you're upsetting my friend and you need to leave. Perhaps you'd do better spending your time explaining to my parents why you've been lying to them."

Everley gasped, and when he turned to look at her, she had her palm over her pretty lips. "It's not what you think," she said to Miller.

"He's right. I lied. Isn't that what you said?" Dylan asked her, his voice full of anger. "That I'm a liar?"

When she removed her hand, her lips were wobbling. "Dylan, please..."

"Just go, before you make it worse." Miller put his hand on Dylan's chest, and another dark mist of fury fell over him. He slapped Miller's hands away, then grabbed the collar of his jacket again, pulling him close enough for him to smell the mint on Miller's breath.

"Don't. Touch. Me." Dylan's voice was thick. "Don't ever fucking touch me."

"Dylan!" Everley sounded frantic. "Let him go."

From the corner of his eye he could see the two journalists watching them avidly. One of them was typing something on their phone. Goddamn it, he was making everything so much worse for Everley. Yet he couldn't stop himself from pushing Miller away with the palm of his hand, making the taller, thinner, man stumble backward.

A sob came from the dressing room. Those sweet, salty tears were running down her cheeks again, and all he could think was that he wanted to lick them. To suck them up like the asshole he was, then kiss her until the sobs turned to gasps as she trembled beneath him.

"Please go," she whispered. "Please, Dylan."

"I'm going," he muttered, because he couldn't look at her when she was like that. Not knowing the dark thoughts in his mind. Without saying a word to Miller, he passed him and the journalists, ignoring the greetings that the cast shouted out to him as he made his way through the backstage hallway to the stage door.

He'd fucked up. And he had no idea how to make things better.

Maybe he couldn't. Wasn't that the worst thought of all?

Miller closed the door softly behind the four of them, and walked over to Everley. "I think we should postpone this interview," he said, his voice low. "You're in no state to talk to Ria and Robert."

She blinked, mortification washing over her. "Oh no, they've come all this way."

Robert shifted his gaze, looking distinctly uncomfortable. "We got to see the show. And maybe we can do a video interview after Christmas."

Ria nodded. "That's a great idea. I know I'd like to get home sooner rather than later. These roads are dark at night."

"Thank you." Miller nodded at them. "I appreciate it." He shook their hands and led them to the door, saying something to them that Everley couldn't hear. Her hands were still shaking, her heart still hammering against her chest.

It was almost impossible to think properly.

Once the journalists had gone, Miller closed the door

again and turned to face her. He looked confused. "So, what the heck is going on?"

"Nothing. Dylan and I had an argument, that's all."

"About not being married?"

Her breath quickened. "I was hoping you hadn't heard it."

"I'm pretty sure the whole theater heard it. You two weren't exactly whispering in here." Miller raised an eyebrow. "So what gives?"

"I can't tell you."

"Why not?"

"Because I feel like I'm betraying Dylan." She knew he wasn't Miller's biggest fan. And as angry as she was with him, sharing this would be a step too far.

Miller leaned against the door, his eyes on hers. "Don't you think you owe me an explanation? I've just sent away two of the top journalists in the entertainment industry. I brought them here as a favor to you. I'm going to have to suck up to them to get them to reschedule the interview, and I'd really like to know why I have to do that."

"You know as much as I do. Dylan and I are divorced."

"How long have you been divorced?"

"A few days."

Miller blinked. "So you'd already filed the paperwork when you came to my parents' house for Thanksgiving?"

She nodded.

"But they thought you were happily married. Dylan told them you were."

"I know." Her voice was small. "I'm sorry."

"So he lied to them, too?"

She inhaled raggedly. "It was my idea. My fault. He made a mistake, when he completed the application details, that's all. It was me who suggested we pretended to be happily married. Maybe I enjoyed it a little too much, I don't know." She pressed her palm to her brow. "But please don't put the blame on him."

Miller shook his head. "I'm going to have to tell my parents. They need to know the truth."

Her stomach churned. "Will they take the donation away?"

Miller shrugged. "I don't know. Maybe."

"But this isn't Dylan's fault. I told you, it's mine. He shouldn't be punished." The thought of the donation he'd worked so hard for being taken from him made her want to be sick. It really had been her who started this lie. Who'd enjoyed playing husband and wife way too much.

She'd thrown herself into it the same way she threw herself into a new role. Except by the end she wasn't acting. She was in love with Dylan Shaw.

And now everything was ruined.

"Look," Miller said, his voice kind. "You need to stop worrying about Dylan and start worrying about yourself. Get the make-up off your face, get changed, then go home and get some sleep. You have another show to do tomorrow."

She thought about going home when Miller left, but the image of her bouncing around those four walls with all these recriminations running through her head was too much to bear. Instead she climbed into her car and switched the ignition on, turning the heating to high as she drove the couple of miles to Holly and Josh's place.

The lights were still on as she pulled into their driveway. It was just after eleven, and she started to wonder if she should have called first.

But Holly was family. And she always knew the right way to look at things. So Everley grabbed her purse and walked up the steps to their inviting front door, a festive wreath hung at eye level, which she rapped on three times.

"Everley," Holly said, when she'd opened the door to see her cousin standing there. "Are you okay?"

"Not really. Am I interrupting? I needed somebody to talk to."

"Of course you're not interrupting. Come in." Holly ushered her inside. "The fire's on. You can warm up there."

"Who is it?" Josh walked out of the living room. His face softened when he saw her standing there. "Everley? Is everything okay?"

Holly shook her head. "No, apparently not. Can you get us a couple of hot chocolates? Maybe add a shot of whiskey for hers?"

Josh winked. "Your wish is my command."

She led Everley to the living room, gesturing to one of the chairs beside the roaring fire. The room was beautifully decorated for the holidays with a pale blue and white theme that stretched from the garland on the fireplace to the shining ornaments on the tree.

Josh brought in three steaming mugs of chocolate – two of them topped with whipped cream and sprinkles, Holly smiled warmly at him.

"So I'm assuming this is about Dylan," Holly said, sipping at her mug, as they sat on the sofas beside the fire.

Everley nodded.

"There are rumors already racing through town. Alaska called me because she went to your house and your car wasn't there. She'd heard that you and Dylan are divorced." Holly grimaced. "Apparently, everybody's talking about it."

Everley squeezed her eyes shut. Of *course* everybody was gossiping. "We've been divorced for a few days. He hadn't told me."

"What?" Holly's brows lifted. "Why not?"

Holly listened intently as Everley filled her in on the sorry tale, her face crinkling with compassion as Everley's eyes filled with tears again. "I know this is mostly my fault. But he should have told me. We can't start a life together if he's basing it on lies."

"He should have told you the truth." Holly nodded. "I bet he's kicking himself now."

"I can understand why he didn't," Josh said. Everley startled at his voice. She'd almost forgotten he was there he'd been so quiet on the sofa.

"Why?" Holly frowned at him.

"Remember when you lied to me? Because you didn't want me to know you and your cousins had stopped my plans for the town?" he said, referring to the previous year when his business had bought Winterville, planning to raze it to the ground, and Holly, Everley, and their cousins had fought him for it. Somewhere in all the madness, Holly and Josh had fallen for each other, but the lie she'd told him had almost broken them apart.

"I didn't tell you because I couldn't," Holly protested.

"There was no law stopping you. And at the time it felt to me like you were siding with your family." A smile tugged at his lips. "Hey, don't look like that. I understand now. But it took a frozen night in a snowstorm for me to come to terms."

Holly sighed. "You're right. I lied to you. And I'm lucky you forgave me."

Josh caught Everley's eye. "Do you know why Dylan lied to you?"

"He didn't want to tell me because he was afraid." Everley looked down at the steam wafting up from her hot chocolate. "He doesn't trust that I love him."

"That sounds feasible," Josh agreed.

"Maybe that's understandable, too," Holly suggested. "He went through a lot with his mom as a child. Being abandoned like that had to take a toll on him. But if he trusts anybody, it's you. I've seen how he looks at you."

"I have, too." Josh nodded. "The man's in love with you."

"But we can't do this again if we're not going to be truthful," Everley told them. "We've hurt each other enough already. I want to be his partner, not somebody he hides things from because he thinks he knows best. I can't have a relationship with somebody who doesn't tell me the truth. I just can't."

Josh snorted. "I'm pretty sure he doesn't think he knows best."

Her phone started to buzz. It wasn't a surprise when she saw his name on the screen. She'd been ignoring it since she'd left the theater, not ready to talk to anybody, and especially not Dylan.

"Is that him?" Holly asked.

Everley nodded. "I can't talk to him right now."

"Let me talk to him," Josh suggested, holding his hand out for her phone. "He probably just wants to know that you're okay."

Everley passed it to him and he accepted the call. "Dylan, it's Josh." He paused, listening to Dylan through the line. "Yeah, she's here and she's safe." Another pause. "I don't think that's a good idea right now. It sounds like you both need a little break. Why don't you call her in the morning?" He looked at Everley.

She sighed heavily. She needed to talk to him, she knew that. But not now. He was right, she was dramatic. She'd shouted when whispering would do. She jumped to conclusions when sometimes she needed to listen.

"Okay, take care. And try to get some sleep." Josh hung up and passed Everley her phone back, giving her a soft smile. "You should probably call Alaska. She'll be worrying."

"You're right. I will."

"Do you want to stay here tonight?" Holly asked her. "The spare bed is made up, and you're in no shape to drive."

"There's a good shot of whiskey in that drink," Josh agreed.

Everley nodded. "That would be good. Thank you." She rubbed her eyes with the palms of her hands. "Ugh, what a night. I can't believe I made such an idiot of myself in front of those journalists."

"There were journalists there?" Holly asked, aghast.

"And Miller Carson." Everley squeezed her eyes shut. "Oh God, I didn't tell you that he's going to tell his parents. And there's a chance Dylan could lose their donation."

"Seriously?" Josh frowned. "Isn't that a little much?"

"We lied to them." Everley swallowed hard. "And their reputation is important. Miller wasn't sure if they'd withdraw or not, but there's a strong possibility." She squeezed her eyes shut. "What if they do? It's all my fault. If I hadn't screeched at Dylan so the whole theater heard they never would have found out."

"It's not your fault," Holly said gently. "It's just bad timing. You and Dylan wanted to stay married, didn't you?"

"We did in the end." Everley sighed.

"And you thought the divorce wouldn't come through until next year. It must have taken Dylan by surprise to hear that it had happened so soon. I guess because you have no children or joint assets they were able to fast track it." Holly knew a lot about divorce. Once upon a time it had been her job to work with divorce lawyers in financial discovery.

"I'm sure it won't come to Dylan losing their donation," Josh said. "And there's nothing you can do about it anyway. One way or another they'll make their decision."

That didn't make her feel any better about it. Worse, really. Everything was so out of control and she hated it. She'd never forgive herself if he really did lose the donation.

She wasn't sure he'd forgive himself, either.

How did it end in such a mess? She hated this feeling of helplessness. As she put her mug back onto the coffee table, a yawn overtook her, making her jaw ache as it stretched her mouth and throat.

Holly smiled. "Why don't you get some sleep, honey?" she suggested. "Everything will look better in the morning. I'll grab you some spare pajamas. Everything else you need is in the guest bathroom. There's a spare toothbrush in there, too."

Everley nodded. She really did feel exhausted. "Thank you," she said, looking at Holly then at Josh. "You guys are amazing, you know that?" She'd go to bed, call Alaska, and hopefully get some much needed sleep.

And tomorrow she'd decide what the heck to do next.

$\maltese$ 30 $\maltese$

Charlie did a double take when he walked into his small kitchen and saw Dylan sitting at the table, nursing a lukewarm mug of coffee.

"Hey," he said, glancing at his watch.

"Hi." Dylan caught his eye.

"Ouch. You look tired. Did you sleep here last night?"

"I laid in bed." Dylan shrugged. He hadn't gotten a whole lot of sleep. The shadows beneath his eyes were a testament to that.

"Why weren't you with Everley?" his dad asked, pouring his own coffee from the half-filled carafe that had been warming on the plate.

"You didn't hear? I was pretty sure the grapevine made it this far in Winterville."

His dad turned around mid-pour, then hissed as a splash of coffee hit his fingers. "Hear what? I went to bed early. And you know I'm not one for gossip."

Dylan lifted a brow at his dad's blatant lie. Along with Dolores and Frank, Charlie was practically the center of the Winterville grapevine. "Everley found out we're divorced."

His dad blinked. "Sorry, what? I thought you two were going to make a go of things?"

"We were. But our divorce came through in the meantime and I lied about it. And now she's not sure what she wants."

"You let her go?" His dad's voice rose an octave. "*Again?*"

"I haven't let her go. I'm waiting for her to wake up and then I'm going to beg her for forgiveness." He filled his dad in on the whole sordid incident. The way he'd responded to her pain, and the angry confrontation with Miller Carson.

Charlie's eyes widened. "You should throw yourself at her feet."

"Okay." Dylan took a sip of coffee.

"And buy her flowers."

"Sure."

"And cut your fingers off and give them to her as an offering."

"What?" Dylan's brow creased.

"I'm just checking that you're listening. I can't believe you've messed this up again. Jesus, Dylan, I practically remarried you two, and now you're divorced? How did you let this happen?"

Dylan blew out a mouthful of air. He'd been asking himself the same thing. How could he have lied to her? The truth was, when he'd finally gotten ahold of Jeff and he'd said that the courts had signed off on the divorce he'd felt his stomach drop. And yeah, maybe there was part of him that was afraid she'd push him away if she knew she was free.

The thought of losing her again made him want to punch something.

"It was supposed to take longer," he mumbled, shaking his head.

His dad checked his watch. "What time are you calling her?"

"At eight. I'm going to see her." He'd beg if he had to. Do whatever it took.

"You can't mess this up again, Dylan. There's only so many chances we get to make things right. You've had more than your share."

"I know that." He raked his fingers through his hair. "I don't deserve her."

"That's not true." His dad's voice was low. "Of course you deserve her. You're a good man. You just don't always think things through. I blame myself for that. Me and your mom, we weren't exactly the best role models when it came to a healthy relationship."

Dylan caught his dad's eye. It wasn't often they talked about his mom. "You were a great role model," he said, his voice soft.

Charlie's lips twitched. "Thank you. But that's not going to help you if you mess this up. I'll be the grouch from hell." He glanced at his watch again. "Why don't we take a walk. We can go into Dolores' café and you can buy Everley her favorite coffee before you see her. It ain't flowers, but they can come later."

"Sure." It beat sitting around here. Dylan stood and grabbed his keys and wallet, following his father into the hallway.

It was time to win back the woman he loved. And this time, he definitely wasn't going to make her cry.

It was right before eight when Dylan knocked on Holly and Josh's door. The air was cool, but there was no snow today. There was some forecasted for tomorrow, but that was fine. It would be Christmas and they had no place to go.

"Merry Christmas Eve," Holly said, as she opened the

door with a smile. It widened when she saw Dylan standing there holding a tray with four coffees.

"I got your order from Dolores. The one at the front on the left is yours."

"If Everley doesn't forgive you, I'll definitely reconsider my marriage to Josh," she teased, letting him walk into the hallway. "Speaking of Everley, she must still be sound asleep. I haven't heard anything from her all morning. Why don't you go into the living room, I'll go wake her up."

Josh walked into the hallway, giving Dylan a welcoming smile.

"I got you a coffee, too," Dylan told him.

"I always accept bribery." Josh took the proffered cup as Holly walked down the hallway to the guest suite. "Come sit down. You look like crap."

"Thanks." Dylan raised a brow.

"That was supposed to sound nicer than it did." Josh gave him an apologetic smile, gesturing at the sofa for him to take a seat. "I'm guessing you didn't sleep much last night."

"How did you know?"

Josh lifted a brow, sitting in the chair next to the fireplace. "I'm married to a Winter girl. I know what they're like. They kind of consume you, don't they?"

Dylan exhaled softly. "Yeah, they do."

"She loves you. I could tell that much from talking to her last night." Josh took a sip of his coffee. "But you lied and it hurt her."

"I know. I'm a damn idiot." His eyes met Josh's. "But I'm not going to hurt her again."

"Of course you are."

Dylan frowned. "What?"

Josh ran his finger around the rim of his coffee cup. "Here's the thing. If you spend your life with somebody, you're probably going to hurt them. Not intentionally, and hopefully not too much, but relationships aren't just sweetness and light. They're discussions and compromise, they're getting sick but being there for each other. They're exhaustion and snapping then asking for forgiveness. It's not possible to avoid hurting the person you love. Not all the time. It's what we do after that's important. And you're here, ready to take your beating like a man."

"You think she's gonna beat me?"

"Metaphorically, yes." Josh grinned. "Another thing I've learned from marrying a Winter. They're almost always right."

"I'll try to remember that." Dylan thought about Josh's words. Was he right? Was it inevitable that you hurt the person you love?

He'd tried to avoid it, and ended up hurting her more. And then he'd gotten excited by her tears and hated himself.

Dammit, he needed to talk to her.

"Um, there's a slight problem," Holly said, walking into the living room. "Everley isn't here."

"What? Where is she?" Dylan's stomach lurched. "Did she go home?"

"You drove past her cottage. Was her car there?" Holly asked.

"No. I would have stopped if it was."

Josh's brow wrinkled with concern. "She has to be somewhere. Maybe she's gone to see Alaska."

"Yeah." Holly nodded. "Or to the theater. She says it's a good place to think."

"Or she could be at your place," Josh said to Dylan. "I wouldn't put it past her to come straight to you to talk."

"Well, there's one way to find out." Holly grabbed her phone and swiped her finger across it, pulling up her contacts and pressing on the screen. She lifted it to her ear, then her brow crumpled as she said, "Hey honey, it's me. Call me back when you can." She swiped her finger to end the call. "It rang to voicemail. Maybe she has it turned off."

Of course she did. She was probably still trying to avoid him. Not that he could blame her. "I'll drive around, she has to be somewhere," he said, trying to ignore the tug in his stomach telling him that something was wrong.

"I'll come with you." Holly met his gaze, and he could tell by the way she was staring at him that she was worried, despite her light tone. "Two people looking for her is better than one, right?"

Josh sighed. "Better make that three."

"She's not here," Casey said, shaking his head as he stared at the four of them. Alaska had joined them on their search after a quick phone call had confirmed that Everley wasn't with her. They'd looked everywhere, and Dylan was starting to panic. "I had to unlock the door myself." Casey tapped his jaw with his thumb. "Have you tried calling her again?"

"Yeah, but she's not picking up." Dylan had tried every few minutes, each sound of the automated voicemail making him feel a little more anxious. "Nobody has seen her at all. Not Dolores, not my dad. And her car is missing."

"I just talked to North," Holly said, her voice low. "He hasn't seen her either. He and Gabe wanted to drop everything and come search but I told them to hold their horses. They're working in the shop right now."

"Hey, I have an idea." A slow smile pulled at Casey's lips. "I have her on my *Find My Friends* app."

"You track her?" Dylan lifted a brow.

"I started doing it when she insisted on walking home from the theater each night after rehearsals." Casey shrugged. "Of course that didn't last long because you decided to be her escort, but I don't think I ever turned it off." He grabbed his phone from his pocket, unlocking it, then found the right app. "Here we go, let's see where she is..." he murmured, as he tapped on the screen. The four of them crowded around him as a map appeared, and a little dot that looked to be moving along a road.

"That's the highway," Dylan said, frowning. "What the hell is she doing on the highway?" He looked at Holly. "Did she say she was going anywhere?"

"No." She shook her head. "She didn't say anything at all."

"She can't be going far," Casey said. "We have a show later. She'll need to be back before then."

Josh looked at Dylan. "Can you think of where she's going?"

"No." Was she running away from him? Had she had enough? Last time they'd split she'd gone to New York. He had a snowflake's chance in hell of finding her there.

But he *would* do anything to find her. He wasn't going to lose her again. He wasn't. Not this time.

The door opened, and Marta walked in. She blinked when she saw the five of them standing in a circle. "Oh hey," she said, a confused smile pulling at her lips. "Everley asked me to take her role today." Every major role was understudied by one of the dancers. "I thought I'd come in early to make sure the costume was okay."

Dylan's chest felt like a python was squeezing it. So she wasn't coming back. Another wave of panic washed through him.

Casey turned to look at her. "You talked to Everley?"

Marta shook her head. "No. She left a message. It was real early too. Does that woman ever sleep?"

"So she's not planning on being here for the show," Casey murmured.

"I don't know. And if she doesn't answer her phone, we can't find out." Holly sounded frustrated.

"Is there a problem?" Marta asked.

Casey shot Dylan a look. They both knew Everley wouldn't want her business being broadcast all over the theater. Not after last night's argument.

"There's no problem," Casey said smoothly. "Why don't we go check that costume out. If any adjustments are needed I'll call somebody in." He handed Dylan his phone. The dot with Everley's name above it was still moving along the highway, further from him.

"That would be great," Marta said brightly, Everley clearly forgotten. A lead role in a show did that to a person.

When they'd gone, Holly looked at Dylan, a frown on her face. "What do we do now?"

"I'm going to drive the highway. Try to find her."

"She's got a couple of hours on you. She'll be long gone," Josh said.

"Yeah, but if he takes Casey's phone he can at least follow her progress," Holly pointed out. "There's not much else we can do, is there?" She looked at Josh. "Do you know that road?"

"I know it. It's the same one we took when we went to the Carson's last month."

Holly's mouth dropped open. "Oh."

His eyes met hers. "What? Do you know something?"

"She was really worried last night. She said something about Miller telling his parents that you weren't married. She got all worked up that you might lose their donation."

Of course she did. That was so Everley, trying to take care of everybody. The tight band around his chest loosened. Maybe she wasn't running to New York.

"So you think she's driving to the Carsons' place?" Alaska asked. "On Christmas Eve?"

Dylan and Holly looked at each other. "Yeah," they both said at once.

"We need to find her," Alaska said. "Which of us has the fastest car?"

"I'll do it. Alone," Dylan said firmly.

Alaska frowned. "But you'll bring her home, right? It's Christmas tomorrow. She has to be here. Not driving halfway across the state."

"Yes, I promise. One way or another, I'll bring her home." And though he hoped to God she would be with him, he couldn't guarantee it. Just because she was trying to save his ass – *again* – it didn't mean anything more than that. Sure, she cared for him, but did she forgive him?

Did he deserve her forgiveness?

He wasn't sure. All he knew was that he wanted it. He wanted her. More than he'd wanted anything in his life.

"It makes sense for some of us to stay here," Holly murmured. "In case she comes back for any reason." She touched Alaska's shoulder. "And you're due to work at twelve. It's Christmas Eve, we need all hands on deck."

Alaska let out a heavy sigh. "You're right," she said, nodding. Then she looked at Dylan, her eyes shining. "Just bring her home, okay?"

"I will, I promise. I'm not coming back without her."

31

Driving all the way to the Carsons' house had seemed like a good idea at five o'clock that morning. But as Everley pulled into their driveway, she was second guessing herself. It was Christmas Eve, and she knew they loved to entertain. Maybe she should have called. Or at least contacted Miller to make sure his parents were home.

She took a deep breath. These were all things she should have thought about hours ago, before leaving Winterville. But the need to do something had come over her. She couldn't just lay in bed feeling anxious about everything anymore. She preferred action to thoughts.

And she wasn't going to let Dylan lose his donation because of her screaming at him in the theater. No way.

Parking the car, she yanked open the door and made her way to the steps leading to the porch. Since Thanksgiving, Grace and Warren had added to the Christmas decorations, and a bright green holly wreath was fixed to the shiny black front door. On each side was a life-sized nutcracker, both in a red coat and golden crown, their black moustaches pointing up to the sky. They were taller than her, and she lifted her brows at one as she knocked at the door.

"Wish me luck," she muttered, her breath turning to vapor in the cold air.

The nutcracker didn't say a word. Just stared up at the sky, unmoved.

The butler opened the door, showing no hint of surprise when he saw her standing there. "May I help you?"

"I'd like to see Mr. and Mrs. Carson," she told him.

"I'm afraid they're not here. They're spending Christmas Eve with friends. Can I take a message?"

Her stomach flipped. "Which friends? Do you know where they are?" she asked. "I need to speak to them today. It's urgent."

"That's impossible, I'm afraid. They won't be taking calls until after the holidays."

Over his shoulder she saw a blur of movement. Wait, was that...

"Miller!" she shouted, over the butler's unmoving shoulder. She rolled onto her tiptoes, waving her hand madly. "Miller, it's me!"

The butler frowned. 'Miss..."

"It's missus," she said firmly. "Mrs. Shaw."

"Mrs. Shaw." The butler inhaled sharply. "The family isn't taking calls until after the holidays."

She could see Miller turn to look at her, surprise etching his face. "Everley?" he asked, walking down the hallway toward them. "What the hell are you doing here?"

"I need to see your parents."

He frowned. "They're not here."

"I know." She smiled at him, so happy to see a friendly face. "Your butler told me. I was just asking where they are. I really need to talk to them right now."

"They're at their friend's house in Freiburg. They stayed

over last night. It's about an hour from here." He lifted a brow. "Did you drive from Winterville this morning?"

"Yeah." She nodded.

"Well, you probably passed them. It's on your way back from here. You want me to give you the address?"

"Would you?"

The butler frowned.

"Sure. What's this about anyway?" Miller gestured for the butler to let her in. "Does it have something to do with last night?"

"I wanted to explain about the divorce face to face. I don't want them to take the donation away from Dylan."

Miller ran his thumb along his jaw. "I haven't told them about the divorce yet. I haven't had a chance."

She felt a wave of relief wash over her. "Even better. I can explain it to them, that it wasn't Dylan's fault."

"Of course it was Dylan's fault." Miller shook his head. "Why are you doing this? After what happened between you two last night I thought you'd never want to talk to him again. He almost ruined your career."

"I think I did that all by myself." She grimaced. "I kind of shouted when I could have talked."

"Doesn't change the fact that he lied to you," Miller pointed out. "So why are you trying to help him now?"

Her breath caught in her throat. "Because I love him." It was simple but true. "And if he loses this donation it'll kill him."

"Damn." Miller shook his head. "He doesn't deserve you, you know?"

"I think he does." Her eyes stung, remembering their last argument. Dylan Shaw was the only one who really knew her. Who understood her need to always be moving, who accepted that she jumped first and asked questions later.

And yes, he'd made the biggest mistake in not telling her.

But she'd jumped to conclusions again. She hadn't let him get a word in last night at the theater. She'd just accused him of being a liar and hadn't listened to his explanations.

She'd told him he was afraid, but the truth was, she was afraid, too.

Afraid of being hurt by him. Afraid her heart would break again. She'd been looking for the slightest hint that he wasn't perfect and when she'd found it she'd rejected him.

It was a self-fulfilling prophecy. And the truth was, it could have been anything. He could have been late to pick her up, or chosen to go to a work meeting instead of going to her show and she probably would have blown up.

Because she didn't trust his love for her. The revelation hit her right in the chest. All those things she'd accused Dylan of were exactly the same for her. Yes, she'd told him she wanted a future with him, but there was a part of her that didn't believe it would happen.

That part thought it would fail the same way their relationship always did. And she'd actively sought out the first mistake he'd made.

Her heart hammered against her chest. She needed to talk to him. To tell him about her realization, to tell him she understood why he was scared.

Because she was, too. But she was more scared of losing him than facing the future by his side.

But first she needed to secure this donation. Without it, he might feel like he had no choice but to go back to Africa.

"Can you give me the address for your parents' friends?" she asked Miller, breathless.

"Sure." He grabbed his phone, scrolling through until he found the right contact, then pressed a button. "I've forwarded it onto you."

"Thank you." She leaned forward to kiss his cheek. "For everything. I owe you a lot."

"I know." He lifted a brow.

"I'll call you after the holidays," she said, giving him a quick hug.

"Yeah, you will. We have those interviews to rearrange," he reminded her.

"You still want me to do them?"

"Of course. It'll be good publicity for you."

She grimaced. "After my performance last night?"

Miller shrugged. "Hey, they were both impressed by your fire. Robert called you 'a real character' which from him is high praise. So you'd better call me."

"I will." She grabbed her phone from her pocket to download the contact he'd sent her, ignoring all of the missed calls from Dylan. She'd fix this first, then they'd talk. "Merry Christmas, Miller."

The little dot on the screen had changed direction. Dylan frowned as he looked at the cellphone he'd put into the cupholder, watching the red dot coming toward him instead of staying still the way it had for the last five minutes.

The car was definitely moving toward him now. From what he could tell, they were about two hours apart. He wondered if he should stop and wait for her to come past, but he wasn't sure he had the patience. He'd drive until he found her then turn around and chase her if he had to. He just needed to know she was okay.

Why was she driving back this way? Had her discussion with the Millers been that short? Had they thrown her out before she could even speak?

His chest tightened. He just wanted to be with her. To hold her. To thank her for loving him because god knew he loved her. She was the love of his life, his soul mate.

And if she didn't feel the same? Well, he'd deal with it. Love her from afar. Do whatever it took to make her happy. Because yes, life wasn't all sunshine and smiles but Everley's should be, dammit.

Minutes passed as he drove along the highway, traffic busier than usual thanks to the holiday. He kept his eyes trained on the road ahead, his jaw tight, his fingers steady as he steered the car toward the location where he hoped to find Everley.

It was almost an hour later when he saw the dot on Casey's screen come within a mile of his location. Relief washed over him. He'd probably see her car within the next few minutes.

Every time he passed a car going the other way, his heart did a little skip. But none of them were her Honda. He glanced at Casey's phone again, frowning when he saw that the red dot had left the road. It almost looked like it was driving across fields.

He glanced at his own location, frowning as his dot almost lined up with hers. Pressing his foot on the brake, he coasted onto the shoulder, looking around to figure out where the hell she could have gone.

Then he saw the small paved road winding between the trees. Glancing back to make sure there were no cars in sight, he quickly executed a U-turn and took a left down the track, his heart beating fast as he saw a car in the distance.

Her car.

He pressed his horn but either she didn't hear him, or didn't want to acknowledge him. He hoped to hell it was the former. In the distance a large house loomed – larger than the Carsons. Why the hell was she driving there?

Only one way to find out. He put his foot down, following Everley and the road, until they both came to a stop in front of the imposing mansion.

Without taking a breath he jumped out of the car, running toward her. Not seeing him, Everley climbed out, grabbing her purse and putting it over her shoulders, then took a deep breath as she looked up at the huge house.

"Evie."

She blinked, a tiny 'v' appearing in her brow as she turned to look at him. "Dylan? What are you doing here?"

It was so damn good to see her face. Her perfect, beautiful face. He stalked toward her, his expression serious, as he cupped her cheeks in his cool palms.

"What are *you* doing here?" he murmured.

"The Carsons are here. I need to talk to them."

He couldn't let her go. Couldn't bear not to touch her. Ever since last night it felt like a part of him had been torn away. His body hummed to have her close again.

"You've spent the morning driving all over West Virginia to look for the Carsons?" he asked her. "It's Christmas Eve. You have a show to do."

"I asked Marta to cover." Her breath caught. "I should call to check that everything is okay." She rummaged through her bag, locating her cell.

"It would help if you weren't diverting to voicemail. I've been calling you all morning. And Marta arrived bright and early for her fitting. It's all under control."

"How do you know?"

"I was at the theater looking for you. That's when Casey had the bright idea of tracking your phone. That's how I found you. But I don't understand why you're doing this. The Carsons aren't your problem, they're mine."

Everley pulled her lip between her teeth. "If you lose that donation it'll be all my fault. Miller only knew because I was shouting at you."

Dylan shook his head. "If I lose it, it's my fault, not yours. Everything that happened I agreed to." He dropped his brow until it was touching hers. "You're crazy, you know that? I can't believe you'd do this for me."

Her eyes watered. "I'd do anything for you."

"Everley? Dylan?"

They looked up to see Grace and Warren standing at the top of the sweeping steps leading up to the ornate mansion. The Carsons looked completely confused to see them on the driveway.

"I need to go explain..." Everley said. She stepped away from him, and he immediately missed her closeness. Missed the feel of her in his arms.

"No. I'll explain. It's my problem. My donation. My mess up." He reached out to touch her cheek again, just because it was impossible not to. "Let me do this, then we can talk, okay?"

She nodded, though it pained her not to be the one solving things. "Okay."

Warren and Grace had made it down the steps. They weren't wearing coats, and Grace was already shivering. Warren put his arm around her and gave Dylan an enquiring glance. "I'm guessing this isn't a courtesy visit?"

"No. There's something important I need to tell you about my application for the donation." It was strange how strong Dylan felt. Yes, this donation was hugely important. But losing it felt nothing compared to losing Everley. "I lied when I said I was married."

"Technically, you didn't," Everley whispered. He tried not to roll his eyes. She couldn't keep quiet for a minute.

"Okay, *technically* we were married, but it was a clerical error. We should have been divorced eight years ago." He looked Warren dead in the eye. "And when I realized I'd made that mistake, I should have told you right away. But instead I came up with this crazy idea that Everley and I should pretend we were still a couple and in love."

Grace blinked. "So you're not married?"

"Our divorce came through last week."

Warren frowned. "Let me get this straight. You two were married, but you were divorcing when you completed the application for the donation?"

Dylan nodded. "Yes. We officially separated all those years ago. The divorce should have gone through back then but it didn't. So we refiled and were waiting for the courts when I came to your place for the interview."

"Why didn't you just tell us that?"

"I don't know," Dylan said truthfully. "I've thought about that a lot, especially today. Maybe I was avoiding any conflict that might lose the donation. Or maybe there was something else."

"Something else?" Warren's brows lifted. "What else could there be?"

"Maybe I was still in love with Everley." Dylan swallowed. "Actually, there's no maybe about it. I *am* still in love with Everley. And that's why I can never be sorry that I lied, because all this pretending led me back to her. It made me realize how much in love with her I am. And how I want to spend the rest of my life being married to this beautiful, funny, slightly unhinged woman."

Everley gasped.

"But you're not married anymore?" Grace asked. Her teeth were starting to chatter. Dylan shrugged his coat off and offered it to her. She blinked and took it, putting the oversized jacket over her shoulders and pulling the woolen fabric around herself.

"No, we're not married anymore." Dylan shook his head. "We're definitely divorced now."

"But you're still a couple?" Grace seemed more confused than ever.

Dylan could feel the heat of Everley's stare on his face.

"No, we're not right now. Because I'm an idiot and messed everything up. But all I can say is that if she'd have me back I'd be there in a heartbeat."

"What did you do to mess it up?" Warren asked. Dylan couldn't tell if he was amused or appalled.

"I didn't tell her we were divorced."

Warren started to laugh. Well there was that question answered. "So you lied to her about your marital status, as well as us? Jesus, what a tangled web."

"I don't understand why you're here on Christmas Eve telling us all this," Grace said softly, still looking cold. "Don't you have a show to do?"

"It's my fault," Everley said. "Miller found out that we were divorced last night and he said he had to tell you. I was afraid you might pull the funding for Dylan's project if you found out. So I wanted to tell you face to face. Explain to you that it was all my fault, not his. I was the one who pushed him to pretend to still be married." She pulled her bottom lip between her teeth. "And if he lost the money I'd feel terrible."

Warren frowned. "You think we'd pull the donation because you two can't decide if you're married or divorced? That's why you drove all the way here on Christmas Eve?"

"How did you know where we were anyway?" Grace asked.

"I went to your house first. Miller told me you were here," Everley said quietly. "And Dylan tracked me down using my phone location."

Warren's shoulders were still shaking, as though he was trying to suppress laughter.

"Everley was trying to do a good deed," Dylan said. "She always tries to do the right thing. She has the biggest heart of anybody I know. That's why I love her so much."

Her breath caught again. He turned to look at her, and she was staring up at him with shining eyes. There was such a look of adoration in her face that it made his whole body heat. "I love you," he said again. "And I'm so sorry I lied."

"Can I suggest something?" Warren said, pulling his own wife close. "Why don't we go inside before somebody's skin freezes off. You two can have something warm to drink and eat. Our friends have plenty to share."

Dylan turned to Everley. "That okay with you?"

"Yeah." Her cheeks were still burning, as though she was completely embarrassed.

He took her hand, folding her cold palm within his own. Damn, he loved this woman. She could protect herself, but he still wanted to protect her. To be the one who always shielded her from the cold.

He pressed his lips to her temple, breathing her in once more. "And then we talk."

Everley had never felt so embarrassed in her life. Driving to the Carsons' house had seemed like such a good idea in the middle of the night when she couldn't sleep because all she could think about was Dylan losing the donation.

But now Warren was laughing and Grace was smiling at them indulgently as they walked up the stairs to the house, Dylan's hand gently pressed into Everley's back.

All she could think about was that she should have stayed in Winterville to talk to Dylan, instead of dragging him all the way out here just to hear that their divorce wasn't a problem in the Carsons' eyes.

"Why don't we go clean up a little?" Grace said as they walked into the magnificently decorated hallway. "Then I'll ask my friends to feed you." She shrugged Dylan's coat off and handed it back to him.

"They really don't have to." Dylan took his coat, folding it over his forearm. "We can get something to eat on the way home."

"Nonsense. This is the most fun I've had all Christmas. It's like a Hallmark movie brought to life." Grace took Everley's hand. "Warren, we'll join you and Dylan in the dining room."

Warren nodded. "Sure."

The bathroom was as expansive as the rest of the house. There were three separate stalls, each with an oak door and tiled in marble. And the sinks had gold taps that shone as though they'd just been buffed.

"You doing okay?" Grace asked her softly as Everley dried her hands on one of the soft fluffy towels.

"I'm feeling a little bit stupid. Especially for disturbing you here."

Grace smiled. "You remind me of Warren when we were younger. He hated waiting around when there was a problem to solve. He had to be in on the action, always running from one place to the next."

"He doesn't seem like that now." Everley put the towel in the hamper.

"That's because he's calmed down. Sometimes problems get solved in the pauses, not in the center of the action. Solutions come when we breathe instead of holding our breath, you know?"

Everley frowned. "Not really."

Grace winked. "I think that's why Dylan's so good for you. He's the pause and you're the action."

"He's the pause?" Everley asked, not understanding.

"He's the deep breath you take before launching yourself forward. You couldn't have movement without oxygen. Both are important. Tell me, do you feel calm whenever he's near?"

Everley sighed. "Yeah, I do."

"Warren says I do the same for him. He says it's like I turn down the volume in his head."

Everley blinked. That was exactly how it felt with Dylan. Like she could finally relax.

"Can I ask you something?" Grace said softly.

"Sure."

"How long did Dylan lie to you about the divorce?"

"For a few days. I found out last night and went crazy. I shouted so loudly that Miller and his journalist friends heard me out in the hallway."

Grace tried to stifle a laugh. "I wish I'd been there to see his face."

Everley squeezed her eyes shut. "I'm so glad you weren't."

"Can I ask you one more question?" Grace asked. "Before we join the men?"

"Okay." Everley met her gaze.

"Why didn't you stay in Winterville to talk to Dylan this morning? Instead of rushing here and there, trying to sort out this donation?"

"Because I didn't want him to lose it."

"But it could have waited until after the holidays," Grace said gently. "You must have known that."

"Maybe I'm as bad as Dylan. He avoids problems, I rush at them like a bull in a china shop." Everley grimaced. "I can't stand having a problem and not solving it."

Grace smiled. "You're definitely like Warren."

Maybe she was. And the truth was, confronting this problem meant she didn't have to panic about her messy relationship with Dylan. Maybe in confronting one problem, she was avoiding another.

Avoiding the pain, the same way that he did, but in the opposite way. She'd been so hurt that he'd lied to her, that instead of sitting with that pain she'd punched it into the distance, preferring to concentrate on his donation instead of the hurt.

And he'd chased her. He'd obviously been to the theater, then Casey had sent him after her. He'd been willing to drive all over the state looking for her if that's what it took. He hadn't been angry. Not even a little. He'd been indulgent. Loving. Told them that she had the biggest heart and that he loved her.

He loved her.

And she loved him, so much. She hated that they'd argued, but maybe clearing the air had been important. Arguments didn't have to lead to separation. Sometimes they brought you closer together.

The same way sometimes simply breathing solved problems.

She looked up at Grace, her mind still full of Dylan. "Would it be really rude if we ate and drove out of here?" she asked her.

Grace grinned. "Of course it wouldn't. You two need to spend some time together."

Thank goodness, because all she wanted to do was be alone with Dylan right now.

$$\text{\textbf{\textasteriskcentered}} \quad 3\,2 \quad \text{\textbf{\textasteriskcentered}}$$

It was midafternoon by the time they'd made it back to Winterville. It felt like the longest drive of her life, knowing that Dylan's car was right behind her but not being able to sit and talk with him.

He'd made it better by calling her every once in a while, mostly to tell her to slow down and keep to the speed limit. She'd ignored him completely because, well, the roads were clear and they needed to get home.

The town was bursting with visitors as she drove around the town square. They were grabbing last minute gifts from the shops that lined the outside, or heading toward the Jingle Bell Theater, ready for the last show before Christmas. And she didn't care that she wasn't starring in it, or that she'd miss out on the best performance of the year, because this was where she wanted to be, pulling up in her driveway, knowing Dylan's car was right behind hers, and climbing out onto the blacktop that was lightly dusted with snow.

"Eighty five miles an hour?" Dylan said, frowning as he walked toward her. "Seriously?"

"I wanted to get home fast."

He tucked a piece of hair behind her ear, his eyes soft. "Yeah, and I wanted to get home in one piece. If I get a ticket in the mail it's on you."

She grinned. "We can do time together. I always look good in stripes." She skipped up the steps to her cottage, sliding the key into the lock.

He rubbed the bridge of his nose with his fingers. "If I end up in jail it'll be for more than just speeding. You drive me crazy, you know that?"

She unlocked the door and they stepped inside, Dylan closing it behind them.

"I know," she said, feeling stupidly happy. "But that's why you love me, isn't it?"

When she turned to look at him, he was staring at her with such love in his eyes that it took her breath away. She'd been kind of joking with her last question, but she could see the answer.

He loved her completely. Her crazy and all.

"Dylan..."

"Evie." He reached out to cup her cheek. "I'm so damn sorry I lied about our divorce."

"No. I'm sorry. I overreacted. I should have listened to why you did it. Instead I went off like a nuclear bomb."

He pressed his lips to her brow, as though breathing her in. "You were right about me being afraid. About me protecting myself. I was afraid you'd react badly so I avoided telling you." He lowered his head until his eyes were in line with hers. "I'm not going to do that again, baby. I promise. I'm working on myself. I want to be the man that deserves you."

"You do deserve me," she breathed. "I just wish you'd believe that."

He ran his finger along her cheekbone. "There's something else I want to tell you."

"Okay?" She tipped her head to the side, loving his touch.

"This is going to sound weird, but it's been playing on my mind and I've promised to be honest with you from now on. So here it is." He swallowed visibly. "When you cry I get aroused."

She went to laugh, but then she realized he was serious. "What?"

"I told my therapist about it, and she thinks it's because that means you care. And that it makes me feel connected to you. But it's true, I get hard when you cry."

"Is that why you almost ran away last night?" She remembered the agony in his eyes when the tears were rolling down her face.

"Yeah. I hate myself for feeling that way." He sighed. "You're hurt and all the blood rushes to where it shouldn't go."

She shook her head. "Maybe it's not that," she said softly. "Maybe it's just nature's way of forcing us to make up. Think about it, I'm crying and all I really want is to feel your arms around me. You're all horny and all you want is to slide inside me. Then we go to bed and all those stupid arguments are forgotten about because all we need is each other."

A half smile pulled at his lips. "You think I get hard because I want make up sex?"

"Maybe?" She tilted her head again, smiling back at him. "Do you want to know something else?"

"Hit me with it."

"I'm an actress," she whispered. "I'm really good at tears. So now I know exactly how to make you excited any time I want to."

He chuckled. "That's manipulation."

"I know." She wiggled her brows. "Most women manipulate with their bodies. I'm going to use my eyes."

He trailed his fingers down her jaw, to her neck. "You can manipulate me any time."

She grinned. "That's good. Because I'm definitely trying it tonight. We can watch *It's A Wonderful Life*. I'm sure to be sobbing at that one." She looked at him, her eyes shining.

"You're making me regret telling you."

"You won't regret it tonight," she said, her voice husky. "I promise."

He pushed his body against hers, and she could feel that he was aroused. She felt desire flicker inside of her like a flame, heating her up. "Do you forgive me?" he murmured, his fingers caressing her neck.

"I do. Do you forgive me?" she asked, her body humming with need for him.

"Always," he said, pulling her closer to him. "I love you so much, Evie. I have from the first time I saw you walking across that square, your ponytail swinging and your face lit up with a huge smile. You brighten my damn life up like a Christmas tree and I never want that to stop."

"Grace told me you were the calm to my storm," she whispered. "And she's right. When you're not with me, I feel lost." She reached up to trace his lips. "I don't want to be lost anymore."

"Then let me find you." His voice was gruff. "Let me protect you. Let me take care of you."

There was a lump in her throat the size of a boulder. "Yes, please," she whispered.

She didn't have to say anything else. He was already pressing his mouth to hers, his lips warm and soft as he pulled her closer to him.

"I love you," he murmured, deepening the kiss, one hand in her hair, the other sliding down her back.

"I love you, too." She curled her arms around his neck,

arching her back and lifting her head to his, kissing him back with so much emotion it felt overwhelming. "So much."

And when they parted, she laughed, because here she was, kissing her ex-husband on Christmas Eve, as the show she'd created went on without her.

But it didn't matter, because she liked this role better. And maybe in a little while she'd cry like a baby just to see how things turned out.

EPILOGUE

Christmas Day was always manic at the Winterville Inn. It was family tradition that all the Winter cousins – and their partners – worked together in the morning and early afternoon, feeding the guests and providing entertainment, as well as giving out gifts and singing until the final coffee had been drunk and the guest retired to the lounge and bar.

Everley tried her best to stifle the yawns that kept wracking her body.

"Are you okay?" Dylan asked, as they helped clean up in the dining room, once the guests had left. "You look tired."

"I spent the night with a sex god," she whispered. "He wouldn't take no for an answer."

Dylan grinned. "You were the one who woke me up at five this morning," he told her, rubbing the back of his neck as though his muscles ached as much as hers.

"That's because I wanted to see if happy tears made you hard," she said.

"Baby, *you* make me hard," he whispered in her ear, his breath making her shiver. "You could be happy or sad, I don't care." He ran his finger down her spine. "Although if you're sad, I'll be doing my best to make you happy again."

"Hey, keep your hands off my cousin until the place is cleaned," Gabe said, grinning at Dylan as he walked past them, carrying a trayful of dirty glasses. "We have to get this place ready for the family dinner this evening."

She blew a kiss at Dylan as she rolled up the used table-cloths and put them in the hamper, ready to be laundered when the staff were back at work. Then she grabbed the cloth and spray, cleaning each tabletop to a shine. When she was done, North, Gabe, Josh, and Dylan carried six of the tables to the center of the dining room. Later, they'd all eat together around one giant table, family style, to celebrate Christmas. Each one of them helped with the cooking – though North insisted that nobody else go near his ham – and then together they'd clean up, before retiring to the staff lounge to exchange gifts and play games.

Her heart felt full because she was surrounded by so many people she loved. Not just her cousins – though they were important enough – but Charlie was joining them tonight for dinner, having spent the day with Dolores and her family, and so were Casey and David. Along with any of the cast who were spending Christmas alone were invited, too. She hated leaving anybody out.

And then tonight, she and Dylan would go back to her cottage and curl up together in her warm, inviting bed. They had a few more days before he was due to go back to Africa. When they weren't kissing last night, they were whispering and making plans to make the most of their time together. The show would continue until mid-January, but only evening performances which gave them the days.

Plus there was Marta. She'd turned out to be a great understudy, and she'd already offered to stand in for Everley for a few shows so she and Dylan could spend more time together.

Sure she had ulterior motives, but you couldn't hate the woman for being ambitious.

"You okay?" Holly asked, sliding her arm through Everley's as they watched the guys rearrange the tables.

"I'm perfect." Everley grinned at her. "I was just thinking how nice it is for us all to be together."

"I know. I love this tradition of spending Christmas night as a family. Remember when Candy used to insist we all wait until evening to open our gifts?"

Everley laughed. "It drove me crazy. I hated the wait."

"Really? I could never tell." Holly's voice was warm. Dylan looked up, his eyes catching Everley's, and winked. "I love the way he looks at you," Holly said softly. "Like he can't believe his luck."

"I can't quite believe mine, either," Everley murmured. It was amazing how easily Dylan fit into their family. He and Josh were laughing about something, then Gabe mock-punched him in the arm. Alaska walked over to where Holly and Everley were standing and put her arm around Holly's waist.

"How's the morning sickness?" Everley asked her.

"Not so bad. Luckily it only happens first thing," Holly said. "Josh brings me a glass of water and some ginger cookies and then I throw them up. After, everything is better."

"Ewww." Everley wrinkled her nose. "That doesn't sound lucky to me."

"It'll be worth it." Holly touched her still-flat stomach.

"Yeah, it will." Everley caught her eye. "Can you believe that this time next year we'll have a baby here with us? Maybe more if Casey and David are here. Another generation to join the mayhem."

"If you and Dylan hurry up, we could have even more," Alaska said hopefully.

Everley laughed. "That's not happening. Not yet, anyway. We have too many things to sort out. I'll be the favorite auntie instead." She was definitely going to be an auntie, despite them only being cousins. Holly had always felt more like her second sister.

Alaska shook her head. "Nope. I'll definitely be the favorite. I'm great at hugs."

"Are we talking favorites?" Gabe asked. She hadn't noticed him walk over to join them. "Because if we are, I'm clearly the favorite uncle. Or cousin. Or whatever the hell I'll be."

"I'm sure North will have something to say about that," Alaska pointed out.

"I'll have something to say about what?" North lifted his head and looked over at them.

"Gabe thinks he's going to be the favorite uncle to Holly and Josh's baby," Alaska told him.

North shook his head. "Gabe's delusional. We'll just let him think that. We all know this baby's going to love his uncle North the most."

"I'm not delusional." Gabe frowned.

"You're building a ski resort from scratch," Everley pointed out. "I'd call that slightly delusional."

She was teasing, again, because Gabe had already started work on the resort plans. He and Josh had split the development into phases, and they had already started recruiting for the construction. She was impressed how quickly they'd moved after the initial plan.

"You'll all be the favorite uncles and aunties," Holly said. "Especially when Josh and I have a date night and need a babysitter."

"Will it involve changing diapers?" Alaska asked.

"I've changed my mind," Gabe said quickly. "North is definitely the favorite uncle."

The next ten minutes were a flurry of activity. When the tables were cleared and re-laid, Everley stepped back to admire their work. The oversized table was set for twenty people. Fresh white tablecloths were complemented by sparkling golden chargers and silverware for starters, main, and desserts. Amber had created the centerpiece – a large wreath of fir, decorated with white mistletoe berries and golden twine, candles mounted all along it to provide sparkle once lit.

"Okay, champagne time," Gabe called out. The guys shooed the girls away, as they opened four bottles and started to fill the flutes they'd prepared earlier. Charlie and Dolores walked in, kissing them all, closely followed by Casey and David, and Everley's friends from the show. Amber was talking with Alaska, as Holly and Everley watched with amusement as the guys bickered about filling the glasses just right.

"A glass of orange juice for my wife," Josh said, slipping the flute into Holly's hands. "Don't worry, I'll drink enough champagne for the both of us."

"I bet you will," Holly said, grimacing.

Gabe passed some flutes to Everley's friends, as North gave Charlie and Dolores theirs. Dylan walked over carrying two flutes, but didn't pass one to Everley yet.

"Does everybody have one?" North called out.

"Yes!"

"Okay, mate, it's over to you." North glanced at Dylan.

Everley blinked. Before she could say a word, Dylan put the glasses he'd been holding on the table, then dropped to his knee, pulling out a small velvet box.

"Everley Winter. Or Shaw. Whichever you prefer," he began, and everybody chuckled. "But for the record, I prefer

Shaw. Just so you know." His eyes flickered to hers. "I feel like the luckiest guy in the world, to have found you in my life not just once, but twice. And this time I'm not going to mess it up."

"Glad to hear it," Charlie called out.

Gabe started to laugh, but Alaska hushed him.

"Beautiful, talented, gorgeous woman. The love of my life. Will you do me the honor of becoming my wife. Again?" Dylan asked softly. "Because if you do, it'll make me the happiest damn man on this planet."

Everley's chest was so tight it was hard to breathe.

"You need to show her the ring first," Charlie shouted. "Let her see what she's getting herself in for."

Dylan bit down a smile and lifted the lid. Inside was a white gold solitaire. He stood and took it out, sliding it onto Everley's finger.

"Wait, is that..." Everley frowned, looking at the gem sparkling against her skin. It couldn't be.

"Your original engagement ring. Yeah." Dylan's brows knitted. "I can get a different one if you think this one's jinxed."

"I gave it back to you," she said. "All those years ago."

"I know." A smile played at his lips. "But I kept it."

Tears stung at her eyes. "I thought you would have sold it. Or thrown it away."

He shook his head. "Never. I would never have done that. So what do you say? Will you be my wife again?"

She caught his eyes, her smile broad. "Yes."

Dylan threaded his fingers into her hair. "Are you sure about this?" he asked her. "I'm a lot to take on."

"So am I," she pointed out. "But I think we've got this."

"I think we do, too." He leaned in, his mouth claiming hers, his fingers curling around her neck to angle her face to his. "I love you so much, Mrs. Shaw." His lips were warm and soft as they kissed, as their family and friends clapped around them.

"I love you, too, Dr. Shaw," she said, her voice tight. "But if you keep looking at me I'm going to cry."

He laughed and held her tighter. "Hold in those tears," he said, brushing her lips with his once more. "We have Christmas to celebrate first."

***

"This looks amazing," Everley said to Gabe as they stood on the slopes of the mountain months later, looking at the buildings under construction. Only the caps of the mountain were covered in snow – everything else was a glorious emerald green. Soon it would start snowing on lower ground again, but for now they'd enjoy the cool, crisp days of fall. "I can't believe it's really happening."

She'd been so impressed by his hard work. To her, Gabe had always been her fun loving cousin. Never serious, always joking, the one that women flocked to for a good time.

But she was seeing a whole new side to him now. He and Josh were working so hard, and she could tell that he was loving every minute.

"Do you miss snowboarding?" she asked him, sliding her fingers between his and squeezing tight.

"Not as much as I thought. I miss the guys and the adrenaline of competing, but I don't miss the constant training. Or the injuries." He winced.

"So you're happy you decided to come home?"

A smile pulled at his lips. "Yeah, I am. I like being here with you guys. I like that I was here for Candace's birth." Holly and Josh had named their baby girl after their grandmother. It had touched them all. His warm eyes met hers.

"And spending time with you and Dylan, too, now that he's back for good."

"We like you being here." She hugged him. "Even if I do have to keep swatting you away from my dancers."

He laughed. "Hey, it's not my fault if they keep making a beeline for me. It's the old Winter charm. They'd make a play for North if he wasn't such a grouch."

"Yeah, well just treat them right, okay? I'm loving how close knit our theater company is." The Jingle Bell Theater was going from strength to strength. In the summer they had a number of repertory companies visiting for a week at a time. Most of the shows had sold out, thanks to the positive publicity that had come from her interview with Miller Carson's friends. He'd turned out to be a real supporter of the Jingle Bell Theater.

And Dylan didn't seem to be too bothered by that.

"Ah, I won't be able to bring them back to my place soon anyway. I have a new roommate coming."

Everley blinked. "You do? Who?"

"Remember my friend Matt?"

"The one you roomed with at competitions?"

Gabe nodded. "Yeah, him."

"Oh, is he coming to stay?" Everley smiled. "I like him."

"Nah, not Matt. His sister. Apparently she's just been through a bad breakup and wants to get out of their hometown. He wanted to know if I could give her a room while she's here."

"He's trusting *you* with his sister?" Everley bit down a grin. "Wow."

"What do you mean, *trusting me?* Of course he's trusting me. What do you think is going to happen?"

Everley shrugged. "The same thing that happens when you come near my dancers."

Gabe huffed and shook his head. "She just found her

fiancé in bed with another woman. I'm pretty sure she's not going to be a problem. And anyway, she's my friend's sister. You don't go there. And if you do, you end up with your balls twisted around your neck."

"Dylan went there. He's North's friend. And yours."

"And technically, you're not our sister." Gabe gave her a sweet smile. "So shut up. I'm doing a friend a favor, that's all. Stop seeing things that aren't there." He slid his arm around her shoulder. "Come on, let's hike back. I know you're dying to see Dylan and I have a hot date tonight."

"With a dancer?"

"Nope, with a beer and a movie." He winked at her. "And since I'll have a roommate soon, that's the closest my place is going to see to action in the next few months."

THE END

DEAR READER

Thank you so much for reading Dylan and Everley's story. If you enjoyed it and you get a chance, I'd be so grateful if you can leave a review. And don't forget to keep an eye out for LEAVE ME BREATHLESS, Gabe and Nicole's story.

I can't wait to share more stories with you.

Yours,

Carrie xx

ALSO BY CARRIE ELKS

THE WINTERVILLE SERIES

A gorgeously wintery small town romance series, featuring six cousins who fight to save the sound their grandmother built.

Welcome to Winterville

Hearts In Winter

Leave Me Breathless

Memories of Mistletoe

Every Shade of Winter

THE SALINGER BROTHERS SERIES

A swoony romantic comedy series featuring six brothers and the strong and smart women who tame them.

Strictly Business

Strictly Pleasure

Strictly For Now

ANGEL SANDS SERIES

A heartwarming small town beach series, full of best friends, hot guys and happily-ever-afters.

Let Me Burn

She's Like the Wind

Sweet Little Lies

Just A Kiss

Baby I'm Yours

Pieces Of Us

Chasing The Sun

Heart And Soul

Lost In Him

THE HEARTBREAK BROTHERS SERIES

A gorgeous small town series about four brothers and the women
who capture their hearts.

Take Me Home

Still The One

A Better Man

Somebody Like You

When We Touch

THE SHAKESPEARE SISTERS SERIES

An epic series about four strong yet vulnerable sisters, and the alpha
men who steal their hearts.

Summer's Lease

A Winter's Tale

Absent in the Spring

By Virtue Fall

THE LOVE IN LONDON SERIES

Three books about strong and sassy women finding love in the big
city.

Coming Down

Broken Chords

Canada Square

STANDALONE

Fix You

An epic romance that spans the decades. Breathtaking and angsty
and all the things in between.

ABOUT THE AUTHOR

Carrie Elks writes contemporary romance with a sizzling edge. Her first book, *Fix You*, has been translated into eight languages and made a surprise appearance on *Big Brother* in Brazil. Luckily for her, it wasn't voted out.

Carrie lives with her husband, two lovely children and a larger-than-life black pug called Plato. When she isn't writing or reading, she can be found baking, drinking an occasional (!) glass of wine, or chatting on social media.

You can find Carrie in all these places
www.carrieelks.com
carrie.elks@mail.com

ACKNOWLEDGMENTS

This is only the second time I've written about a couple who are already married (even if they didn't know it) and it was SO MUCH FUN to put Everley and Dylan's story onto paper. There's something so delicious about second chance romances, and when you add the complication of a marriage it makes for a fun, romantic and emotional ride. I really hope you enjoyed it.

Hearts In Winter wouldn't be here if it wasn't for the following people. Rose David, editor extraordinaire. Mich from Proofreading by Mich, Marian - beta reader and amazing error spotter. And of course the amazing Kirsty from Pretty Little Design co who created this gorgeous cover.

Thank you all for being part of my team. You make my life and my work so much better.

Thank you to my agent, Meire Dias, of the Bookcase agency, and Flavia who always gives me so much support and kindness.

My PA, Amanda, is amazing. You rock, lady!

Ash, Ella and Olly - your support and patience with me is unending. Thank you for your love and all those cups of tea.

And to my reader group, The Water Cooler, thank you for all your support and appreciation. We have a lot of fun, and it's my favorite place to blow off steam.

Finally to you, the reader. THANK YOU for picking up this, and any of my other books. I hope I helped you escape for a little while. I'm grateful for you giving me a chance.

Keep reading!
    Carrie x